Chef's Kiss at the Chalet

Sookie Snow writes small-town, seasonal romance. A lover of all things cozy, sweet and spiced, she is at her happiest curled up by the fire with a hot chocolate and a swoon-worthy romance – HEA guaranteed.

Chef's Kiss at the Chalet

SOOKIE SNOW

PAN BOOKS

First published 2025 by Pan Books
an imprint of Pan Macmillan
The Smithson, 6 Briset Street, London EC1M 5NR
EU representative: Macmillan Publishers Ireland Ltd, 1st Floor,
The Liffey Trust Centre, 117–126 Sheriff Street Upper,
Dublin 1 D01 YC43
Associated companies throughout the world

ISBN 978-1-0350-8033-5

135798642

A CIP catalogue record for this book is available from the British Library.

Typeset in Legacy Serif ITC Pro by Six Red Marbles UK, Thetford, Norfolk
Printed and bound in the UK using 100% Renewable Electricity by CPI Group (UK) Ltd

MIX
Paper | Supporting
responsible forestry
FSC® C116313

Visit **www.panmacmillan.com** to read more about
all our books and to buy them.

*For the nostalgic romance girlies,
this one's for you.*

BE WHISKED AWAY TO MAPLEWOOD CREEK . . .

There She Goes – The La's
Kiss Me – Sixpence None The Richer
'tis the damn season – Taylor Swift
That's So True – Gracie Abrams
Dreams – The Cranberries
Suddenly I See – KT Tunstall
Sweater Weather – The Neighbourhood
From Eden – Hozier
Bloom – The Paper Kites
Where'd All the Time Go? – Dr. Dog
Fade Into You – Mazzy Star
Out of Reach – Gabrielle
Chasing Cars – Snow Patrol

Chapter 1

I swiped my phone screen to refresh my email for what felt like the hundredth time in two minutes. My fingers trembled, more from nerves than the chilly mountain air that zipped through the front door of The Denver Drip. We were slammed at the coffee shop I managed, and my heart sank a little at each new customer who appeared at the counter to tear me from my obsessive email stalking.

"Hi, welcome," I greeted the young power couple who popped in every morning on their way to work. "The usual?"

"And a protein ball, please," the woman in the designer cardigan set answered, sweeping her auburn hair behind her ear as her brand-new engagement ring sparkled under the fluorescent overhead lights.

"Make mine a triple shot," her short, handsome beau added.

They were eerily similar, this preppy pair of J.Crew-clad professionals. One of those couples who start to look like siblings, slowly morphing into the same person.

Once they had been served, an elderly woman with cat hairs on her coat ordered an English breakfast tea and a scone, taking them to the table beside the window to watch the side-walk traffic.

Next up was Frank, a regular, no-frills-added, black-coffee drinker. He was a true unicorn at the high-end shop, known more for its creative espresso drinks, as well as sandwiches and gourmet pastries care of yours truly. The modern decor met somewhere at the intersection of Scandinavian minimalist and overgrown greenhouse: wood accents and white subway tiles, with copious potted plants and hanging vines over the thrifted leather armchairs and cozy reading nooks. Quickly, mechanically, I poured Frank's drink and went back to staring at the clock, willing the thin, black second hand to move a little faster.

At ten on the dot, I would find out if my application to the prestigious Academy of Culinary Excellence in London had been accepted. Not only my dream program, but my dream city. Ever since I'd applied in June to continue my culinary education, I had waited for the day their decision would arrive. Now that it was here, I dreaded the answer. Raising my hopes only meant I had farther to fall if I failed.

"Any news?" Hannah asked, pouring oat milk and matcha over ice.

The perennially upbeat blonde, with tiny studs in her ear cartilage and a butterfly tattoo on the back of her neck, was a senior at my alma mater, The Kent School, and worked here a few days a week. She was also well versed in my application saga.

"Nothing yet." I shook my head and tapped my phone where it sat on the counter while I dashed between ringing up customers and plating profiteroles and pains au chocolat. "Good or bad, I'll know in thirty minutes."

She patted my back. "It'll work out. I'm sure of it. You're so talented, Elle."

"You have to say that. I make the schedule and can give you all the worst shifts," I teased, laughing when she looked affronted. "Kidding. I appreciate the vote of confidence."

"Seriously though, as someone going through the college application process, I know the stress is endless. I can't imagine doing it at your age."

"Oof." I cringed at her teasing. Insert knife and twist. "Kick me while I'm down. Twenty-seven is hardly ancient, you know."

She laughed as two more customers entered. Sighing, I reminded myself that taking care of them helped the clock creep closer to decision time. I was trying not to pace, not to get caught up in the *what if*s while I constructed a bagel sandwich with homemade mint yogurt spread.

"That looks amazing." Another customer picking up her croissant gawked at the sandwich as I handed it over. "Can I get one of those too?"

"Coming right up," I said automatically, barely pausing to breathe as I went back to the register to put in the ticket.

The compliments were better than caffeine to keep me on my feet, darting back and forth behind the counter while I tried to fend off the doubt spiral brewing in my head. That voice that told me I wasn't good enough and never would be.

Each time Hannah walked by, she gave me a reassuring smile, a pat on the arm, or whispered, "You've got this."

I appreciated the support, but I was immune to her infectious positivity today. Not that I considered myself a pessimist—just realistic. The program was one of the most competitive in the world. Only a tiny fraction of applicants made it in each year. Despite my glowing academic transcript and the pastry diploma I'd already received from Auguste Escoffier School of Culinary Arts, the odds were stacked against me. Still, I hoped the admissions office would read my heartfelt personal essay and understand my passion. They wouldn't find another student who worked harder or wanted it more. In that regard, I backed myself against anyone.

Again, I refreshed my email app. And again, I felt a creeping sense of dread inside.

"If I don't get in . . ." I muttered to myself.

Hannah jabbed me playfully in the arm with an espresso spoon.

"Um, ow." I rubbed my arm and laughed. "You don't need to resort to violence."

"Oh, please." She planted her hands on her hips. "You don't need to be all morose and dejected. Manifest it."

"Manifest it?" I said, skeptically. "Sure. I'll get right on that."

"If you only think in negative terms, you're going to keep living in a negative space and what good will that do?" She pulled pastries from the display case and boxed them up for a to-go order. "I think if you believe that you're deserving, acknowledge that you've been dealt a shitty hand and deserve something good, then maybe it'll happen."

"Power of positive thinking," I mocked playfully.

She was oblivious to my sarcasm. "Exactly."

"You're wise beyond your years."

She laughed. "Yeah, well, remember that when you do next month's schedule."

"Ah, I see how it is."

Hannah yanked me in for a quick hug. We were both sweaty, my wavy black ponytail sticking to the side of her face.

"I don't know if I've ever said it," I told her as we pulled away, "but I'm glad the alumni office matched us up."

I first met Hannah as her mentor, but I'd come to think of her as family. Like me, she had received a full-ride scholarship to The Kent School, part of an award funded by former recipients to continue to provide opportunities to the next generations. Without that scholarship, I never could've afforded the prestigious institution.

"I'm grateful too." Hannah sniffed and blew out a deep breath. "You're like the big sister that I never wanted." Pushing me back, she wiped a stray tear away and rolled her shoulders with a pouty grin.

It was at my five-year reunion that the alumni office approached me about mentoring Hannah as she was entering her sophomore year, and I readily agreed. We had both grown up with similar hardships: single parents and never enough money, spending too much of our childhoods as caregivers when the universe dumped more on us than our fair share. I admired so much the way Hannah never let any of it make her cynical. She made it look easy.

"Seriously," she said. "You've got a few minutes before the email that will change your life. Think good thoughts. Manifest that shit."

"You should put that on a T-shirt."

"I could probably pay for college that way." She laughed and shoved me toward the back room. "Go take a break. I can handle things out here. Come back with good news."

Slipping into the small, cluttered room, I closed the door

and sank into the worn leather chair at the desk, glancing at the clock on the wall above me.

"Five minutes. Good thoughts only," I told myself. "I can do this."

In a way, I'd come to want this as much for Hannah as I did for myself. It just meant so much to her to see me succeed. I felt a responsibility to show her good things were possible. Big dreams weren't out of reach for people like us.

I didn't believe in luck or manifesting. Only effort. It was perseverance that earned me that Kent scholarship. And dedication that allowed me to excel academically while I was there. Nothing ever came easy. I busted my ass studying, cramming until dawn, always doing that much more than my peers. I wasn't interested in simply keeping my head above water. I wanted to be *great*. Still, I worried that maybe some things would always be out of reach. It was hard to feel deserving when you were used to going without.

So, I started to rationalize the worst-case scenario. If I didn't get into ACE, it just meant that I had to do another two-year associate degree at Escoffier. That wouldn't be the end of the world. Still good enough to build a client base and perhaps land a private chef position in Aspen or Boulder. It wouldn't be London, but I could make it work.

Then I heard Hannah's voice in my head telling me that was quitter talk.

And in my rationalizing, I'd also missed the alert notifying me of a new email. It was five after ten, and I'd distracted myself into not noticing the banner that had appeared on my phone.

The subject line simply read "Application Decision."

"Here we go."

Using my thumb on my old iPhone, I took a deep breath and clicked the email app.

Congratulations, Chef-in-Training!

I read and re-read the first line three times before an enormous grin broke out on my face and I called for Hannah.

When she burst through the door, I handed her the phone so she could read the message for herself. I was a wobbly and runny-nosed mess that mixed tears and laughter.

"I told you! You manifested that shit!" she shouted before beginning to read the opening paragraph aloud. "Congratulations, Eleanor! On behalf of the entire Admissions Committee, we are pleased to notify you of your acceptance to the Academy of Culinary Excellence in London for the spring entry date. ACE is located in one of the world's food and hospitality capitals, and our position as a premier culinary college offers unbeatable opportunities for participation in internships, research, events and cultural programs. Your ACE education is an investment in your future, and we cannot wait to help you get started."

Hannah handed me back the phone, jumping up and down and shrieking, "Holy shit! You did it, Elle!"

"I can't believe it," I breathed, reading through the first paragraph again before moving on to the nitty-gritty details. "It looks like I'll get an acceptance packet in the mail tomorrow, with all of the information on housing, tuition, etc."

Hannah gave me a concerned look, her blue eyes turning serious. "You're not scheduled to work tomorrow, but maybe you should come in so you're not pacing a hole in your apartment floor."

I knew what she was getting at. I had indicated on my application that I would require financial aid to cover tuition. The total cost of that tuition, and how much of it the school would be willing to cover, were details yet to be ironed out. Getting into ACE had been step one. Paying for it was my next hurdle.

"You know, I have no idea how housing works at ACE," I said. "Especially since I am considered an international student."

Hannah nodded. "Plus, you'll need to sort out a work and student visa application. Flights and . . ." She paused, her face breaking out into a huge smile. "Forget all that for now. This is really happening. I am so happy for you."

While she pulled me into a backbreaking hug, I made a mental list of what needed to be done.

I broke the hug, but kept my hands placed on her shoulders. "I've got my good news. Now we need to manifest your dream college acceptance."

"Deal," she said. "For now, come and give me a hand out there. We're swamped." She pulled me toward the door, and sure enough, there was a line backing up into the dining room.

Tomorrow was the first day of a new start.

Chapter 2

Waking up before sunrise on the couch in my shoebox apartment above the Latin market, I had the worst crick in my neck and a headache from falling asleep with my contacts in. Last thing I remembered, I was watching a Korean cooking competition on Netflix. Now I had a throw pillow full of drool and mascara crusted on my eyelids.

On the rare occasion I had the chance to sleep in, I found it impossible. I was too accustomed to the routine of waking up at four to open the coffee shop promptly at five, with just enough time to shower, slam down a quick breakfast and get to work. My body was a machine that found habits hard to break. Add in the excitement, stress and apprehension about the ACE packet that would arrive by first-class mail today, and it was a miracle I slept at all.

After I dragged myself to the bathroom then gulped down a cup of coffee, I reflected that I probably should've listened to Hannah and gone into work, if only to save the linoleum from my pacing footsteps. I occupied myself by mindlessly scrolling Instagram. Next, I bagged up some clothes for a trip to the

Laundromat later. I even dusted the apartment from top to bottom, before I stopped short of talking myself into stripping and waxing the floors like a psychopath.

Instead, I pulled three eggs from my fridge to prepare an omelet.

A proper French-style omelet was deceptively simple. It started with soaking the eggs in warm water to bring them up to room temperature. Warm eggs meant a shorter cook time, which was part of the secret to a perfect, slightly custardy center. When the eggs were ready, I cracked them into a small bowl, gave them a good whisk and seasoned with salt and pepper before pouring them into a buttered non-stick pan. I stirred slightly with a silicone spatula until they started to curd and then folded the omelet over one third of the way as the bottom began to turn golden brown. I folded another third, tilting the pan and tucking the remaining curd inside the envelope I had created, before sliding the whole thing onto my plate to garnish with a little fresh chive and tarragon.

As I ate, I sat with my phone to look up everything I could about the London neighborhood where ACE was located. The website described London in six zones. ACE was in Zone 1, where the rents were some of the highest in the city. They suggested venturing out to Zone 2 or 3, but it would add a significant commute to my day, and even those neighborhoods looked like a stretch for my limited budget. The alternative was looking for a roommate situation. Though after living on my own for a while now, I wasn't enthused about the idea of sharing.

While rents in Denver weren't cheap, I managed to get by.

The coffee shop owner let me pick up overtime shifts when I needed them and I had even started taking the occasional pastry gig for catering events to bolster my ACE tuition fund.

My current apartment was what creative realtors would call "cozy" or "snug." Meaning tiny. The bedroom was barely large enough for a queen mattress and dresser, and the living-dining combo room made my two-seater couch look enormous. The winning feature for me had been the kitchen, with generous counter space and new appliances. The former landlord had been in the middle of a renovation to flip the place until they went bankrupt and sold off the building.

It was like a metaphor for myself. A little worse for wear and held together by bubble gum and grit, but every extra penny I had went into that damn kitchen, from quality pans to better ingredients than had any right to be found in these humble surroundings.

Around lunchtime, I was curled up on the couch watching the street outside when I saw the mail truck pull up to the curb. I darted to the door and quickly shoved my feet into a pair of shoes. I realized as soon as I made it to the stairwell that I should've grabbed a coat too. It was an especially frigid day in November and the landlord didn't turn on the heat in the lobby until Thanksgiving.

By the time I skidded into the foyer, the mail carrier was just beginning to drop off the packages near the cluster of mailboxes. I waited anxiously while he nodded his head to the music playing in his earbuds, completely oblivious to my presence. The moment he stepped away, I unlocked my box and grabbed the small bundle of envelopes before hurrying back upstairs.

I tossed every other piece of mail onto my coffee table before settling back onto the couch with my legs tucked underneath me, and gingerly opening the thick, white envelope, clearly marked with the ACE logo. I slid out the stack of papers and skimmed through the pages, searching for the financial aid letter, while a tiny seed of panic began sprouting in my gut. My eyes widened at the first glimpse of a pound sign. I swallowed hard.

The letter stated that the program had received an especially large number of requests for financial assistance for the upcoming term. To accommodate as many students as possible, approved applicants would receive a smaller portion of total tuition than previous years. They were pleased to inform me that I was awarded £20,000, or roughly half of the total tuition. And that still didn't include my flights, visa applications or accommodation in London. Even with my hard-earned savings, I was going to come up short by almost thirty grand.

"Damn," I spat.

I jumped to my feet and resumed pacing. My nerves were frayed. I needed a massive influx of cash, and fast, or I'd lose my spot and my dreams would be up in smoke. All the overtime shifts and catering gigs in the world wouldn't cover the gap soon enough. This was knocking-over-a-bank levels of urgent.

As my pacing reached the kitchen, I paused at the fridge, where a tattered business card was held beneath a magnet.

Megan Wheelan, Hannah's mom, was the founder and director of Culinary Connection, a specialized recruitment firm in Denver for industry professionals that was growing fast. Starting out as just a boutique business that served the Greater Denver communities, it had since expanded its network and reach to the West Coast. Megan's hope was that in two years she would be in half the states in the country. It was the perfect home-based business she'd started while recovering from cancer treatment, a way to ease herself back into the workforce without the stress of a commute and with flexibility to make her doctors' appointments. Essentially, Megan and her team served as a culinary job-placement service. Hospitality workers in hotels, sous, executive, and pastry chefs, managerial staff, you name it. She was also instrumental in throwing catering jobs my way when she came across them.

I padded back into the living room to find my phone. Megan picked up after a few rings.

"Elle, hello!"

"Hey! Not sure if you've spoken to Han yet, but I got into ACE!"

"Yes, she told me when she got home last night. Congrats! I'm so happy for you."

I tucked myself back on the couch and slid the packet of papers to the side. "Yeah, well, now comes the hard part."

"Oh? What's the hard part? Leaving Denver behind while you work your magic in Jolly Old England?" She laughed to herself at the cartoonish accent she affected.

"Funny you should say that, because I actually do need some magic."

Reading the trepidation in my voice, her tone grew serious. "I'm not sure how I can help, but I promise I'll try."

"If you could keep an ear to the ground for any high-paying

jobs, I'd really appreciate it. The tuition is going to be a stretch."

"Oh, no. Did the financial aid fall through?"

"Not entirely, but it's well below what I'd hoped. I've got some savings, and I can stagger some of the payments, but I'm still falling more than a little short."

"For you, anything." Her voice perked up, determined, a mama bear springing into action. "I'll be in touch if anything comes up."

"Thanks, Megan. I owe you."

"You don't," she told me firmly. "You've always taken care of my Han. I'll keep you posted."

The wait was horrendous. I spent the next couple of days in a persistent state of anxiety that manifested in twice double-charging customers at the coffee shop. I burnt breakfast sandwiches and screwed up even the simplest orders. My mind was entirely elsewhere. I thought about having to give up my spot at ACE and spending another year at the Drip with no plans and no direction. Hannah kept reminding me that if I put out positivity, the universe would provide, but I had serious doubts about the universe's track record.

Then on Sunday, just before midnight, things started to look up. I had just finished cleaning my kitchen after spending my entire day off from the shop preparing hors d'oeuvres for an upcoming catering gig and baking two dozen chocolate croissants for Megan's breakfast meeting when my phone buzzed with a text from the woman herself.

Megan: Found a potential job.
We can discuss tomorrow.

Me: Any hints? I'm dying here.
PS The croissants are finished.

Megan: I know I ordered them for
the office . . .
But I might just keep them all for me.

Me: That's cold, but I do know
how much you love them.
The suspense is killing me!

Megan: You're worse than Hannah.

Me: Don't let Hannah hear you say that.
She won't let me live it down. One hint.

Megan: Pays well but . . .

Me: You can't leave me on a but!

Megan: It's in Maplewood Creek.

Me: Where?

Megan: Maplewood Creek. Suburb
of Aspen. Potentially tricky client.

Before responding, I googled Maplewood Creek, Colorado, and let out a low whistle at the median salary and home prices.

Though, calling these buildings "homes" was probably offensive to the owners.

Mansion chalets? Chalet mansions?

Either way, the town was fancy, which made sense if it was in such close proximity to Aspen. The photos online were like something out of a Christmas movie: snow-covered rooftops nestled within the valley, buildings down the main street framed by twinkling lights, brochure-ready families ice-skating in the square and strolling past the shops with steaming cups of hot cocoa.

It was a small town, but in the middle of a huge resurgence, thanks to a number of wealthy families buying up mountainside property to build luxurious, state-of-the-art chalets. That meant plenty of upscale restaurants accommodating a wealthy clientele, demand for private chefs, and the nearby ski resorts would have hotel kitchens and catering, with plenty of opportunity for making tips. It also appeared that the population wasn't year-round, which meant short-term work during the ski season.

Perfect.

I started to imagine what life in a resort town might be like. There had to be plenty of hours for the taking in the high season. And good tips, hopefully. Maybe even the added benefit of access to the amenities from time to time. The idea started to grow on me.

Me: I'll get the details from you tomorrow, but unless they're some sort of crazy Hannibal Lecter type, count me in.

Chapter 3

The following day, I swung by Megan's house on the way to the coffee shop. She lived in the childhood home she'd inherited from her parents. It was situated in an older suburb that hadn't yet been gentrified and where the lower property values allowed for larger square footage than comparable neighborhoods. This had given her the flexibility to turn a den and spare bedroom into office space for the two young assistants she'd brought on to help with the workload now that the business was really taking off. But most of the time, they all congregated in the large, cozy kitchen.

"Come on in," Megan said, escorting me inside with the boxes of pastries. She took them from my arms and laid them out on the kitchen counter. "Han's already left to open the Drip and my girls aren't in yet."

The house wasn't fancy—Megan was still focused on investing everything in the growth and success of Culinary Connection. But, despite the old paint and dented baseboards, she kept the place immaculate and always had cute little touches dotted about, like fresh flowers and seasonally appropriate kitchen towels on display.

Megan poured me a cup of coffee and dug into the croissants as we sat at her dining-room table.

"Lay it on me," I said, eager to hear the details of this mysterious job. "What's the gig?"

"Hello to you too," she scoffed playfully.

Megan had short blond hair that had grown back a few shades darker than Hannah's after the chemo and radiation treatments. Once she'd felt well enough to put away the robes and pajamas, she always dressed like she was going into a real corporate office, even if she wasn't leaving the house. Today she was wearing a crisp, collared shirt and blazer, with gold stud earrings.

The truth was, if Hannah was my little sister, then Megan was my big sister. I'd lost my mom years ago to Huntington's disease and I'd since found some of the maternal nurturing I missed so dearly in Megan. It was a relationship between the three of us that I had come to really rely on these last few years.

"Don't get too excited, I don't know if this is going to be something that you're interested in. It's an unconventional request."

"Color me cautiously intrigued."

Megan didn't do out-of-the-box with her company. Her placements were always straightforward, fair and the consistency of her five-star reviews were what kept industry leaders knocking on her door.

"I'll warn you, I haven't had time to investigate this job fully yet, as it literally came in last night, right before I texted you."

"Okay . . ." My trepidation grew. I imagined the worst.

Megan took a bite of her croissant and moaned with pleasure. She quickly took another while I waited impatiently for the details.

"First of all, they need someone who can start immediately," she said.

Oh. I had to give the coffee shop ample notice. They had been good to me for years and I didn't want to screw the owner over, no matter how great this potential gig was.

"How soon is soon?"

Megan washed down her croissant with a sip of coffee. "She asked if tomorrow was an option."

"Tomorrow?" I yelped, laughing as I waited for her to say it was a joke. "Tell me you're kidding."

"I am not. Full disclosure . . ."

My stomach dropped.

"They're a tad high maintenance," Megan warned.

I was already pulling up Google on my phone. "What's the client's name?"

She swallowed another greedy bite of croissant and got up to grab herself another one. "It's the Hawthorne family and you'll need to sign an NDA."

"An NDA?" My heart beat a little faster.

"Standard practice with a client in this income bracket," Megan told me. She came back to sit at the table. "The last girl quit in forty-eight hours after a screaming match because of an underbaked soufflé."

I laughed nervously. "What exactly are they looking for?"

"A chalet girl."

"A what?"

"I know, I had to look it up," she said. "The term is a throwback from the sixties, but it's sort of like a private chef, party planner and ski bunny all rolled into one."

"They're not going to make me put that on a name tag, are they?"

Megan snorted. "Did I mention that the pay is good?"

"You did, but tell me more."

"It's really good."

"Like specifically, how good?" Hopefulness crept into my voice.

"Based on what you told me you'd need for London, it would take care of your tuition and then some. I've asked for a complete salary package and we'll make sure the contract is ironclad, just in case. I should have it all by this afternoon. It would just be for the season. Three months, tops."

My heart swelled in my chest. Three months. I could learn to tolerate just about anything for three months. Demanding clients and eccentric tastes didn't worry me. I was good at putting on a brave face. But, I hesitated at the thought of leaving the coffee shop high and dry. It felt a little like absconding in the middle of the night. Then again, this was my future. The key to unlocking my dreams. I couldn't live my life for everyone else, or I'd never get off this runaway merry-go-round with no end in sight.

Megan reached across the table, placing her hand on mine. "This is an amazing opportunity for you, Elle. Impress them, which I know you can do, and your networking opportunities will blow wide open. The sky's the limit. Worth tolerating a couple of red flags, in my professional opinion."

London and all her opportunities called to me. It wasn't something I could ignore.

"Let me know as soon as you get the info," I said. "I'm in."

The following afternoon, we were standing in the parking lot saying goodbye.

"Keep me posted when you get there," Megan said as she arranged my suitcases in the trunk of my car outside my apartment.

Hannah pushed a scraper over my windshield in an attempt to clear the lightly falling snow. A storm was headed in the same direction as me and I had to get on the road now if I wanted to beat it to Maplewood Creek.

"I'll text you both when I arrive," I promised, pulling Megan into a hug. "Thanks again for everything you did. I'm so grateful."

Megan had managed to find a replacement to take over my role at The Denver Drip, which was a huge help to the owner. She had also negotiated with the Hawthornes to get me a signing bonus because of the short notice for the job, enough to finance my travel and visa applications for London.

"Remember what I said," Megan told me, adjusting her scarf against the cold. "If there's anything untoward, you call me immediately."

"I'm sure it'll be fine." I laughed, nervous at the warning. It was a little late for second thoughts.

"Just in case. You have a contingency clause in the contract if Mrs. Hawthorne turns out to be as difficult as the last girl said."

"Stop, Mom," Hannah pleaded. "You're freaking her out. It's going to be great!"

"Absolutely," I said, willing my voice to sound confident and not as shaky as I felt. I would manifest this if it was the last thing I did.

"You will be amazing," Megan said, holding out her arms for a hug. "Careful on the roads, alright?"

I gave her a tight squeeze in return. "Will do. Thank you again."

"My turn!" Hannah slammed into me as soon as Megan and I released our hug, nearly knocking the wind from my chest. "I'll miss you. Call and tell me all about it. I want to hear everything, okay?"

"I promise," I laughed, blowing her hair from my face as a gust of wind enveloped us.

Hannah squeezed tighter and wouldn't let go. "And take pictures. Lots of pictures. I want to see this chalet."

"I'll see what I can do."

"Oh!" She abruptly pulled away to grab a Thermos from Megan's car and handed it to me. "Almost forgot. You'll need caffeine for the road."

"Take care of each other, okay? And try not to burn the place down while I'm gone."

Hannah smiled angelically. "No promises."

When there was nothing left but stalling, I got into my car and blinked back a tear or two as I waved to them both through the window. Standing arm in arm, Megan and Hannah kept waving in the rearview mirror until I pulled out of the parking lot and we couldn't see each other anymore.

Eyes on the road ahead, I took a deep breath. I guess part

of me never thought I would get this far, that'd I'd ever really find a reason to leave Denver and strike out on my own. Maplewood Creek wasn't exactly London, but I was getting closer. One giant leap on the adventure of a lifetime.

Now I just had to convince myself I wasn't terrified.

Chapter 4

Twenty minutes west of Denver, the crowded city streets gave way to suburbs, then rural valleys. Buildings and cars became scarcer as the looming snowcapped mountains filled my windshield. And with them, the rapidly greying skies of the approaching weather. Usually, I loved storms: getting cozy on the couch with hot cider and fuzzy socks, wrapping up in blankets by candlelight, eating all the ice cream in case the power went out. On the road, however, the conditions were less enchanting.

The snowstorm moved quickly, from a light dusting to huge cotton balls falling from the sky. Forceful gusts of wind blew sideways, jostling my old Subaru station wagon around on the winding highway. Ice began to harden on my windshield and several times I considered pulling over to wait out the worst of the storm, but I needed to make it to the Hawthornes' chalet tonight. Megan said Mrs. Hawthorne had been emphatic on that point.

As I dipped into the valley, tires crunching over several inches of snow and ice, my cell reception went from spotty to zero. The GPS map on my phone no longer pretended to know where I was and I almost missed the exit for Maplewood Creek. I made a last-second lane change into a wall of solid white that completely obscured the road signs.

I had hoped the valley might provide some measure of cover from the storm. Instead, the mountains seemed only to create a tunnel effect that channeled the worst of the weather straight on top of me. I'd lived my whole life in Colorado and was no stranger to blizzards, but this one had me white-knuckling the steering wheel.

My attention flicked between the windshield and the clock on the dash. Keen to reach the chalet on time, I pushed the car faster. Probably faster than was strictly prudent. I was desperately searching for street signs, any indication I was going the right way. I was the only car on the road and that was never a good sign.

Suddenly, the car thumped. A pothole maybe. Or a curb? I gripped the wheel as the tires skidded. I was in a spin and entirely out of control, whirling in a whiteout and desperately begging not to come to a halt inside some frightened family's living room. Then, with a violent jolt, I came to a dead stop. A pile of snow collapsed onto the hood of my car. I sat there shaking a moment, adrenaline pumping through my veins, while I caught my breath.

It was just a snowdrift, I realized. Nothing catastrophic. After I gathered my wits, I very carefully put the car in reverse and gave it the slightest bit of gas, downshifting to give the wheels more torque. If I dug in too deep, I'd be sleeping in my car until a tow truck found me in the morning buried under a foot of snow.

Careful. Easy does it.

The crunch of ice cracking beneath my tires brought a massive wave of relief. I was free of the drift and back on my way. However, I didn't make it even a mile down the road before flashing red and blue lights blocked my path.

A police officer bundled up in a heavy winter coat and Day-Glo vest stepped out of his SUV and flagged me down. He hurried up to my window and I cracked it just a couple of inches.

"Sorry, ma'am. This way's closed. You're going to have to turn around."

"But I have to get up the mountain," I said. Snow blew in through my window and immediately collected on my center console, melting in the blast of the heater.

"Too dangerous. We already had to pull people out getting stuck on the way up."

Panic rose from my gut, queasy and urgent.

"You don't understand. I'm starting a new job today and I absolutely have to get to the Hawthorne chalet tonight. Please. I've got all-wheel drive. I can make it."

"I'm sorry, but I can't let you through. Even if you could climb those roads, there's abandoned cars blocking the way."

"But . . ." My mind began to spiral. I should have left sooner. I should have gotten ahead of the storm. That's what Mrs. Hawthorne would say. No excuses. If I'd been better prepared . . . "Where am I supposed to go?"

"You can find lodging in town. Just down that way. They'll get you set up for the night, and you can be on your way tomorrow after the roads are cleared. Go on now," he said, freezing and clearly annoyed to be standing outside in the middle of this storm.

The officer hurried back to his SUV and even flipped on the siren a couple of times to move me along.

Dejected, I followed his directions and took a left toward the center of town. It wasn't long before a lighted sign appeared as a beacon, mocking me in the snowy night. A B&B called The Snowdrift Inn. Fitting.

I pulled into the parking lot of the red farmhouse-style building, then dragged my suitcase through the deep snow, up to the wraparound porch and through the front door. Inside, it smelled of mulled wine and cinnamon cookies. Plaid sofas surrounded a roaring fireplace. The reception area was lit with beautiful Tiffany-style lamps on each of the tables, giving every inch of the room a soft glow.

At the reception desk, made up of an old dining room set with the hutch sitting behind a long, narrow oak table, an older Black gentleman was watching *Jeopardy* reruns on an even older television. There was nothing hi-definition about anything here. It was cozy with a capital C.

"Hello, dear. How can I help you on this extra-chilly evening?" he asked, taking the duct-taped remote and lowering the volume from rock-concert level to slightly less earsplitting.

"Hi, I'm hoping you have a room available?" I felt guilty asking. It wasn't like I'd turned up at a roadside motel. There was no reason to believe a tiny B&B would have a last-minute vacancy. "It's just for the night. The road up the mountain is blocked and I've got nowhere else to go."

"Of course," he said cheerfully. "We have a lovely single room right upstairs. It has a Jack and Jill bathroom that it shares with another single, but I haven't seen that guest since very early this morning."

"Not a problem," I told him. At this stage, I'd have been grateful if he let me sleep on one of the reception area sofas. "I'll take whatever I can get."

As soon as I was able to put my stuff down, I'd have to give Megan a call and beg her to smooth things over with Mrs. Hawthorne, who was no doubt sitting in her comfy chalet grousing about her chalet girl no-show.

"He's an old friend of the family. I suspect he spent the day on the slopes." The old man paused, glancing out the window again. "May have decided to stay at one of the cabins up there if it was too difficult to get back down."

"Thank you," I sighed, unwrapping the scarf from around my neck. "I know it's getting late, but is there anywhere I can grab dinner?"

He frowned. "I wish I knew you were coming. I would have saved our pot roast for you. It was delicious."

At that point, I felt my stomach growl. "Any chance there's something still open in this weather?"

He chuckled, a low, wheezy bark that reminded me of a cartoon cat. "We're used to this weather, dear. Around here, we're always open."

My stomach erupted in another loud growl.

"Two buildings down," he said, pointing in the general direction. "There's a bar called The Foggy Goggle. Get a burger. You won't regret it."

"Thanks, uh, Mr . . .?"

"Wagner. Peter Wagner." He handed me a room key. "But you can call me Pops. Everyone in Maplewood Creek does."

"Alright. Thanks, Pops. I'll see you in the morning, then."

"Breakfast is between eight and ten."

Inside my room, the radiator groaned to life as I shrugged off my snow-covered coat. The mattress sagged when I flopped onto it. I pulled out my phone and tried several times to call or text Megan, but nothing was getting through. When I tried her on the room's landline, it went to voicemail.

"Megan, hey, it's Elle. I'm stuck in town. The road is blocked, and I can't get up the mountain. I'm staying the night at The Snowdrift Inn. This is the number to reach me. Cell reception in the valley is shit. Hopefully I still have a job, but I'll wait to hear from you if I should just turn around tomorrow and come on home. Call me back when you get this. I'm running out to get some dinner, but I'll be back soon."

At least the room was comfortable. Not overly polished, modern or elaborate, but I immediately felt right at home. There was a small electric fireplace in the corner, with various ornaments and a stack of books positioned on the mantle.

I decided to wash up, then pop out for an hour to eat, yawning as I got up to head to the adjoining bathroom.

There was a double vanity in there, with two sinks. On the right side, I saw a mess of men's grooming products, with the caps scattered and white foam overflowing from the can of shaving cream. There were tiny hairs in the sink and the electric-blue remnants of toothpaste around the drain. The idea to tame the mess might have briefly flitted through my head if I hadn't been so hungry. I got a little chaotic when I hadn't eaten.

After a quick freshen up, I headed back out into the snow.

The Foggy Goggle wasn't unlike many Denver bars. A large stone fireplace occupied most of one wall. A live band played on a small stage at the far end of the room. It wasn't crowded, but there was enough of a buzz to make it lively.

Sidling up to the bar, I eased onto a stool near the roaring fire, letting the chatter, rock music, and clinking glasses wash over me. I wasn't sure how much free time I would have to spend in town, if by some miracle I still had a job tomorrow, but this place would be on the list to revisit.

"Hey there, what can I get started for you?" the bartender asked, handing over a food menu. "We've got a great mulled cider. It's got a real kick to it, but ideal for this weather."

"Oh, that sounds perfect. And Pops at The Snowdrift suggested a burger. Which one would you recommend?"

He smiled. "Any allergies?"

I shook my head.

"In that case, one Greek burger coming up. Lamb, tzatziki, and feta. It's outstanding."

My mouth watered at the thought. After putting in my order, he stepped away, tending to the other patrons. I passed the time nervously awaiting a ping from Megan as I watched the signal bars jump from zero to two and back again. When my food arrived, I pocketed my phone and dug in like I hadn't eaten in days.

"How is everything?" the bartender asked, smiling at the animal way I attacked the burger.

"So good," I mumbled with a full mouth, hand covering my face.

He laughed and refilled my water glass. "Another cider?"

What the hell. For better or worse, I was stuck here, and I

suppose I was already preparing myself for bad news. If this was the last time I was ever in Maplewood Creek, I had better make the most of it.

"Hit me," I said.

After demolishing the burger, and most of my second drink, I turned on my stool to watch the band play a little. That was when I noticed him. He was playing pool and chatting animatedly with some other people in the billiards area. Every few minutes, he would send a furtive glance my way, just a subtle tilt of his head in my direction. I thought at first it was my imagination, or he was just waiting on a long-overdue drink from the bartender. I'd never been quick on the uptake when it came to deciphering signals from guys.

Case in point, it was Hannah who had to tell me when the hot UPS guy was interested. Apparently, when a guy came into the coffee shop every day "to use the bathroom" it was code for he liked the girl behind the counter. Meanwhile, I'd just thought he had a weak bladder.

Two ciders in, I was feeling pretty relaxed. Maybe too relaxed, considering my life's ambition might've already slipped through my fingers, ripped away by a poorly timed blizzard. Mr. Pool Player, with his dark blond, tousled hair and piercing eyes, fully captured my attention. Leaning against the billiards table, he rolled up his flannel sleeves to reveal strong, muscular forearms. I watched the way he lined up a shot, sliding the cue through long fingers.

Was it warm in here?

Like he could hear my thoughts shouting at him from across the room, his eyes found mine once more. His lips curled into the slightest smile. He took his shot and missed, laughing at himself while his buddies ribbed him and ordered him to the bar for another round. Empties in hand, he sauntered toward me with the slow, practiced stride of a man who was skilled at bar-flirting.

"Who's winning?" I asked when he came to stand beside me.

Casually, he leaned on the bar. "Let's say, me."

He flashed another smile that brought out two deep dimples in his cheeks. I guessed that he was just a few years older than me, with the first hints of laugh lines around his mouth. What struck me most, though, was his eyes. Light brown with flecks of black peppered around the center. The kind of eyes that held on and didn't let go.

"Let's say," I repeated, smitten with the sight of him. As eye candy went, the guy ticked all the boxes.

"Mind if I join you?"

"Go for it," I replied, gesturing to the stool beside me. "I'm Eleanor."

I held out my hand for him to shake and he took it firmly. A good sign. I hated when men limp-wristed me, like I was a delicate flower they might crush. To me, a good handshake was as sure a sign of things to come as the bread in a restaurant. Because crappy bread never failed to predict a disappointing meal.

"Funny," he said, holding on to my hand just a second longer than necessary. "You don't *look* like an Eleanor."

"What does an Eleanor look like exactly?"

"Well, *my* Eleanor, I call her Nan, she's about five feet, zero inches, and feisty. Shocking white hair and drinks like a fish. She also has a tendency of pinching my cheeks so hard that I look like I'm wearing makeup."

"So, I have the same name as your grandmother," I said, narrowing my eyes as I bit back a grin.

He opened his mouth and snapped it shut again, bashful. "You know what? Forget I said that. Let's start over." He held out his hand to shake mine again. "Hi, I'm Charles. I'd love to buy you a drink."

"Well, Charles, I'm Eleanor. Which is a perfectly fine name. And I'm already on my second cider, but if you insist . . ."

The bartender was quick on the turnaround and already had one on deck for me. We were becoming fast friends.

"So, now that we're acquainted," Charles said, "what brings you to Maplewood Creek?"

"Work. Theoretically. If I'm not fired already."

His brow furrowed with concern. "Why's that?"

Sipping my drink, I waved off the question. "Nothing. No point dwelling on it."

I didn't want to be a buzzkill. Whatever happened with the Hawthornes tomorrow, it was out of my control. I'd only tie myself in knots worrying about it now.

"What about you?" I asked.

"I guess you could say I'm in the family business."

"Ooh," I hummed. "Mysterious. Care to elaborate?"

Charles shrugged. "I promise it would be terribly boring."

"Ah, well. Then don't." I clinked my glass to his and took another gulp.

The cider really was very good. I was relaxed now, as our banter all but erased dread of Megan's phone call. Almost.

"So, this job you probably don't have in the morning," he said.

"Cheffing for a family on the mountain." Because under no circumstances would I be adopting the title of chalet girl.

"A private chef?" He sat up straighter and played at smoothing the creases of his shirt. "Very fancy."

I laughed, a little embarrassed. "Stop."

He had tall-man confidence, which was good, to a point. It was surprisingly difficult to find a guy at the optimal height. I was on the taller side myself, so guys shorter than me often got a complex about it. And guys taller than me tended toward arrogance. Neither was attractive. Charles, so far, was edging toward the Goldilocks zone.

"I've always wanted to learn to cook," he said.

"What's stopping you? Even cavemen mastered the basics."

"Suppose I'm just unusually unteachable." The corner of his mouth turned up in a self-deprecating smirk. "Except for macaroni and cheese. It's the one thing I can competently manage."

"You can tell a lot about a person by their signature dish," I told him.

"Yeah? What does mine say?"

I took another swig of my drink and shook my head. "Let's say . . . it's stalwart. Conventional, but in a comforting way. If also a little bad for you."

"Huh." He finished his beer and held up his hand to the bartender for another. "You got all that from mac and cheese?"

I shrugged. "Off the top of my head."

"Alright, let me give it a try." He furrowed his brow, concentrating, as he motioned for me to lob him the pitch. "What's yours?"

"Osso buco."

35

He rubbed his chin, seeming to think on it a good long while, until he threw up his hands and admitted, "Yeah, I don't even know what that is."

"It's an Italian dish. Veal shanks braised with white wine and vegetables. Usually served over something like risotto or polenta."

His brows perked up. "Okay, that sounds amazing. You'll have to make it for me sometime."

"Oh yeah?" I said over the rim of my drink. "Angling for a second date already?"

Charles winked. "I like my chances."

"What if I said that now I'm completely turned off?"

His smile widened, full of perfect white teeth.

"I'd say, don't write me off before you've tried my mac and cheese."

We talked for nearly two hours, about everything, anything, and nothing at all. Our conversation was effortless. And as we sat there, his body gradually slid closer to mine, our knees touching between our stools, his hand finding reasons to brush my arm or graze my leg. Our faces grew closer and closer until barely a cocktail napkin could fit between us. The whole room seemed to shimmer.

"I suppose you're staying nearby?" he said.

Maybe it was the drinks, or the way his navy flannel fit perfectly over his broad shoulders, but as the bar began to thin out and edged toward closing time, part of me desperately wanted to take him up on the implied invitation.

"I am," I said, glancing at the clock on my phone. "And I'd better get back. One way or another, I have an early morning."

Whether I would be meeting my new employers or making the long drive back to Denver, I had to get some sleep tonight.

"Just a nightcap then?" He gave my knee a playful squeeze and held up his hand to the bartender for the check.

"I really wish I could." I put some money down on the bar and slid my jacket on. "It was very nice talking to you. You don't know how much I needed the company."

"Can I at least walk you home?" he offered, frowning at the cash on the bar as he stood.

"Trust me," I said. "You did everything right. And under normal circumstances, I might even let you *carry* me home."

I reached up on my toes to give him a kiss on the cheek. When I did, he gently wrapped his arms around my waist and held on.

"No pressure, but I'd at least like to get your number," he whispered in my ear. "Let me call you tomorrow. Breakfast."

By now, I was used to letting men go where dating was concerned. Work always came first. I had no time to go out with the girls to the bar, no time to date, dashing from one shift at the coffee shop to another catering gig. Shower, sleep, rinse and repeat, from sunup to sundown. I found it was easier to keep most people—and especially guys—at a distance when I knew I couldn't make myself available. I suppose I'd gotten comfortable with deprivation.

"It was great to meet you, Charles." I slipped out of his grasp and headed for the door.

Someday, when I had my feet under me, I'd date to my heart's content and find someone great. Bring home a charming man with come-hither eyes. Meeting a great guy at the wrong time meant he wasn't Mr. Right.

Outside, the snow had finally stopped. It had left several inches of perfect, undisturbed powder that blanketed the quaint town and created mounds on top of buried cars. The icy crystals sparkled beneath twinkling lights, and a clear sky of infinite stars.

Back at The Snowdrift Inn, the reception desk was vacant and most of the lights downstairs were off, except for a few strategically placed lamps to light the way upstairs. In my room, I peeled off my clothes and headed to the bathroom to jump in the shower. I put on my pajamas and brushed my teeth. As I rubbed in some body lotion, I heard the door to the next room open and shut, and the sounds of someone rustling around on their side of the wall.

I hurried to finish up in the bathroom and was reaching for the handle on my side of the room, just as my neighbor opened the door on theirs.

"Well . . ." Charles wore a loose T-shirt and plaid pajama bottoms that hung low on his narrow hips. "I think this is a sign, don't you?"

His eyes smoldered, his smile all mischief and desire.

"This just isn't fair," I sighed, utterly defeated.

"Technically," he said, "you followed me. I'm pretty sure I checked in first."

"Guess you've got me there."

One-night stands weren't usually my thing, but there was something about Charles. I didn't know what. An easy, undeniable gravity that pulled me in from across the room. Like the second I got trapped in this town, I was helpless to escape him.

"So . . ." He leaned over me until I was pressed against the doorframe. "What do we do about this?"

It felt like he could sense my stomach doing flips, nervous acrobatics while he sat in the audience, smirking with a box of popcorn. It almost made me hate him a little. Because I didn't like feeling out of control, and this guy was making me want to do all kinds of things against my better judgment.

I tried for aloof. "Oh, I'm done in the restroom, so it's all yours."

Charles chuckled. "How about a game?"

"A game?" I snorted. "I think it's a little late for Scrabble."

His mouth pulled into a teasing smirk. "I was thinking more like cards."

"You want to play cards?" I repeated, incredulous. "It's like, 2 a.m."

"Come on. One game? Maybe I'll even let you win."

I scoffed. "Let me? What would I win?"

His grin grew wider. "Lady's choice."

I could feel any remaining self-control slipping away. Maybe this was the perfect opportunity for some fun, two people just passing through, never to cross paths again. Clean. Simple.

"Alright," I said, pulse thrumming. "But you have to call me Elle."

I'm not sure which one of us leaned in first, but our lips finally met right there in the bathroom doorway. His kiss was gentle as he cupped the side of my face, then combed his fingers through my hair. I lifted slightly on my toes and wound my arms around his neck, liking the way we fit together in this moment, made all the more romantic by the spontaneity. The recklessness. I wasn't thinking, just reacting to him and the way my body swayed in his direction.

Charles pulled back then, resting his forehead against mine as we stood in the soft glow of the bathroom light. I glanced up into his shimmering eyes as his lips pulled into a slight smirk.

"Huh," he said.

"Huh?"

His smile drew wider. "Yeah."

I shoved playfully at his chest. "What's that supposed to mean?"

Charles shrugged. "It means forget the cards. Let me try that again."

With both hands, he pulled my hips against his. When his lips met mine again, they were hungry, our breathing becoming deep and rushed. I pulled us toward my room as we fumbled through the doorway, each step increasing my impatience. Maybe it was those mulled ciders, or just the way he smelled, but I felt my entire body flush with urgency. And as his mouth became more forceful against mine, I knew he felt the same need.

Charles walked me toward the bed, where I crawled backward to the headboard. He sat back on his heels a moment and pulled his shirt over his head. His smooth, chiseled chest heaved with each breath. My eyes wandered down his abs to the drawstring tied at the top of his pajama pants as he leaned over me, parting my legs.

"Your eyes have a little green in them," he whispered, pressing his forehead to mine.

It was the strangest thing to say, and yet somehow romantic. Disarming. I rarely felt so seen by another person.

As our tongues met, I untied his drawstring then dragged

my hands over his abs, skimming soft skin and the firm ridges of his muscles.

His lips explored my neck, my chest, as I melted into his touch and surrendered to the moment. I let him lift my T-shirt over my head and watched his eyes sweep over my naked form. His gaze was admiring, almost reverent.

"You're staring," I said, excited and still a little nervous.

"Can you blame me? You're gorgeous."

Again, our mouths met, and I had the oddest sense of familiarity with him. The way our tongues anticipated each other wasn't like two strangers, but lovers reunited. He hitched my leg up around his hips and pressed himself between my legs, letting me feel his erection. My head sunk deeper into the feathery pillows while my hands learned the ways his muscles flexed in his back. I felt his heart beating against my chest like an echo.

His warm mouth left mine to seek my breasts, palming one in his hand while his tongue teased the other. He took his time to stir my nerves into a frenzy of anticipation, while I clung on to anything I could find. His shoulders. His hair. Hands fumbling for purchase to steady myself, like going over the peak of a rollercoaster. Weightless.

When Charles raised his head from my chest, I tried to coax his lips back to mine. Instead, he slid lower, kissing between my breasts. He slowly grazed his mouth down my stomach, peppering the heated, sensitive skin with gentle kisses until he glanced up at me for confirmation, before hooking two fingers into the waistband of my underwear to pull it free of my legs.

I watched as he spread open my knees to settle between

them, kissing a line down each thigh before meeting my center with his tongue. My eyes drifted shut while my hands clutched at the sheets and my hips rolled to meet every movement of his mouth. In those moments, I forgot myself entirely. For the first time in ages, nothing else mattered. Not London or ACE. Not my dwindling bank account. Least of all the job I may not even have tomorrow. I was entirely consumed with Charles, with how he lured my body closer to ecstasy.

And when I couldn't wait any longer, I pushed his pajama pants down to free him from the fabric, too impossibly turned on not to have him inside me. I took his hand, sucking one finger, then placing him between my legs to feel me. Charles groaned against my lips, moving his hand up and down softly and steadily. Then, when I bit his lip, he found my entrance and pushed forward, setting my body on fire.

Chapter 5

I jolted awake with the sunrise. Already I'd slept later than usual, and now I glanced over my shoulder to find a naked man nestled snugly under the covers beside me, sleepy bed hair falling over his forehead. Somehow, he was even more handsome this way. His eyes were closed, lips lightly parted, chest rising and falling with gentle breaths. But I couldn't linger over the image. No matter how much I wanted to snuggle up under the sheets with him.

Grabbing my T-shirt off the floor, I scrambled out of bed and hunted for my phone. The screen lit up with a dozen texts and missed calls that had come in last night once I finally got cell reception again.

Megan: Don't worry, I'm on it.

Megan: Glad you're safe.

Megan: Update. Hawthornes are also delayed en route due to the storm.

Megan: They won't arrive at the chalet until afternoon, pending road conditions. Family will want lunch waiting.

Megan: You can use the gate code to enter the property. Text me in the morning to let me know you're alive.

Megan had sent over a code for the gate and a note that the property manager would meet me there. I was so relieved that I sunk to the floor at the foot of the bed and curled into a ball for a quick stress cry before I hauled myself up and into the shower.

Charles didn't stir while I brushed my teeth and got dressed. I packed up my clothes and texted Megan to say that I'd got her messages and would be on my way as soon as I confirmed the roads were open.

"Hey," Charles mumbled suddenly, sheets rustling as he sat up against the headboard. "Going somewhere?"

"Heading downstairs to ask if the roads are open yet. Stay as long as you need."

He scratched at his scalp and rubbed the sleep from his eyes. "Suppose I can head on back to my room."

Charles squinted against the glare of the sun reflecting off the freshly fallen snow. He turned his head, groaning.

"Sorry to take off. Turns out I'm not fired, so I've still got a chance to get my shit together before I screw this up."

I'd always said you learn a lot about a person by how they

handle a hangover. There were the hair-of-the-dog types, who woke up nursing a Bloody Mary. Or the well-prepared ones, with Advil and water ready at the bedside. Personally, I prided myself on the mind-over-matter approach. If I didn't mind the headache and slightly queasy stomach, it didn't matter. I simply never had the luxury to wallow in bed.

"I'm happy for you." Charles dragged himself out of bed, pulling on his bottoms commando-style. "Suppose that means you'll be sticking around for a while."

"Yeah, but assuming you are too, let's not make it awkward," I said, shamelessly memorizing the planes of his bare chest as the hazy images of last night tumbled around in my head. "I'm going to be working a ton and this . . ." I gestured between us. "Isn't really part of the plan. So, let's not make it a thing."

"A thing?" He watched me from the edge of the bed as I gathered my stuff and shrugged on my jacket. "Surely you must clock out at some point."

"Not sure I ever learned how." I paused to give him a reassuring smile. "This was fun. You're wonderful. But you've got a face I could get used to, and I don't see how I'd have time for that. It's a distraction I can't afford."

He nodded, thinking on that. "You find me distracting."

"Big time."

"I could work on that," he offered. "Being less distracting. You'd be amazed how growing up in my family has trained me to blend into the background."

"I find that incredibly hard to believe," I told him frankly. "You kind of stick out in a crowd."

"I do?" he said, wincing.

"You're lousy with charisma. Filthy, really."

And tall. Devastatingly attractive. With an irresistible aura that grabbed me from across the room. All the qualities that would turn one date into constantly glancing at my phone for the next text. The next call. Leaving early and going in late. I could already envision the domino effect that would lead to professional disaster. He was trouble, no doubt about it.

"Can I at least get your number?" he asked.

Luggage in hand, I approached him at the bed and pressed my lips to his briefly before pulling away.

"We'll always have the blizzard," I told him, and marched myself out of the room before I forgot why anything else mattered.

Downstairs, a Black woman about my age stood behind the reception desk. Her nametag said Delilah and she had long blond hair fixed up in a dozen thick braids that zigzagged around her head.

"Good morning," she said cheerfully. "You're still a bit early for breakfast. If you're hungry, I can give you a recommendation in town."

"Do you know, by any chance, if the road up the mountain is clear yet?"

She nodded with a smile. "Plows went out last night after the snow tapered off. It should be open, but you'll still want to take care with the ice. Gets pretty slippery going up."

"Great. Thanks. I'll go ahead and check out now then, if that's alright."

"Of course." She prepared an invoice for me and I slid her my credit card. "How was everything?"

"Terrific." I blushed to myself, grabbing a mint from the

dish on the table. "You've got a wonderful place here. Tell Pops I said thanks again. He's a real lifesaver."

"Will do. Hope you can come back and see us again soon," she said, and handed me a paper map of the town. "Just in case. Cell reception is pretty hit and miss around here."

I gratefully pocketed the map. "No kidding."

Leaving The Snowdrift, I decided to skip breakfast and head straight to the chalet. With lunch to prepare for the Hawthornes' arrival and no idea what the state of the kitchen or provisions might be, I had to give myself all the time I could get. One benefit of being the chef: it's never too hard to scrounge for a snack.

Slowly, I hauled myself up the icy mountain. It was truly a spectacular view, climbing through the pine trees with the snow-covered valley below, the clear blue sky growing impossibly larger outside my windshield. I took it as a sign that I was out of the woods, so to speak. A new day. A little hiccup out of the way, and back on track.

The Hawthornes' chalet was known as The Viceroy, according to the additional information Megan had sent. All the estates on the mountain had similarly pretentious names, apparently. The Viceroy was on North Mountain, aka the highest peak in Maplewood Creek. It was about a forty-minute drive from The Snowdrift up to the top, then another fifteen minutes to navigate the neighborhood they were in. Gated and gorgeous, of course.

Each home I passed on the way up had a wall of windows that invited in the natural scenery. At a stop sign, I marveled at a beautiful home of stone and wood with a drastic roof angle that pitched in three places. It was angular and modern, yet somehow it still fit in with the rural atmosphere around it. My GPS alerted me that I would have to make the next turn. There, two large pillars rose up from the ground on either side. In the center was a large wrought-iron gate with a plaque that read "Vantage Summit."

Mounted to a pole was a small silver box with a keypad attached. Punching in the code that Megan had sent, I waited until the large gates swung open so I could drive inside the development. It was, for the most part, exactly like any gated community back in Denver, but the deeper into the development I traveled, the larger and more imposing the homes got. When the GPS finally alerted me to 95023 Summit Pass Road, I saw the small rural postal box ahead. Beyond that was a gravel road. I drove for five minutes before the trees thinned.

"Holy shit," I breathed, my mouth falling open at the sight of the house before me.

To call The Viceroy stunning would be a gross understatement. The entire front of the chalet was filled with at least sixty windows of every shape and size. Six massive fieldstone pillars rose up from the ground to support three full floors of rooms. It appeared that the upper two levels had balconies jutting out in the front to use, perhaps, in warmer weather, unless you were really daring and sat out in the chilly winter air.

The surrounding trees were mature, but they looked like they were strategically placed at intervals around the house, each one seemingly planted to frame the home perfectly. As I drove up, I turned into the circular driveway and around to the back of the property, where Megan had left instructions to find a pair of cottages for staff. Waiting for me was a woman in her forties. She wore jeans and a sweater, which I took to mean that the Hawthornes at least weren't overly picky about uniforms.

"Hi," I said, jumping out of my car. I met her on the cleared stone pathway to the first cottage and stuck out my hand to shake hers. "I'm Eleanor Evans. I'm the new chef. I mean, chalet girl."

She smiled tightly. "You're early. That's good. I'm Ali, the Hawthornes' house manager. Megan informed me you were also delayed by the storm last night."

"So sorry about that again," I offered, contrite.

"Not at all. I only just made it up the mountain this morning as well. I'm afraid everything is a bit behind schedule now, so we'll have to skip the full tour and take you right to the kitchen."

No time to get my bearings. Just right into the fire.

"Sounds great," I said, because today chipper was my middle name.

"You may deposit your belongings inside, then please follow me."

The cottage apartments mimicked the style of the main house, although much smaller and less ornate. I quickly dug my luggage out of the trunk and shoved everything inside the front door, without sparing even a moment to glance inside.

"This way," Ali called.

She was tall and slender, her presence made more severe by her perfect posture. Her light brown hair was pulled neatly into a French twist that I admired from behind while I scurried to keep up with her fast pace as she strode toward the main house along the stone path.

"Ordinarily, you'd enter the house through the staff

entrance from your cottage, but I'll take you around to the front door so you can get a sense of the property."

My boots crunched across the snow as I followed her toward the front door, which was at least twelve feet tall and made of a solid piece of oak. It wasn't overly polished or finished, but looked like it had been hewn from a tree and put straight onto the house with hinges.

"The Hawthornes aren't due until this afternoon," Ali said, leading us inside. "I'm here to help you get settled in. You're aware they'll require lunch when they arrive?"

"Yes," I said, following her through the grand foyer.

"Good. I hope you enjoy your work here."

"I'm looking forward to getting started," I answered, wondering how many times she had to say this exact phrase to new staff after the Hawthornes ran the others off.

Much like the exterior of the chalet, the interior was rustic yet luxurious. The walls in the entryway were a soft, buttery white, with one accent wall created entirely of fieldstone. Inset into the stone wall was a large, square window with the most breathtaking view of the Front Range of the Rockies that I had ever seen. From the ceiling hung a two-tiered, circular chandelier with horns jutting out from the top to hold the light bulbs.

We went through a door beside the massive double staircase off the entrance. It wasn't hidden, per se, but it wasn't obvious either.

"This is the easiest access point to the staff area."

"Have you worked for the Hawthorne family long?" I asked, careful to keep pace and not fall behind as Ali marched along.

"It's been nearly a decade now. I manage all of their

properties, so I come and go depending on what they need or which house has to be tended to next."

She walked me through a series of austere hallways that were solely for staff use, like the hidden tunnels of Disney World. Through here, we had access to the entire chalet for housekeeping and other duties, while remaining out of the way of guests and the family.

"What brings you to us?" Ali asked. "I understand it's your first time in this type of position?"

"It is, though I've been in catering for years and have worked in several restaurants," I said. "This is a new opportunity for me. I'm very excited to be here."

"It's not usually too busy at this property."

"Does the family have many homes?"

"A fair few, though Mr. and Mrs. Hawthorne only venture to a couple during the winter months. I believe this is Mr. Hawthorne's favorite, but Mrs. Hawthorne isn't particularly fond of it. She was a champion skier back in the day, but she hasn't strapped in for years. Ah, here we are."

Ali pushed through a pair of swinging double doors. The centerpiece of the kitchen was a large island, with a stunning marble countertop that would be perfect to roll out my croissant dough. The walls were a rich bluish-black under the pendant lights that hung above the island. My heart skipped at the gorgeous silver and black La Cornue stove and the twin walk-in fridge and freezer.

"Unfortunately, the provisioners couldn't stock the kitchen last night," Ali informed me. "So, you'll have to make do with what you can find in the pantry and freezer. After lunch, you can shop for dinner at the market in town."

My stomach hit the floor. Blood rushed out of my face while my fingers began to tingle. "You mean, th-there's no fresh produce at all?"

"I'm afraid not. Will you be able to manage?"

"Of course," I said, sounding maniacally cheerful. "No problem at all. I'll make it work. Any allergies or preferences I should be aware of?"

"No allergies. I'm sure whatever you make will be suitable."

That sounded like a trap.

Ali gave another tight smile. "Please find me if you have any questions. Otherwise, I'll leave you to it."

Alone, I sat on the edge of a counter to take several deep breaths. A full-blown panic attack threatened to erupt while I looked around at the big empty kitchen that had just become my battleground. This was real. I was here for the next three months. For better or worse.

All I had to do now was plan and prepare a perfect welcome lunch.

Chapter 6

I started with a quick inventory. The pantry had plenty of shelf-stable dry goods and canned foods. The freezer was stocked like a fallout shelter to feed a village through the apocalypse, with plenty of meat, fish, and bags of pre-diced frozen fruit and veggies. None of which would make an ideal first impression for a gourmet lunch. The high water content in frozen veggies meant everything tended to taste flat and bland, like the inside of a plastic bag. Similarly, frozen meat never achieved the right tenderness again. It affected the composition of the tissue fiber.

Then there was the refrigerator. The smell that erupted from that walk-in nearly knocked me sideways. There were pounds of spoiled produce and mold bordering on a full civilization. Nothing could happen until I cleaned out the fridge, took out the trash, washed, and sterilized the walk-in, all of which took another two hours off my prep time.

When I'd taken stock of what I had to work with, I decided the least offensive ingredients at my disposal were some frozen Yukon Gold potatoes and spinach, chicken thighs, and white rice. The pantry had panko breadcrumbs and a generous array of nuts and spices. The best way to redeem a frozen protein was to deep-fry it. To me, that said one thing: chicken katsu with massaman curry over rice, with spinach and potatoes. Because when all else fails, throw copious amounts of seasoning at it, blend and pray.

It was a humble dish. Certainly not what I'd envisioned serving to the family for their first meal. And there was a voice screaming in the back of my head that I might be making a terrible mistake. But I didn't have time to hear it. Not over the louder sound of the clock ticking like my heart banging in my chest. There just wasn't time for second-guessing. I needed to pick a direction and go with it.

Strangely, as I pulled my ingredients together and got some pans heating on the stove, the apprehension and anxiety started to melt away. The first thing was to get my coriander and cumin seeds toasting in a pan with some peanuts. Then I ground the mixture and added it to some red curry paste. Next, I pounded out my chicken thighs and set them to marinate in a bowl with some gochujang and fish sauce. In a pan, I combined my curry paste with coconut milk, then added dried lime leaves and set it to simmer. While that bubbled away, I thought about an appetizer.

Normally, I'd serve a salad or some kind of fresh component to balance the fattiness of the curry, but my only produce came courtesy of the freezer. Then I saw the frozen peaches and raspberries. I decided on a tart peach and raspberry sorbet as a sort of palate cleanser. It was those sorts of pivots, the opportunity for creativity and improvisation, that gave me such a spark of excitement in the kitchen. It was never mundane when I was able to think on my feet and solve problems. I had stopped seeing this dinner as an emergency, but more like a game. I even found myself having fun. Because the kitchen really was my happy place. Turning disparate ingredients into a cohesive meal was my simple joy.

I brought the spinach and potatoes up to temperature in separate pans, then dried as much moisture from the greens as I could before adding them to my curry. I diced the potatoes and threw them in too, then set the rice going in the rice cooker.

Then, because I had time, I made some quick roti before dredging and breading my chicken thighs and frying them off, just as Ali returned to tell me the family had arrived and would be seated for lunch shortly. She was setting four places. I'd prepared enough for eight, just in case.

"Would you care to try some?" I offered. "I can make you a bowl."

Ali glanced back to the doorway, then lifted her chin. "Yes, alright. Thank you."

I placed rice in a bowl and ladled on the curry. Next, I seasoned and sliced the katsu chicken, placed it carefully on top and garnished with a piece of roti on the side. I handed Ali a fork at the kitchen island where she stood, and she took a tentative bite. Then another. She mixed the rice further into the sauce and stabbed a piece of chicken to get a little bit of everything in one bite.

"This is quite delicious," she said stiffly. "Very good."

I began to second-guess myself. "You don't think it's too much starch on starch? Potatoes *and* rice?"

She shook her head, dabbing at the corner of her mouth to

wipe away some stray curry. "Not at all. Good for this sort of weather. And it balances the heat of the sauce."

I smiled. That had been the idea. Always better to err on the side of caution, when I still didn't know the family's tolerance for spicy food.

"I'll just finish this," she said, hugging the bowl close to her. "If you don't mind."

"Not at all. I'm going to start plating."

I'd always found food to be the great icebreaker. With any luck, it would work on the Hawthornes as well.

On the kitchen island, I set out four bowls on top of plates, and filled each with the rice, curry, and sliced chicken topping. Then I folded pieces of roti to set on each plate beside the curry. Just as I did so, two more staff members I hadn't even known were in the house entered the kitchen.

"Are they seated?" Ali asked.

A young man, barely in his twenties, nodded, so I went ahead and prepared a quenelle of sorbet on a porcelain soup spoon for each diner.

"For regular service, the waitstaff will run the plates," Ali explained to me.

"In that case, these go out first," I told the guy and girl, pointing them to the sorbet spoons.

They each took two and left the kitchen.

"I'll have you join us with the main course to briefly explain the dish," Ali said to me.

"Is there time to freshen up before I meet them?" I glanced at my reflection in the stainless steel door of the freezer. "I look hideous."

My hair was a frizzy mess and I had curry splatters on

my jeans. Not the best first impression to make on my new employers.

Ali gave me an appraising glance and barely concealed her grimace. "You'll be fine. Keep your words brief and to the point. Mrs. Hawthorne hates rambling. And speak up. No muttering. Other than that . . ." She grabbed a napkin and wiped a spot of bright orange curry from my cheek. "You'll be fine."

Every time she said *fine*, I felt my knees buckle.

A couple of minutes later, the waitstaff returned with the empty sorbet spoons. That was our cue.

Ali set her bowl aside and quickly dabbed her face with a paper towel, straightening her posture as she took two bowls of curry. I followed her with the other two, back through the staff corridor to the formal dining room, where the rustic decor continued. The main feature of the room was a solid oak table that might've come from the brother of the tree that gave up the front door. At the far end of the table, an older man with graying hair, who I took to be Mr. Hawthorne, sat at the head in a green quarter-zip sweater over an Oxford shirt. He had a friendly smile that lit up at the arrival of the main course.

"Well, doesn't that smell great!" he said, watching us enter.

Ali set a bowl in front of Mr. Hawthorne as I placed one in front of his wife at the opposite end of the table.

"Curry?" Mrs. Hawthorne was in her early sixties, an immaculately polished, blonde woman in a black turtleneck with piercing blue eyes and an angular face. She glanced down her nose at the food and sniffed.

I wasn't sure how to interpret the reaction, except that a

bubble formed in my throat and I suddenly had the uncontrollable urge to cough. Which is just about the worst first impression you can make at a meal service.

"Remember that lamb curry we had in Amsterdam last year," Mr. Hawthorne said. "Incredible."

"I remember you spent the whole trip in the hotel room with a terrible flu," his wife remarked flatly.

"Yes, but the lamb curry made the trip worth it," he answered with a laugh.

I held my breath as I set a plate in front of the younger blonde at the table, perhaps in her thirties, with her hair in perfect ski-bunny curls. Their daughter, if the family features were any tell. She wore a white, long-sleeved cashmere crop top with matching leggings and had her face buried in her phone, thumbs moving furiously over the screen.

"Dad always gets sick when we travel," she said. "I told you to drink more green juice."

Relieved to have delivered their food safely, I glanced quickly at the fourth member of the party and nearly passed out then and there. The bowl wobbled loudly on the plate as I let go. Because seated directly across from the daughter was a thirty-something man with dark blond hair and two dimples that froze mid-smile and faltered as our eyes met across the dinner table.

"Why does the color have anything to do with it?" Mr. Hawthorne joked, earning an eyeroll from his daughter.

Finally, Ali's eyes sought mine and widened, urging me to get on with it.

"Y-you have a massaman curry," I told the table, voice

trembling. I cleared my throat, but nothing would dislodge the boulder that was growing larger just behind my tongue.

Charles's eyes locked with mine in a brief moment of mutual horror before we both quickly looked away. I felt the blood drain from my face. My vision went blurry and a loud ringing filled my ears.

"Um . . . served over white rice with, uh, spinach and potato," I fumbled to continue nervously. "On top is gochujang-marinated chicken katsu."

"Please enjoy," Ali said, her expression urging me to back the hell away from the table so the daughter could pick up her utensils without me practically standing in her curry.

As delicately as possible, I bolted out of the dining room and practically sprinted to the kitchen. Ali entered a moment later, her face puzzled.

"What's wrong? I thought everything turned out quite well, considering."

"Who is that other man in there?" I asked very quietly, like they might have the kitchen bugged.

Her brow furrowed. "Charles Hawthorne. Why do you ask?"

Because I was utter toast.

Chapter 7

"I don't know why I expected the Hawthorne children to be, you know, kids," I lied, scrambling to disguise my embarrassment.

It wasn't a great cover, but Ali seemed satisfied. Or at least disinterested in the monumental meltdown that was currently underway inside my head.

"As it stands, the family will take some time after lunch to rest and settle in. Dinner is tentatively set for eight this evening," she told me, returning to finish the last of her lunch still waiting on the counter. "That should give you ample time to shop in town for any provisions you'll require."

"Great," I said, only half hearing while I piled pans in the sink to begin washing up.

My head was like a subway station of panic, train cars darting back and forth with new thoughts of existential dread every few seconds. I thought about how I might accomplish entirely avoiding face time with the family for the next three months. Becoming a kitchen hermit that only traversed the darkened halls of the staff quarters in the dead of night. The Phantom of the Chalet.

A mask wasn't a bad idea, actually. Maybe cut and dye my hair. Get a disfiguring face tattoo.

"First, after we've cleared lunch, you'll meet with Mrs. Hawthorne."

Great.

So, after I'd scrubbed the kitchen from top to bottom, Ali escorted me to an office that smelled of leather and cedar. Floor-to-ceiling bookshelves lined the walls. In the center was an enormous mahogany desk polished to a mirror shine. I was left to wait in a wingback chair for a few minutes, wallowing in dread that at any moment Charles would walk in to corner me.

What would I say to him? Would he tell his family he'd nailed the help last night? How long before the rest of the staff knew about it? And where were they hiding the additional employees that seemed to appear like Oompa-Loompas from hidden doorways?

Mrs. Hawthorne strode in with the brusque efficiency of a downhill slalom skier.

"Hello," I said, standing to attention like I thought I'd woken up in boot camp. "I'm Eleanor Evans. Elle, if you prefer."

She took a seat behind the desk with a curt nod, her ocean-blue eyes staring fixedly at me.

"Thank you for taking the time to meet with me," I said.

Mrs. Hawthorne arched one perfectly sculpted brow. "Your firm highly recommended you. Ms. Wheelan seemed to suggest that you were almost too qualified for such a position."

Megan must've given them the hard sell to get me this gig. Maybe pumped me up a little too much.

"I have a diverse background of experience to offer," I told her, attempting to skate around what felt like a trap she'd set for me. "I assure you, I'm grateful to be here."

Her lips remained thinned to a sharp line. "We expect a strong work ethic from our staff, Miss Evans."

"Absolutely," I agreed. "I've never been afraid of hard work."

"Good." She nodded tightly. "Now, let's discuss lunch today."

I swallowed hard, bracing myself.

"While your flavors were pleasing, I expect a more polished and elevated presentation in the future. You have fine dining experience, correct?"

"I do," I answered, trying not to sound wounded, even as her words stung me right in the chest. I would've loved to put out something fancier, but I had been working with limited ingredients. I wondered whether Mrs. Hawthorne was aware of that fact.

"Then let's aim to show it. We always have room to improve. I trust you'll continue to challenge yourself to do so while you're here."

"Of course." My smile was forced, while her expression remained indifferent. "You'll get my very best moving forward."

"I'm sure."

Mrs. Hawthorne clearly wasn't the type to hand out idle praise, though she at least seemed satisfied that I wasn't a complete disaster. If only because she wasn't privy to what I got up to with her son last night. Or that he was propositioning women in his pajamas at 2 a.m. But I digressed.

"Your role as our chalet girl will include managing the

kitchen, preparing our meals, catering events, and ensuring the chalet remains well stocked and organized at all times. We will have guests on occasion, and you'll be expected to accommodate their needs as well. This is not a nine-to-five position, you understand. Flexibility is key."

"Understood," I replied quickly, meeting Mrs. Hawthorne's gaze. "I'm prepared for that."

"Ali will go over rules and procedures with you, but there is one point I must stress. Our family values discretion, Miss Evans."

Her voice turned sincere. The hardness in her eyes faltered somewhat. This was personal to her.

"Our privacy is precious," she said. "I have zero tolerance for gossip."

I found the statement oddly comforting. Maybe it was wishful thinking, but perhaps my secret was safe too. I wouldn't be the chalet girl with the scarlet letter. It was flimsy reassurance, but enough to unclench my muscles for now.

"Yes, ma'am."

With that, her tone became brisk once more. "We've had several chalet girls over the years, and few have remained through the season. I do hope you last longer than they did."

I lifted my chin. One thing working in restaurant kitchens had taught me was to show backbone. Head chefs pounced on weakness. Show the slightest crack and they would hammer you until you broke. But make yourself impenetrable and you'd earn their respect.

"I always honor my commitments, Mrs. Hawthorne. This job is important to me."

"And why is that?" Mrs. Hawthorne asked, narrowing her eyes.

"I was recently accepted to the Academy of Culinary Excellence in London to continue my training. It's a very prestigious school, with only a small percentage of students accepted each year. This job will allow me the financial security I need to attend."

Something flickered in Mrs. Hawthorne's expression— approval, perhaps—but it was gone as quickly as it came.

"Then I wish you luck," she said simply. "We look forward to seeing what you prepare for dinner."

Ali came to collect me once Mrs. Hawthorne had left. As interviews went, I suppose it wasn't so bad. Megan had warned me the family could be difficult, but so far, I'd seen much worse. Excluding the one glaring issue of my late-night antics with Charles last night.

We reconvened in the kitchen to plan for dinner. Ali informed me that the family would expect a coursed, plated meal with dessert. They were not great fans of family style service, so it was best to avoid that entirely. Otherwise, there were no allergies or dietary requirements to be aware of.

"I've included a credit card you can use for anything you require and a map of good places in town to shop," she told me, sliding a large manila envelope across the island to me. It was heavy and stuffed with several bulky items. "The marketplace includes several local producers, so I'd suggest you start there, but feel free to use your discretion."

"Perfect, thank you."

"There is a staff vehicle in bay three of the garage for official use. Keys are in the envelope as well. If you run into any problems, my number is already programmed into your staff phone. Remember, dinner is at eight."

For the last two days, getting to this house had been my top priority. Now, knowing Charles was lurking somewhere inside it, I couldn't wait to leave. A trip to town was a welcome excuse to get a little distance.

Chapter 8

When I opened the garage door to bay three, I nearly dropped the envelope. A shiny black Land Rover stood waiting to tear up the mountain roads. I launched myself at it like a girl reunited with her childhood pony, sunk into the supple leather seat and turned on the butt heater. Man, it even smelled better than normal cars. Rich and new, a huge upgrade from my battered old station wagon.

After taking a minute to figure out the onboard navigation system, I plugged in the address for the marketplace and let the pleasant noise of the GPS over the speakers guide me away from The Viceroy. The artificial voice sounded like the leading man from a British rom-com, and for a few miles I imagined how some hilarious Hollywood hijinks might ensue from the disaster of my blizzard-based one-night stand.

If only life were so easily resolved with a little comic relief and well-timed scene cuts.

In town, the square buzzed with activity from the small boutiques and bustling cafes. With my window down slightly, the crisp winter air carried the scent of roasted chestnuts from a corner store that had an outdoor stove set up on the sidewalk. A young family played in the snow nearby, their toddler wobbling about in a thick, puffy jacket as the dad coaxed them to build a tiny snowman.

Several signs along the busy street guided the way to the marketplace, eventually leading me to a parking lot in front of a picture-perfect red barn with white gingerbread trim. I wasn't sure what I had expected to find inside, but I was utterly charmed by the layout of more than a dozen stalls, like an indoor farmers' market, selling everything from fresh produce and local honey to baked goods and artisanal olive oil. All of the stalls were outfitted with seasonal decor and trays of free samples to entice the strolling shoppers.

A young man in a suede apron and flannel shirt handed me a canvas tote as I walked inside. I shivered slightly at the cold and wrapped my scarf tighter around my neck. This was truly a repurposed barn, totally at the mercy of the elements. A few tall heaters like those you'd find on any Denver restaurant patio were spaced along the wide aisle between the stalls, but any warmth they provided quickly rose into the tall rafters above, where exposed beams looked nearly as old as the majestic mountain range outside.

Yet the weather clearly didn't deter any patrons. The market was thrumming with activity, kids clamoring around the candy stall and moms sipping tiny plastic glasses of red wine next door.

I decided my first order of business was to track down some hot chocolate and a snack, as I saw several people carrying steaming paper cups and pastries wrapped in wax paper. Following my nose led me to a stall decked out in a gingerbread house motif. Display cases made of old wooden crates were filled with gingerbread men and women wrapped in snowflake-print plastic with curly red ribbons, and there was even a caramel fountain, where the young lady behind the counter dipped apples for waiting children.

"What can I get you?" she asked, flipping the dangling bell of her elf hat behind her ear.

"A hot cocoa and, um, a gingerbread man, I guess."

"The best in the Rockies," she said, like I needed convincing.

"Better give me two then."

I brought my treats to a picnic table decorated with holly and potted poinsettias, where I sat to watch the bustling market and listen to the hum of Christmas music filling the air. It was the reset I needed, sipping the rich, chocolatey cocoa adorned with one giant homemade marshmallow, and nibbling on the fragrantly sweet and spicy arm of a gingerbread man. It had been a stressful morning, and the dressing-down by Mrs. Hawthorne after lunch had left my confidence a bit shaken. At least she hadn't mentioned Charles. Every time his name popped into my head, my stomach twisted again.

No. For as long as it took me to enjoy my snack, I would forget about him. And the family. Just enjoy the scenery, and think about putting together the perfect dinner for tonight. This was my chance to show off a little. And produce-shopping was one of my favorite parts.

So, when I'd finished my drink and tucked my second gingerbread cookie into my tote for later, I began my stroll through the stalls to find inspiration for tonight.

"Try a sample," a vendor called to me. "Best apples in the county."

Well, that got my attention. I approached the woman with curly red hair at the first stall and gladly accepted a slice from among the bushels of bright, shiny red apples. There were soil-dusted potatoes, verdant cucumbers, ruby beets, and plump tomatoes still sprinkled with drops of morning dew.

"We grow everything right here in Maplewood Creek," she told me. "Family owned and all organic."

She was about my age and full of animated energy, despite the persistent chill. Dressed in olive overalls and a blue peasant top, the cold seemed not to faze her one bit.

I crunched into the sweet apple slice and it burst with juicy freshness on my tongue.

"Mmm," I hummed. "Delicious. Thank you."

"Mia Grant," she said, introducing herself. "First time to Maplewood Creek?"

"Am I that obvious?" I was a Colorado native, so I didn't think I had the same blinking tourist sign above my head as the southerners who'd never seen snow or mountains before.

"It's a small town," she told me. "We tend to get a lot of regulars and I've met 'em all over the years."

"You grew up here?"

"Fourth-generation farmer," she said, nodding proudly.

"I'm Eleanor. Private chef for a family up the mountain."

"Oh," she said knowingly. Then, with a conspiratorial whisper, "Which one?"

Mrs. Hawthorne had cautioned me against gossip, but I didn't think this counted.

"The Hawthornes . . .?" I didn't know why it came out like a question. Except that maybe I was curious what her reaction might be.

"Oh, yeah," she laughed. "They're a lot."

Mia certainly wasn't shy.

"I only just started today." And as first impressions went, I'd call it a mixed bag.

"As just about anyone in town will tell you, Caroline rules the roost. And her husband, Benedict, well, he works eighty hours a week to get away from her. At least, that's what everyone says. Amelia is not-so-slowly turning into her mother. And Charles . . ." She shrugged as my ears perked up. "I haven't seen him in years. Close to a decade, I think. No one has."

"Really?" Strange. I'd seen him just last night, looking not at all shy in public.

Then again, if he'd been away so long, it was possible people didn't recognize him. Who I took for friends of his around the pool table might just have been new acquaintances.

"Last I heard," Mia said, "he was living in Denver, being rich and fabulous and running the family company, though Benedict is still the face of it."

I wasn't exactly up on the society pages in Denver, so I wasn't surprised I'd never heard of him. It's not like we were running in similar social circles.

"But then, that sort of tracks for Charles," she mused to herself. "He's never been a high-profile kind of guy. More behind the scenes of the Hawthorne empire. His parents and sister have always been the ones that thrive in the public eye."

"You must know them pretty well." I helped myself to one more apple slice as I glanced over Mia's produce and started making menu lists in my head.

Her lips thinned, nostrils flaring. "As well as anyone, I suppose." Then Mia changed the subject, perking up again. "Are you hunting for anything specific today?"

"A little of everything," I said. "Stocking up, really. Thought I'd see what was available and hopefully get some inspiration. I do make a gourmet ratatouille that I'd love to serve later this week."

Her face brightened with an excited smile. "Our eggplants will blow your mind."

Mia fixed me up with several bags of produce, containing all kinds of fruits, vegetables, and herbs. Everything I'd need to get through the next few days.

"What else can I help you find? I'll point you to the good stuff," she said with a wink.

A breeze brought the scent of nutty cheese to my nostrils from somewhere in the marketplace. "I'm not sure yet, but cheese always calls my name."

Mia laughed softly. "A woman after my own heart. I know just the place. My friend Agnes has a cheese shop a few stalls over. Let me show you."

Mia put a "back in five minutes" sign out on her display table and beckoned me to follow her to an eclectic little stall of mismatched odds and ends: dozens of small tea plates in all patterns and colors, a few chalkboards with handwriting in upper and lowercase letters that looked a bit like ransom notes from a serial killer, and bright primary-colored, large-bulb Christmas lights, mixed with tiny multi-colored ones that could have been from St. Patrick's Day.

"Mia!" The merry-looking older woman behind the counter waved us over. She had a riot of greying curls and wore Doc Martens splattered in paint. "Who's your friend?"

"Aggie, this is Eleanor. She's got a company credit card and I told her you could help her do some damage."

She laughed, wiping her hands on the apron over her ample chest. "I think I can manage that. What's your poison?"

"I could use the staples, and maybe a few adventurous options as well."

Aggie snapped her fingers, smiling. "I like your style. We can definitely do adventurous. Give me a sec."

She folded together a small white box from a flat piece of cardboard, and began filling it with a collection of supple, colorful, and fragrant cheeses.

"This. Looks. Divine." I took the proffered box, laughing to myself at the hand-drawn label that affixed the lid. It looked like a child's drawing of a goat with wings.

"Your shop's name is Praise Cheesus?"

She nodded proudly. "It is. My daddy was a minister, and while I'm not entirely religious, he sure is and he named the shop. I love it, and people remember it."

"Brilliant. That's good branding." I grabbed a toothpick of blue cheese from the sample tray and took a bite. My eyes closed and I groaned happily. "This is amazing. What's your secret?"

Mia chuckled, leaning against the stall. "Don't get her started. You'll be here all day."

"You know, Mia," Aggie began, pulling Mia and me closer to the stall so she could whisper, "I was planning to come find you later. The market's been buzzing with a bit of gossip you might find interesting."

Mia raised an eyebrow, her curiosity piqued. "Oh? Do tell."

"Word is Charles Hawthorne is back in town," Aggie said.

"Well, you're looking at their new chef," Mia said, deflecting her surprise. "What do you say, Elle? Seen him skulking about that massive house yet?"

I smiled nervously, face flushing red. "It's only my first day. I wouldn't even know what he looked like."

"His family's been keeping quiet about it," Aggie interjected. "But people are talking."

Mia shrugged. "I'll believe it when I see it."

"Why is it a big deal that he's back?" I asked, flummoxed by their interest. "Is there something I should know?"

Aggie smirked. "You could say he has a reputation. Or, well, he did. Been a while now, I suppose. People change."

Mia scoffed. "Do they?"

Their exchange made me wary. It was fine that I didn't know anything about this guy when he was just a one-night stand from a bar. Now, I worried I'd tangled myself in a larger web that would soon make me the target of small-town gossip, and threaten my already tenuous grip on my current employment.

"What sort of reputation?" I insisted, almost afraid to hear the answer.

Aggie's eyes sparkled with curiosity. "Maybe you'll find out firsthand. You will be in the thick of it up there."

"Me?" I shook my head. "I'm not getting involved. I'll be keeping my head down and my ears closed."

Mia crossed her arms, leaning against the counter. "Charles Hawthorne, back in Maplewood Creek. Never thought I'd see the day."

Chapter 9

Back at the chalet, I stocked the kitchen with the new provisions, then spent a few minutes planning my dinner menu. Though I had been able to score some veal shanks from the local butcher, I thought twice about serving my osso buco after mentioning it to Charles last night. It felt somehow like a confession. As if putting that meal out would alert the whole family to my sordid little secret. A completely irrational thought, I knew. Still, it gave me the ick.

Instead, I'd do a different version of it, with braised short ribs over polenta and an olive and herb gremolata. I'd pair that with a simple warm salad of local winter vegetables to start, then finish off the meal with my Earl Grey tiramisu. Which meant I had to get my short ribs braising now.

I set to work, giving the short ribs a quick, hard sear, then adding them to a Dutch oven with a dry red wine and vegetables, while I ducked back out to my cottage to take a shower and change for dinner service. It was the first chance I'd had to investigate my new digs for the next three months. Assuming Charles didn't have me dismissed by his mother before then. Imagine his mortification at his blizzard bar-hookup sticking around like a bad rash for the whole ski season. How uncouth of me.

I might've saved him the trouble, only I needed this job more than I valued my pride. So, I decided the plan was to lay low. Make myself invisible, as he'd once said. Blend into the background and let him forget we'd ever met.

A wreath of holly with a red bow adorned the front door as I let myself inside the cottage and pushed my bags clear of the front door. I was impressed with the attention to detail for something that wasn't part of the main house. It was a one-story, ranch-style building, with a small front porch that was artfully decorated. The entryway held a small half-moon table, with a tiny bowl on top for keys or change. A free-standing coat tree was just beside the door. Tossing my coat on it, I stepped out of my boots and wandered farther inside.

It was an open-concept space with every modern amenity I could have possibly needed. A pine garland decorated the mantel over the fireplace, where a stack of firewood was provided. There were cozy knit blankets artfully draped over the sofa and fuzzy pillows I couldn't wait to fall into. The kitchen was stark white and not too big. It was the perfect size for this space, and just for me. Custom windows framed the view of the snowcapped Rockies on one side and the main house on the other. The colors in the bedroom were a cozy and inviting shade of blue, and I felt instantly at peace in the space, despite the pressure and tension waiting for me in pretty much every other area of The Viceroy.

After I was cleaned up and dressed, I took a minute to call Megan.

"You made it!" she exclaimed when she answered. "I was worried the fire department would be digging you out of the snow on the side of the highway."

"For a minute there, I was too."

"So, how is it? Gorgeous, I bet. I suppose you've met the family by now. How are they?"

Oh, yeah. We'd met.

"So far, so good," I told her brightly.

Because Megan had done me a huge favor getting this job. I wasn't about to complain and throw it back in her face. It was my own dumb fault for not getting the full picture, or even a surname, before I spent the night with the handsome stranger from the bar. I wouldn't be making that mistake again.

"Oh, I'm so glad. I know I warned you that Mrs. Hawthorne can be a little intimidating, but you're more than up to the task."

"No sweat," I said. "Anyway, I just wanted to say thank you again. I'll make you and Hannah proud."

"You always do, Elle."

That little reassurance from home put an immediate smile on my face. It was the extra boost I needed to remember that this wasn't the end of the world. Most of the time there would be no need for me to interact heavily with the family. I could stick to the kitchen and let the waitstaff run the plates. And when I did need something, there was Ali and Mrs. Hawthorne. A whole hierarchy before I'd have any good reason to run into Charles again.

I was about to head out when there was a light knock at the door. I quickly buttoned my black chef's coat and pulled my hair back into a ponytail before answering. Amelia stood on the doorstep in a thick, cream cable-knit sweater and matching leggings with a headband that held her short, bouncy blond curls away from her face.

"Hi," I said, a little surprised and perhaps grateful it wasn't her brother coming to hunt me down. "I was just changing for dinner. Is there something you need?"

"Oh, no, nothing urgent," she hurried to say, smiling kindly. "I'm sorry to bother you, I just wanted to see whether next time you were in town, I could request a few things for the kitchen."

"Of course." I stepped back from the door to invite her in. "I'd be happy to pick up whatever you need."

It honestly made my job easier when the client told me exactly what they wanted. The less guessing I did, the happier we'd all be.

"Please, have a seat." I led us to the kitchen table. "Can I get you a tea or coffee?"

It was sort of habit to offer, but I quickly realized I hadn't even considered stocking my own kitchen yet. I wasn't sure if there was anything in the cabinets.

"Oh, no, that's sweet. I'm okay. I don't want to take up too much of your time. I know you're busy," Amelia said, pulling a piece of family stationery from her pocket, where I could see she'd jotted down a list in neat handwriting.

"It's just a few things you can only get in town, and I always crave them when we visit. One of them is a strange request, but The Snowdrift Inn makes these special cookies. I don't know what they do to them, but they're amazing and they won't ship them, no matter how much you pay. Trust me, I've tried. I even offered to send a private jet once," she said, laughing at her own audacity. "They drive a real hard bargain over there."

I amused myself picturing Pops and Delilah in the kitchen, dosing some Pillsbury cookies with THC or just straight, uncut cocaine.

"No problem at all. I think I can manage that."

"So, how are you settling in?" she asked. "Is the hot water working okay? Sometimes they forget to turn the water heater on in these cottages."

I was more than a little taken aback at Amelia. She wasn't at all what I expected. Not that I'd had much to go on, other than first impressions at lunch and Mia's brief comments at the marketplace. I suppose I'd assumed she would take after her mother, two imposing figures that could make a polar bear shiver.

"Everything's perfect, thank you."

"So, is this your first time as a private chef?"

Was it that apparent? I felt self-conscious, wondering what faux pas had given me away. And how many more I'd make before I caught on to the cultural cues.

"It is. So I'll happily take all the feedback I can get," I offered.

Her answering smile gave me some small encouragement.

"Despite the impression I'm sure my mother's given you, you're doing great so far."

She was probably just being nice, but I appreciated the effort either way.

"I hope you'll come to consider yourself part of our family," she said. "I know, maybe that sounds naive or disingenuous when you're paid to be here. I really mean it, though. When you live with people, share a home with them every day, it's more than just a job, right? We have to commit to a level of trust that goes both ways."

Amelia had her own intensity, I began to understand. Different from her mother's, and just as potent. The overwhelming friendliness was a lot, but it covered a deeper sincerity.

"Family is everything," she said. "We take care of one another. So, I hope you know you can always come to me if you need something or there's a problem. And I'll ask you to give us the same respect."

"Of course," I told her soberly.

"Great," she said, standing. "I won't keep you then. Thank you . . ." She held out her hand to shake.

"Eleanor."

"Great to meet you, Eleanor. Welcome to the team."

Once Amelia left, it was time to check in on my short ribs. They were looking good, so I got to steeping the tea. Earl Grey was a delicate flavor, so I needed a lot of it to break through the sweetness of ladyfingers and mascarpone cream. Next, I ground more of the loose tea in a spice mill and whipped it into a bowl with eggs, salt, and sugar over a double boiler. I then set that aside to work on my mascarpone cream, combining chilled heavy cream with mascarpone, salt, sugar, and vanilla bean. When that was nice and fluffy, I folded in the Earl Grey egg mixture and put the whole thing in the fridge. By then it was time to pour my tea into a wide dish, to add some Grand Marnier, then toss the whole thing into the blast chiller to cool it down.

I was about to get started on the warm winter salad when I turned from the stove to find someone sneaking up behind me.

"Oh my God," I breathed, startled, clutching a rag to my chest. "I didn't hear you come in."

Mr. Hawthorne went to the refrigerator and pulled out a bottle of orange juice. "Don't mind me. Anytime we travel, I always feel like I'm getting sick. I'm trying to knock it out before it takes hold."

"I could make you some fresh-squeezed," I offered. It felt like bad form to have the client hunting around in the kitchen for what they wanted.

Mr. Hawthorne waved me off. "I'm not even here. You didn't see me."

"Alright. But while you're not here, are there any special requests for upcoming meals? I'm happy to make anything you like."

He looked taken aback by my question. "I'm not sure anyone has ever asked me that before. Caroline usually handles all the menus. I had a heart attack a few years ago, so she's keen for me to eat healthier, but I refuse to go on some kind of miserable, restrictive diet."

Shit. I thought about the fried chicken, red meat, and copious amounts of butter I was serving this man. That was all I needed. Bang the son and kill the father. What sort of messed up version of fuck, marry, kill was I perpetuating on this family?

"I can try to make you healthier versions of your favorites, if you want. It's no trouble."

Mr. Hawthorne gave me a noncommittal nod as he poured himself a glass of juice. He gulped it down, then poured another.

"I do love a good banana bread," he said after a moment. "See what you can do with that."

He took the second glass of juice with him and left. I decided that Mr. Hawthorne was a bit aloof, but friendly. Clearly Mrs. Hawthorne was the hard-ass of the family. So, it was her I'd endeavor to impress.

That meant not screwing up this polenta. The trick was constant stirring. Aggressive, obsessive stirring. After my salad and gremolata were prepped, my ladyfingers were soaked, and my tiramisu was setting up in the fridge, I poured all my attention into babying that polenta into the perfect creamy base for the short ribs.

At quarter to eight, Ali entered the kitchen. I decided changing for dinner had been a good move on my part when she showed up in a crisp, black button-down shirt, black trousers, and leather loafers.

"The family is starting to gather for drinks," she informed me. "How are you doing on time?"

"Right on schedule."

I pulled out my short ribs to rest and dressed the warm salad. The dessert needed all the time it could get to set up, so I'd portion it once they started clearing the main course. And because I always made extra, I quickly fixed Ali a plate with a little of everything on it.

"Let me know if you think it needs salt," I offered.

She didn't need to know that this was my way of winning her favor. Plus, I was now mortally terrified of inducing a heart attack in Mr. Hawthorne by oversalting my dishes.

Ali grabbed a fork and dug in.

"Oh, this meat is so tender," she said, watching it crumble under her fork.

"Thank you."

She hummed and fanned her mouth, the food still very hot.

"The seasoning is perfect," she said, swallowing. "Don't touch a thing."

With that, I began plating. The salad first, which the wait-staff came to collect. And while the family ate that, I composed a creamy pool of polenta with short rib in the center and a generous heaping of gremolata.

"Would you like to introduce the main course again?" Ali asked when they came back to collect the next course.

"No, I don't think so. I need to portion out the tiramisu. Better if I hang back," I said.

Thankfully, she didn't object. So, after dessert was served and dinner concluded, I sighed with relief that I'd made it a whole meal without another run-in with the Prodigal Son.

Maybe this wouldn't be so hard after all.

Chapter 10

Breakfast the next morning wasn't until 8 a.m., which was sleeping in for me. I was up at six to shower and dress, then make myself some coffee and toast in the primary kitchen, since I had failed to stock my own. I knew there was a staff meeting at eight too, which Ali had said I wasn't required to attend, so while I was making breakfast for the Hawthornes, I whipped up a simple spread for the crew too. Ali arrived first.

"You're early," she said, walking in with a clipboard. "Excellent."

"I wasn't sure if I'm supposed to serve staff meals as well," I told her, pouring her a cup of coffee.

"No, it's not necessary." She helped herself to some toast and jam with a few pieces of fruit. "Though if you did, I'm certain no one would complain. It's been a long time since we've had anyone on a consistent basis in your position."

Ali sipped her coffee at the island. While she mostly had a stringently professional demeanor, I sensed food was the key to her candor.

"While I'm waiting on the others," she said, "I'll go ahead

and let you know the family is out of the house all day and will return later for dinner."

Ali handed me a few sheets of paper, which outlined the family's schedule for the week; who would be in the house and for which meals. Also, if anyone would be with them as a guest.

"This week won't be too busy. Mr. Hawthorne is traveling and Mrs. Hawthorne often goes with him. Amelia and Charles will only be here sporadically, but it's best to have something prepped for them at all times, particularly for Amelia when she comes home. There's usually a guest or two with her when she is here."

"Understood," I said, taking the sheets of paper.

"Your first event will be in two weeks. The Hawthornes throw an annual Thanksgiving dinner that's become famous. Mrs. Hawthorne will need to approve your menu. Your budget is listed on the next page there, plus a few suggestions based on the guests. Can you start drafting a menu?"

My stomach flipped. "Yes. I'll get going right away."

"Good." She nodded tightly. "Oh, and for Amelia tonight, she often likes some late-night charcuterie to nibble on when she's entertaining."

"No problem." I pulled a pen from my white daytime chef's coat and made a note on one of the pages Ali gave me. "I can handle that."

"I'm not sure if you've had a chance to walk the property yet, but Amelia stays in one of the outbuildings."

"Does she come here for her snacks, or do we deliver to her house?"

Ali popped a grape in her mouth, shaking her head. "You

don't have to worry about that. Someone from the house staff will deliver whatever she asks for."

Seemed simple enough. And with the whole day to prepare for dinner, I decided some grocery shopping of my own was in order.

As I washed up our coffee cups, several more staff members entered to marvel at the food waiting for them. They dug in before Ali ushered them all out to the hallway to start their meeting.

It was an odd dynamic, not really interacting with, or even formally introducing myself to, the rest of the team. I wondered if that was a product of them all expecting me to run back down the mountain screaming, as my predecessors had done. No point making friends if they didn't think I'd stick around. Though what I'd seen of the family so far didn't send up especially red warning flags.

Well, the obvious notwithstanding.

Perhaps I was missing something, or the faint whistling in the distance was the other shoe about to drop, but I was feeling encouraged that I could make this gig work. Charles was nowhere to be seen. And it was only three months after all. I could do that standing on my head.

When the kitchen was spotless again, I went to my cottage to change back into regular clothes, then hopped in the Land Rover for a trip into town. Savoring the luxury of the heated seat, I sat for a while and aimlessly scrolled through Instagram. Many of my friends from Escoffier had been in the private chef business for a few years now and my feed was filled with generic posts of pretty food in immaculate kitchens. The content was simple, following their daily lives as chefs in these beautiful high-end spaces. A former classmate had already amassed over 20,000 followers with content that I, too, could easily post.

Admiring the snow glistening in the ethereal morning light, I thought *why not?*

Playing with the settings a little to get that edgy look to the photo, I snapped a few shots of the stunning view, making sure not to get any buildings that could identify exactly where I was, other than it was clearly the Rocky Mountains.

I thought about Mrs. Hawthorne's warning. Surely she wouldn't be thrilled with me posting publicly from their property? They had gates and thick garden walls for a reason, after all. To be safe, I needed to edit my profile name and location so that I could have been any private chef in any part of Colorado. I looked around for inspiration, and spied a pair of skis leaning against one of the garage doors.

"The ski chef, the slope chef, the chalet chef," I mused aloud to myself.

Ugh. Garbage.

But then I glanced at the shopping list I'd jotted down on the papers Ali gave me. Brie was top of the list because, according to Ali, Mrs. Hawthorne loved it, and I thought it would be a nice way to butter her up. If that was at all possible.

Glancing back up at the skis, I had a sudden moment of inspiration. Après Brie?

I searched the silly play on words on Instagram. Nothing popped up, so I quickly changed my username to @ApresBrie. It wasn't like I had any followers who would notice. I hardly ever posted.

Uploading the mountain-scenery photo, I added the

customary excessive number of hashtags to try to get noticed. Later, I would take a few foodie photos, and maybe stitch together a video from dinner prep that creatively cropped out any evidence of whose kitchen I was cooking in. It would be my little secret. An outlet to share what I was doing with the protection of anonymity. After all, if I ever wanted to go into business for myself, I had to get used to a little self-promotion. Baby steps.

My first stop was The Snowdrift Inn to ask about Amelia's cookies. Inside, the foyer smelled like bacon and French toast. Everything was now decorated for the season, with autumn leaves and little porcelain turkey figurines dotted around. Garlands draped with twinkling lights lined the banister and mantel over the fireplace.

"You're back," Pops said, cheerfully approaching the reception desk. "Good to see you again."

"Good morning. You've certainly been busy."

He grinned proudly. "Well, I try to get things started a little at a time leading up to the holidays. I'm not as young as I used to be, and it takes me quite a while to get all the decorations up."

"Doesn't anyone help you?" I asked.

He nodded. "Oh, yes. Don't worry about me. But I try to pull my weight. I'm not too old." He said the last sentence a bit louder than the rest, as if trying to ensure someone other than me heard it.

"You're young at heart, but I'm not letting you on the ladders anymore." Delilah came down the stairs, toting a heavy pipe wrench.

"Hi again," I said, waving.

She gave me an oddly puzzled look as she went to duck behind the reception desk for something.

"We met yesterday morning when I was checking out," I reminded her.

"Oh," she said knowingly, smirking at Pops. "That was Delilah. My twin sister. I'm Bea. Nice to meet you."

"My granddaughters," Pops told me proudly.

"Bea, we're running low on soy milk." Delilah—for real this time, I hoped—entered from around the corner. "These guests are drinking a ton of it." She noticed me and nodded warmly. "Oh, hi. You're back."

Identical twins. I was a bit whiplashed.

"What can we do for you?" Pops asked.

"Well, apparently you have rare and highly coveted cookies. I've been sent to acquire them by any means necessary."

Bea rolled her eyes. "Let me guess. You're working for the Hawthornes."

"Wow," I said with a chuckle. "That is a very good guess."

"Amelia," Delilah said, looking slightly annoyed. "She's got a problem."

"Apparently," I admitted. "You'd really be helping me out though, if I could get some for her."

"Oh, go on," Pops told the girls, chiding their sour expressions. "What's one more batch?"

"I've got a toilet to fix." Bea took her wrench and hurried back upstairs.

Delilah huffed. "Fine," she said to her grandfather. "But I don't want to see you outside on that ladder again."

"I'm just using the step stool to do the front windows." Pops pulled a cardboard box from behind the reception desk.

"No way," she argued, grabbing the box. "Give me those. It's too icy out there for that. You'll break your neck. Go see if you can scrounge up some more non-dairy milk for the vegans. They're getting cranky in there."

"Oh, now you're the boss, I see." Pops lifted his chin, sauntering away from the desk. "Telling me what to do like I ain't been running this place since before your mama was born," he muttered to himself as he left the room, playfully affronted.

"Guess he's not ready to give up the garland just yet," I said to Delilah.

She sighed, shaking her head. "He will sulk a little, but eventually he'll remember that we're just trying to keep him safe. He had a bad fall a few years back. Maybe we're a little overprotective."

"He's fortunate to have family who look out for him," I told her.

I knew exactly how difficult it was to take on that caretaker role. And how frustrating it could be when they didn't always want the help. My mom had been fiercely independent. She hated being waited on. Sometimes I'd find her in the kitchen in the middle of the night, burners going and everything, because it was the only time I wasn't there to tell her to sit back down and let me do it. She couldn't stand letting go of that autonomy.

"Yeah," Delilah scoffed. "Try telling him that."

"So, what else have you got in there?" I asked, nodding at the box of decorations.

"These are our sprinkles," she replied, plucking a small bow out of the box. They were in every size from teeny-tiny that could have fit on the end of a pencil, to a few that were large enough to fit on a front door or the top of a tree.

"Sprinkles?" I questioned, running my fingers over the soft velvet.

"My nan used to say that nothing was finished until it had sprinkles on it. Need to decorate the tree? Add sprinkles. Garland? Sprinkles. They could be anything from bows to ribbon to small jingle bells. It didn't matter during the holidays, as long as every square inch of available space was covered and beautiful. If it was coated in glitter too, even better."

Pops stood in the doorway again, with a wistful and misty look in his eye. If I had to wager, I would have guessed that Nan was Pops's wife. "Delilah and Bea agree with me that in November we will always start decorating. As soon as Halloween is over and pumpkins are stored away, we move on to generic autumn, with a smidge of Christmas decorations, before going the whole hog starting December first."

"I really want to see what 'the whole hog' entails," I admitted. "Sounds like my kind of decorations."

Pops beamed. "You'll have a lot of opportunities to see the decorations. The whole town has a competition every year, and the Lifties vote for their favorites. The winner receives a trophy, but it's the bragging rights that we all want."

"Lifties?" I asked, confused.

Delilah rolled her eyes, just as Bea came back down the stairs.

"It's the term the lifers in town use for the tourists," she said, coming over to stand beside Pops. Though she looked identical to her sister, I noticed that Bea carried herself differently. She was a little more abrupt, dressed simply and practically in a denim shirt and brown leather boots. She also had a nose ring, which I filed away for identifying her easily in future. "Because they come for skiing and then leave. Get it?"

"Like chair lifts," I said, catching on.

"Pops here . . ." Bea put her arm around his shoulder and squeezed, "was born and raised in Maplewood Creek, so he's a lifer."

He nodded. "Yes, ma'am. I met my wife here fifty-seven years ago at Christmastime. She was a Liftie and she fell in love with the town."

Delilah looked affronted. "You mean, with you. She fell in love with you."

She was obviously the romantic of the sisters, bundled up in an oversized sweater and sporting carefully applied lip gloss and eyeshadow.

"Eventually," Pops said with a wink. "Girls, that's a story for another day. Say, Elle. While you're here, stay for some breakfast."

"Oh, no, I couldn't bother you. I've got some errands to run anyway."

Pops scoffed. "You've got to wait for your cookies anyway. It's no trouble at all. You paid for a room, remember. That comes with a breakfast."

Well, he had a point. I never argued with an elder.

He led me into a lovely dining area that was probably once a living room that they had converted into a breakfast or dinner nook for guests. A large window overlooked the main street of Maplewood Creek and highlighted the beautiful mountain view. The space itself was another cozy, well-appointed room, with a fireplace along one wall that was surrounded by bookshelves full of framed pictures, novels and knickknacks.

My stomach rumbled. That toast and coffee now felt like a very long time ago.

"I'll be right back with a special treat," Pops said, beaming. "Sweet and salty should do the trick."

He pulled out a chair for me at a four-person table near the fireplace. Right behind him, Delilah picked up the coffee pot from the sideboard and brought it over.

"So, Elle. Why Maplewood Creek?" she asked.

"It was sort of a spur-of-the-moment thing," I said, sipping the coffee.

It was delicious. Weird to say, given my previous employer, but I wasn't much of a coffee person. I consumed it mostly for utilitarian purposes, rather than enjoyment. But this was actually . . . incredible. Maybe there was something to that cocaine theory.

"I was accepted to culinary school in London, so I'm saving up to cover tuition and living expenses. A friend of mine found the job for me."

"First time working for the Hawthornes, then." Bea set a plate in front of me. "Here you go. Snowbird Special."

The breakfast consisted of a single perfectly fried egg, two triangles of whole wheat toast with jelly and butter, three slices of bacon, and a silver-dollar-sized pancake with a drizzle of syrup. Adorable, and exactly what I wanted.

"Do you know the Hawthornes well?" I asked the twins. "I get the impression they're sort of infamous around here."

They shared a knowing glance. "You could say that."

"Amelia's mostly okay," Bea elaborated. "As long as you don't get on her bad side."

"I've only talked to her once." I wondered what the bad side looked like. If she was anything like her mother, it must be formidable. "She seems nice enough."

Again, they eyed each other, silently speaking in twin language.

"Yeah," Delilah said.

Bea shrugged. "Nice."

"And Charles hasn't been around in ages, so of course the rumor mill is working overtime now that he's back," Delilah added unprompted.

"Why's that?" I asked, then instantly regretted it, wondering if the question made me sound too curious.

"Charlie gets a bad rap and small towns have long memories," Bea answered. "Personally, I think people talk when they're bored and more of them should learn to mind their business. Anyway, the Hawthorne grandparents and Pops go way back. Good people."

There was something more to it, but they wouldn't elaborate. Which was probably for the best. Gossip clause and all that.

Chapter 11

Given my conversation with Mr. Hawthorne, I decided dinner tonight required something lighter. I picked up some gorgeous rainbow trout in town, and prepared it with a lobster broth, topped with poached lobster, capers, parsley, and lemon zest. I threw together a crisp arugula salad with a citrusy vinaigrette to start, then finished with a classic crème brûlée.

The bonus of being alone in the kitchen meant I was able to create some content for my new Après Brie account. People on the foodie side of Instagram went crazy for an artsy picture, so I paid special attention to the perfect lighting and background, opting for a close-up on the marble island. Not enough to reveal anything identifiable about the kitchen, but very upscale.

"They're very happy in there," Ali told me after supervising delivery of their dessert to the table.

I wiped up a few spills from the counter while she dug back into her fish, still waiting, half-eaten, on the island. It had become our routine.

"Great. Glad they like it." I began collecting pans to wash in the sink.

Doing dishes was my meditation. Simple, mindless work that let my brain wander. My cool-down time.

"Oh, by the way," Ali said, still eating on her feet. I wondered if she slept standing up on a charging station as well. "Charles requested to meet with you."

I dropped a sauté pan and it clattered in the sink, splashing me with lobster broth.

"What?" I said, alarmed. My pulse instantly started racing. "Charles, why?"

"He didn't say." She was fully consumed in her meal.

"When?" I wiped broth off my face with a paper towel.

"I suppose after dinner. He said he'd come find you."

Good luck with that, I thought to myself.

As soon as the waitstaff came back with the dessert plates, I was furiously washing and scrubbing to get the kitchen spotless before Charles could track me down. With dinner done, I would be off the clock and could make myself scarce. If he thought I couldn't hide from him, he was sorely mistaken.

"Are you alright?" Ali asked as I grabbed her plate and utensils out from under her the second every last bite was gone. I must've looked a little manic.

"Of course," I said, taking them to the sink. "Fantastic."

She gave me a troubled glance, then decided it wasn't her problem. "Alright. Good night."

After Ali left, I wiped down that kitchen like someone was chasing me, then practically sprinted back to my cottage. I planned to shower, then make myself a grilled cheese and soup, but first I tossed myself onto the couch to rest a minute. I shut my eyes.

My phone buzzed in my pocket, the gentle vibration waking me from a nap I hadn't realized I needed. When I glanced at the clock, it was nearly 11.30 p.m.

> **Ali:** Don't forget charcuterie for Amelia and her guests tonight.

Holy shit.

I jumped off the couch. In my rush to leave the house before Charles could track me down, I'd totally forgotten to prep Amelia's late-night snack.

I dashed back to the kitchen and pulled out all the necessary components to throw together a charcuterie board that, hopefully, didn't look like it was composed at the last minute. Having no idea what time Amelia would be back, I simply worked as quickly as I could.

Around midnight, I heard the back door outside the kitchen open and shut, and the rustling sounds of someone discarding their jacket on the hook and kicking their boots off in the mudroom. Just before their shadow crept beneath the door, I placed the last bunch of grapes on the plate.

"Oh, you're up late." Amelia paused in the doorway, wearing just a pair of yoga pants and a baggy sweater. Her short blond hair was pulled up in a bouncy ponytail. "I thought I was being sneaky."

"Your charcuterie is ready. I would've sent it out to you," I said apologetically. Surely it was not a good look for the client to come hunting for their order. "Was no one around?"

"Oh, no." Her expression turned regretful. "Our plans changed and I came home early. I didn't even think to say something. And you went to all this effort. I'm so sorry."

It was slightly annoying, but that was the nature of the job. What did Mrs. Hawthorne say? Be flexible. I couldn't expect the family to run like a restaurant.

"No trouble," I lied. "Can I get you anything else?"

Her smile turned shy. "I was sort of hoping there might be a sweet treat lying around?"

As luck would have it, I'd picked up some muffins at the marketplace this afternoon. I planned to bake for breakfast most days, but it was always good to have a backup.

"Blueberry or coffee crumble?"

Amelia's ocean-blue eyes, just like her mother's, perked up with delight. "Blueberry."

I walked to the pantry and pulled two out. "Toasted?"

"Toasted?" she asked, baffled.

"It's my favorite way to have them."

I pulled out a frying pan and got to work. I scooped butter into the warmed pan, sliced the muffins and proceeded to place the halves into the melted butter. The sweet, fruity scent filled the kitchen. When they were golden brown, I plated the halves and pushed it toward her.

"Enjoy."

Amelia inhaled deeply before blowing on the muffin and taking a generous bite. She hummed at the taste and fanned her mouth as she chewed. I went to the fridge and poured her a glass of milk.

"You're right," she said after a sip. "This is the only way to eat a muffin."

I thought she might take her snack with her, but instead she remained at the counter, eating leisurely.

"I hope I didn't ruin your breakfast plans," Amelia said, nodding at the half-empty box of muffins.

"I've got lots of options. Any special requests?"

"Chocolate croissants are my absolute favorite," she said. "But that's probably a huge imposition."

"Absolutely not," I told her stupidly.

I didn't know why those words flew out of my mouth. I guess it was my instinct to say yes. The client is always right and whatnot. But croissants were hugely labor-intensive. I'd be up all night.

"Charles loves them too," she said, picking another bite off her muffin to pop in her mouth. "We used to eat our weight in them on vacation when we were kids. But he hasn't been up here with the family in ages. I think it'd really make his day."

Her voice turned wistful. Her eyes were a bit sad, even as she spoke of him fondly. I got the impression she'd missed her brother. And it meant a lot to Amelia that he felt welcome.

Maybe it was because Amelia had been so kind to me, but it suddenly became important to me, too.

"Do you see him often?" I asked, taking the frying pan to the sink to wash up.

She shrugged. "Not as much as I'd like. I spend most of the year in LA or New York and Charlie's in Denver. He likes to make himself scarce, you know."

I didn't, but I couldn't deny I was interested.

"Do you always get together for the holidays?"

"The family has been coming up here forever. Since back when my grandparents had a place here. My mom first learned to ski on this mountain." She laughed to herself, a memory forming behind her eyes. "When we were little, we'd spend the whole season building this massive snow fort. And inevitably Charles's friends would be goofing off, and would end up destroying it. Taking turns sledding down the hill to smash into it. Then he'd be up first thing in the morning rebuilding it for us."

"Sounds nice," I said.

"Charles, though . . ." Her voice drifted off as I glanced back from the sink to look at her. "I don't know. Grew out of it, I guess."

"I can't imagine outgrowing a place like this," I said. As far as I could tell, it was perfect. "Did something happen?"

I regretted the question as soon as I asked it.

Amelia's expression turned guarded. "No, nothing in particular. Anyway, I should get some sleep, it's late."

She abruptly finished her milk and picked up her plate to leave. I'd overstepped, and now it was awkward. Nice as Amelia was, we weren't friends. She was, by extension, my employer. A certain professional distance was required.

Still, I didn't have time to linger on it. I'd promised Amelia croissants. So, I put on a pot of coffee and pulled a bag of flour from the pantry to get to work. This was about to be a long night.

Chapter 12

"Why. Won't. You. Rise?" I growled through gritted teeth, poking at the spoiled croissant dough with exhausted frustration.

Then, to add insult to injury, my stomach rumbled, but I had to ignore it. I was too busy prepping, and stressing. I had been at this for hours, and my normally steady hands were trembling, nerves and hunger making everything worse. I wiped a smear of flour across my forehead and blinked back tears of aggravation.

"Okay, dough. We've got one more shot at this and you can't fail me now," I said, wagging a finger at the ingredients lined up before me.

Just then, the sound of the back door opening caught my attention. It was followed by boots stomping on the tiles and I nervously looked at my watch. It was nearly 2 a.m. Who else could be lurking around at this hour?

The kitchen door swung open to reveal Charles dusting snow from his shoulders. The sight of those dimples and broad shoulders sent an immediate jolt through my body that I wasn't prepared for. Like getting smacked in the head with a staggeringly handsome snowball. Which then made me acutely aware of myself to an uncomfortable degree.

"Oh." Charles stopped short at the threshold to the kitchen. He pulled off his beanie cap and shook the frost from his hair. Flakes of snow fell to his blue flannel shirt and melted. "Hi."

"Um, hi."

We both stood there, awkward and silent like a couple of racoons caught in the porch lights while rummaging through the trash cans. And the only thing I could think was I must look horrendous right now. I was sweating, covered in egg and flour, trying my best to plaster on a neutral expression. How did one approach this encounter in a professional manner, after I'd done my best to avoid him thus far?

"I've clearly interrupted something." He glanced around at the catastrophe that had consumed the kitchen. "Or we've been robbed by the Cookie Monster."

I don't know if it was what he said that set me off, or the adorable grin that grew over his lips when he said it, but suddenly a switch flipped inside me.

"Seriously?" I scoffed at his irritatingly charming attempt at defusing the tension. Like that grin had gotten him out of plenty of trouble, and I was just another bump on the golden road that was his perfect life.

"Excuse me?" he said.

I mean, where the hell did he get off, pretending that finding each other here wasn't massively humiliating? Especially for me.

The anger bubbled up inside me, boiling over. I'd run right up on the tipping point, and it was all coming out now.

"Of course you're here right now." I wadded up the wet dough from the flour-covered island. It was useless now. "Because that's all I need."

"Rough night?" he asked, clearing his throat and rolling up his sleeves to reveal well-toned forearms.

"That's all you have to say to me?" My hands still wrist-deep in dough, I considered throwing it at him. "Unbelievable."

Charles sighed. "I suppose we're due a conversation."

"You think?" I laughed sarcastically.

He helped himself to the wine rack, pulling out a bottle of red and easily finding a bottle opener in a drawer. "To be fair, I did try to have the conversation earlier tonight, but you vanished. I was just as surprised as you were the other day. More so, maybe."

"Doubt that."

Next, he found two wine glasses and poured, placing one next to me. I left it sitting there beside my little ant hill of flour while he sipped his.

"I'm not sure why you're angry with me," he said, eyeing me flirtatiously over the rim of his glass, like we were back at The Foggy Goggle.

"Because I am," was my very mature response.

I was in no mood for his charms. Even if I couldn't stop picturing his head on the pillow beside mine. Our foreheads pressed together while his heart beat against my chest.

Damn it. Why had I picked that exact moment to become the spontaneous type?

Because I thought for sure I would never see this tiny mountain town or this gorgeous man ever again.

"Well, then how can I make amends?" Charles leaned against

the opposite side of the island from me, with those eyes like a lock-picker's kit. He'd never met a door they couldn't open. And now I sort of hated them.

"Leave Maplewood Creek and don't come back 'til I'm gone?" I offered hopefully.

"Let's put a pin in that idea."

"Then how about leaving my kitchen?"

Charles arched an eyebrow. "It's your kitchen now, huh?"

I sighed, wiping a flour-covered hand across my forehead again. "Take a look around. Do I seem a little in the shit at the moment?"

I was thoroughly exasperated. At my absolute wits' end.

Appraising me, he straightened up, concern sobering his expression. "What's the problem?"

"Amelia said you both love chocolate croissants, so I promised to have some ready for tomorrow. Only my dough isn't cooperating. I've been at this for hours and everything's gone wrong. I can't figure it out."

"What are they supposed to look like?" He inspected the wad of abused dough.

"Puffy. If you poke it with your finger, it should bounce back. I've made these dozens of times, but something's gone horribly wrong."

"You've got an altitude problem," he said.

"Are you trying to be funny?"

Charles held his hands up in surrender. "Happens all the time up here. A, uh, former employee who worked here a long time ago taught me that baking is tricky at this altitude. Less oxygen, lower air pressure. It messes with the dough."

I scoffed. "I'm from Colorado. It's never happened to me before. I make these all the time in Denver."

"We're at almost 11,000 feet above sea level," he said. "That's double that of Denver."

"Shit. You're right," I said, deflating.

I'd spent two hours killing myself over these damn croissants and it'd never occurred to me I might have to tweak the recipe. I thought exhaustion had made me delirious. I slumped against the counter.

"We can fix it," he said.

My eyes lifted to his. Something about the soft sincerity in his voice grabbed me. Like he had reached out his hand to pull me from rising waters, I could breathe again, the frustration and exhaustion dissipating with his calm encouragement.

"Yeah?" I said, enjoying his use of the word "we" far too much.

His smile was immediate. "Like you said, they're my favorite."

Smothering a grin, I swept the bad dough into the garbage.

"Okay," I breathed, trying to tamp down the giddiness that was rolling through me. "If you don't mind, I really could use the help."

"Yes, chef." He went to the sink and washed his hands, shooting me a wink over his shoulder.

"You need less yeast and more liquid," he said. "The altitude dries things out, makes them behave differently."

"I should've thought of that. I'm seriously kicking myself." I gathered another batch of ingredients to make a final attempt at this dough, then set up the stand mixer. "Croissants are a few steps more advanced than mac and cheese. Who did you say taught you how to bake?"

He had a faraway look in his eyes while he dried his hands. "A friend from a long time ago. When I was a kid. Anyway. Where do you need me?"

There was an ease to our conversation. Even the way we moved around one another in the kitchen seemed effortless. I placed the recipe in the center of the island, and we took turns adding the ingredients to the mixing bowl in order, ensuring that we cut back on the yeast and added a little more milk. In the mixer, the dough pulled away from the sides of the bowl just as it should.

"I think this one's a winner," I told him. "Thank you. I was really at the end of my rope there for a minute."

"Lucky I came along." He bumped my shoulder playfully. "What's next?"

"The fun part."

From the fridge I took several sticks of high-fat Irish butter and lined them up together between a couple of sheets of parchment paper. Then I took out a large rolling pin.

"That's not for me, is it?" He pretended to shrink away when I raised it over the island where my butter waited.

"Not unless you piss me off," I laughed.

I started beating the butter until it began to form a flat, even sheet.

"Remind me not to get on your bad side," he said, watching the slight joy I took in the noisy violence. Truthfully, I needed the catharsis.

We had to wait a while for the dough to rise and cool in

the fridge, so I took the glass of wine he'd left waiting and rewarded myself with a large gulp.

"So . . ." he said, sliding up next to me to lean back against the island. His forearm brushed mine and sent little shivers across my skin. "How are you getting on so far?"

I gave him a sideways glance. "Other than a mild pastry meltdown?"

"Other than that."

"Yeah, great," I said. "Couldn't be better."

Charles shook his head. "You've got kind of a sarcastic streak, don't you?"

"No," I said with sarcastic exaggeration.

He bit back a laugh. "Uh-huh. What else should I know about you?"

"What do you mean, what else? Like, can I juggle flaming swords and balance a poodle on my nose?"

"For starters," he said. "Sure."

I sighed and lifted myself to sit on the edge of the counter. "Well, I have a scar from the time I caught a stray hockey puck to the shin at the rec center in fifth grade. I can't stand it when people call it 'expresso.' And I have a strict rule against sleeping with my employers." I flashed an accusing smirk at Charles. "Your turn."

I wanted to ask him why his return had the whole town talking. My imagination conjured up all sorts of scenarios that could earn a handsome man like this a "reputation." Then I remembered Amelia's reaction to my prodding, and decided it was better to keep my curiosity to myself.

His brow furrowed as he nodded to himself, thinking. "Hmm. Let's see. I also have a scar and I'm not going to tell you where. I love saying 'expresso.' And in my defense, I have an otherwise spotless record with regards to inter-office liaisons."

"You think you're being funny right now, but you're not."

"Alright," he said, straightening. "Let me have it."

"How could you not have said something sooner?" I accused, my voice rising with a renewed vigor.

"Say what? We're hardly the only family on this mountain employing a private chef. How was I supposed to know?"

"Still, you could've warned me. Like, hey, I'm one of those fancy well-to-dos and wouldn't it be crazy if you were serving my meals tomorrow?"

He bowed his head, thinking on that. "I probably wouldn't have used the phrase 'fancy well-to-dos' but, alright, I see your point. Mistakes were made."

"Yeah," I scoffed. "You can say that again."

Truthfully, I wasn't even that mad at him. It was the situation that had me frustrated. And maybe my own impulsiveness a little. A split-second decision had stirred up all this trouble, when the real goal was making some money so I could get to London. I'd lost sight of that in the moment. Never again.

"I get this is really bothering you," he said gently. "I'm sorry for that. Sincerely. Tell me what I can do to fix it."

"Leave the country?" I suggested with a bitter smile.

"That's a thought. On the other hand, I could really pull a dick move and offer to buy you out of your contract. Save you the continued awkwardness."

I snorted a laugh, glancing up and double taking at his earnest eyes. "You're kidding."

He shrugged.

"Just like that. You'd write me a check."

"I mean, it sounds a little uncouth when you say it that way. But I do feel terrible it's made you uncomfortable."

For just a second, the thought was a tempting one. Take the money and run. I'd be set for ACE and wouldn't have to spend the rest of the season worried our secret would get me sent packing early if his mother found out. Yet sitting here, waiting on our dough and having a moment to talk as real people, my resentment evaporated. And I remembered why I'd dragged him back to my room that night in the first place.

"Tell you what," I said. "Just promise me you'll keep our secret, and we'll call it square."

His eyes lit up. "Yeah?"

I held up my pinky finger. "Swear?"

He hooked his pinky with mine. "Cross my heart."

At least that was one less thing I had to worry about. Now, if only I could reason with these croissants.

"What do you think about coffee?" Charles said suddenly.

"I think I'm good with the wine."

"No, I mean with me. In town."

"A date? That's a little presumptuous, don't you think? This is already a rather fragile truce."

He shrugged. "Why not?"

"You're insane."

"Try not to hold it against me," he said, smirking.

"Your mother would fire me on the spot. Not to mention it's just wholly inappropriate. I'm your employee."

"No," he said, holding up a finger. "As you said, you're my mother's employee. I'm more like an interested third party."

I scoffed, rolling my eyes. "Everything I said in the hotel room is still true. I'm working, and you're distracting."

"What if we played for it?" he said. "I'm sure I could scrounge up a deck of cards."

"Yeah, and look how that turned out last time."

He licked his lips, dragging his eyes over me. "Oh, I remember."

Heat flushed across my face and my breath caught in my throat a moment before I turned and grabbed his arm, shoving him toward the door.

"Well, thanks for your help. I think I'm all set here for now. Off you go."

He stood, dazed, at the threshold of the kitchen. "You're kicking me out of my own house?"

"Nope. Just the kitchen. Good night."

The door slammed in his face while I went to the island and gulped down the last of his wine, and mine. Every nerve in my body was buzzing. My fingertips tingled. And I desperately wished I'd never laid eyes on Charles Hawthorne.

Chapter 13

I woke the next morning to my phone's alarm, blushing at the unbidden images of Charles in my dreams, wearing nothing but smudges of dough on his face and that infuriating grin that dared me to ignore him. He'd be easier to dismiss if he were a typical entitled asshole, but so far, I'd seen only kindness and humor. Where the hell did he get off being so damn approachable anyway? It went entirely against type. Not okay.

If there was one benefit to our little cooking class last night, it did relieve some of the anxiety I'd harbored over our first awkward conversation as chef and client. Honestly, in some ways, it couldn't have gone better. But that only reinforced how much harder I'd have to work to maintain the boundary. Especially if Charles was determined to trample all over it.

Getting dressed, I pulled my black hair into a messy bun and slid on a stretchy black headband, because I hated getting hair in my face while I was working. My typical kitchen attire was my white daytime chef's coat with a simple white T-shirt underneath and a pair of jeans and sneakers. Nothing that begged male attention. Which was perfect for hiding from Charles's advances.

Much as we'd both like to pretend there was no conflict of interest here, he was off limits. And there was just no point entertaining any ideas otherwise. Like it or not, he would only be a fond blizzard memory. And a cautionary tale.

Despite only a couple of hours' sleep, I was in the kitchen to prep before seven. Mr. and Mrs. Hawthorne got in from traveling early this morning, so breakfast had been changed to brunch. I first sent the waitstaff out with fruit, bacon, and the basket of chocolate croissants, while I poached some fresh crab legs for a variation on eggs Benedict.

"These are incredible," Ali said, standing over the island to enjoy my pains au chocolat. "How on earth did you have time to make them?"

While she still carried herself like an upright rake, Ali's demeanor had softened considerably, so long as I kept her plied with food.

"I had a little help," I admitted, though she wasn't really listening.

While the crab cooked, I concentrated on my hollandaise. It was deceptively simple to make, and even easier to ruin. In a bowl, I cracked seven eggs, then processed them with an immersion blender for a couple of minutes. Next, I poured in melted butter while continuing to blend, allowing both to perfectly emulsify. The key was constant movement and not too much butter. A little this way or that, and the sauce would separate, ruining it. Then I added a pinch of salt, cayenne, and a squeeze of fresh lemon. When my crab and poached eggs were ready, I assembled everything on a warm, toasted

English muffin, doused with hollandaise, and topped with fresh microgreens and a few fried capers.

And just for good measure, I prepared Mr. Hawthorne some low-fat, low-sodium oatmeal with macerated berries and cinnamon as an option. Even if he chose not to eat it, I wanted him and his wife to know I was making the effort.

"Quickly," I told the waitstaff when they came to collect the dishes. "Don't let them get cold."

So far, feedback from the family had been sparse but largely positive. I was encouraged that it meant I hadn't managed to screw anything up yet. Not that I doubted myself, but food makes people finicky. Too hot. Too cold. Too spicy. Too bland. There were a million ways to fall just short, and far fewer to succeed. And I had to succeed.

So, following brunch, when Ali told me Mrs. Hawthorne wanted to discuss the major events that were coming up, I was hopeful I might get some sense of her satisfaction with me thus far.

"I have a friend in Denver," I told her as we sat in the office with the big, imposing desk and immaculate view of the mountains. "Megan Wheelan. She's the owner of the firm you used to hire me. I'd like to work with her to staff the events."

Mrs. Hawthorne looked over her reading glasses and leveled me with her chilling stare. "I suppose that's acceptable. Ms. Wheelan knows our requirements and already has our NDA on file. We need to have them here in time for Ali to train them. If we don't have space in the cottages, we can ask Mr. Wagner to provide rooms at The Snowdrift."

Nodding, I jotted a reminder in my notebook to contact

Bea and Delilah at the inn. Ali had warned me that Mrs. Hawthorne looked approvingly at always having something to write on in these meetings.

"This is particularly important," she stressed. "An announcement is coming soon from my husband about my son's future role in the company. These next few events *must* be perfect."

I swallowed, a nervous bubble lodging itself in my throat. "Understood, Mrs. Hawthorne. I will do my best."

"Not just your best," she insisted. "Perfection. There mustn't be any distractions."

It seemed I hadn't yet broken through Mrs. Hawthorne's tough exterior. Or else if I had, it only concealed a much tougher center.

"Of course," I answered.

"And Ms. Evans," she added. "The hollandaise was slightly split this morning. Let's try harder next time, yes?"

My stomach dropped. I must've been pale enough to see through as all the blood drained from my face.

"I'm so sorry. Yes, of course."

"That'll be all," she said, dismissing me.

I fumbled to stand and shuffled out of the room, dumbstruck.

She hated my hollandaise. No one had ever criticized my hollandaise before. I didn't understand what could've gone wrong. Did the sauce break in transit to the dining room? Did I not add enough lemon? Too much? My head spun.

I'd had tough bosses before. It usually took a lot to throw me off my game. But this time, her words went through me like buckshot. I had to redeem myself to Mrs. Hawthorne. So, what could I make that would regain her respect?

After brunch, I made a shopping list for dinner and headed back down the mountain in the Land Rover for more provisions. I had an idea about a vegetable-forward pasta dish, but I'd let the produce speak to me. Otherwise, maybe a lean protein like elk or venison. Perhaps a ravioli with butternut squash. I decided I'd stroll the shops in the center of town and see what else was available beyond the marketplace.

Something special. Something I couldn't screw up.

Maplewood Creek's snowy town square sparkled under the early afternoon sun as I drove through. Families of tourists in new ski wear strolled the sidewalks with shopping bags and kids in tow. Handwritten chalkboard signs beckoned pedestrians with seasonal sales and promotions. As I searched for an open space to park along the curb, my eyes followed the flow of people walking with steaming coffee cups from the roastery a couple of blocks up. After sneaking the Land Rover into a space, I popped in to check it out.

The Toasted Bean was packed, with several people in line and more occupying nearly every small table. Around the store, shelves of bagged coffee beans and accessories were artfully displayed among winter decorations and tiny gift boxes ready to take home.

"Does Ali know you've escaped?"

The soft, coy voice whispered in my ear from behind as I stood in line to order. I shivered slightly, telling myself it was from cold rather than pleasure, as I turned around to see Charles towering over me in a black quarter-zip sweater and designer coat. His hair peeked out from under his beanie cap as he unwound the scarf from around his neck.

"Tracking the Land Rover now?" I answered, turning back toward the menu behind the counter. "Or are you going to tell me it's just a coincidence?"

"I saw the SUV and decided to come say hi."

"Uh-huh."

I mean, I loved that he had come to find me away from the chalet. Even if I couldn't say so. But it wasn't helping with the distraction problem.

"Let me buy you a coffee," he said, coming to stand beside me when I refused to look at him.

"You're butting."

"What?" he laughed.

"You're butting in," I said, nodding over my shoulder. "There's a line."

His unflappable grin grew wider. "Alright, let me have cuts."

"Sorry, can't do it. Wouldn't be fair to everyone else."

Charles shook his head at me. "You really won't let me buy you coffee? It's like the absolute minimum effort of friendship. We can be friends, can't we?"

My tongue turned sour at the sound of the word friend. It sent a strange wave of revulsion through my whole body.

"I don't know," I said, trying for aloof. I wouldn't let this man wear me down. Not when his mother was so very scary. "Can you?"

"I'd like to try," he said, eyeing me persuasively as I stepped up to the counter.

Concerned he might make a scene otherwise, I rolled my eyes and sighed. "Chai latte."

His answering smile was triumphant. "Chai latte and a black coffee, please," he told the barista. "See? Look at us. Practically chums."

"Whatever." I smothered a smile as I went to the far end of the counter to wait.

Despite my panic at Mrs. Hawthorne's criticism, my mood had drastically improved with Charles's arrival. Even if I wouldn't let him know that.

"I thought our croissants turned out pretty well," he said, squeezing in tight beside me to let other patrons come and go as we wedged ourselves in beside the wall. "Dad had three. Mother was livid."

I winced. "Should I not have made them?"

He waved off my concern. "That's their fight. Don't sweat it."

Still, I should be more careful. Even if she hadn't said as much in our meeting, I guessed the argument had contributed to her bad mood with me generally.

"Well, thank you again for the help," I told him sincerely. Because he'd found me just short of a meltdown last night. "I was a little frazzled."

"So, are you seeing anyone?"

I laughed, throwing my hands up. "That's your segue?"

Charles put on an innocent face and shrugged. "We're friends now, right? I'm taking an interest. Getting to know you. If there's someone waiting back in Denver . . ."

"Chai latte and black coffee!" the barista called cheerily.

I grabbed my cup and handed Charles his as I headed toward the door and back outside onto the sidewalk.

"No one waiting in Denver," I told him, walking a little

too fast. "Although seems a little late for that question, doesn't it?"

He licked his lips and bit back a smile, almost blushing. I knew because the implied memories made my own face a little warmer too.

"So, where to now?" he asked as I walked in no particular direction past storefronts.

"Don't you have plans of your own?"

"Nope. I'm all yours."

I rolled my eyes at the innuendo. "That was cheesy."

"Cheesy works," he countered. "People like cheesy. It's disarming."

"Yeah?" I said, glancing up at him as I sipped my chai. "How's that working out for you?"

"Pretty well so far."

God, he was so sure of himself. And I hated that it looked so good on him.

As we wandered along the narrow streets, I was fully aware of the constant brush of his gloved hands against mine. The urge to reach out and take one was strong. The whole experience felt very domestic, which was not a usual feeling for me. My dating life, which only ever existed in fits and starts, usually amounted to sporadic dates with people I'd meet at work, until one of us ended up losing interest.

With Charles, he'd gotten under my skin. Made me feel things. Like the way he changed the air when he walked into a room. How my body always bent slightly in his direction. It was sort of infuriating.

"So . . ." I said, unable to shake him and struggling for how to fill the loaded silence. "Have you been coming to Maplewood Creek for a long time?"

The quaint shops, trimmed with twinkling lights, and holiday decor lining the snow-covered paths gave the town an almost storybook charm. It had all the appeal and none of the expensive headache of larger ski towns like Vail and Aspen. The perfect hideaway retreat.

"I used to spend summers here as a kid," Charles said with fondness. "And every Christmas. It's changed so much and yet not at all. It's one of my favorite places. Especially this time of year."

"Yeah, why's that?"

"The holidays in town are just a dream. If that makes sense. Chaotic, sure, with so many extra people, but there's a sense of joy and contentment that no other place on Earth has for me at Christmastime."

There was a sense of nostalgia in his voice, even longing. Something romantic about the way he talked about this place, with all the sincerity and innocence we have as kids when special places take root in our hearts. It was a different side of Charles I hadn't expected. It hinted at something deeper than the flirty banter and cocky charm. And only made it harder to pretend I was immune to him.

"What about you?" he asked. "Where's your perfect Christmas?"

"I'm usually in a kitchen somewhere," I told him.

"That sounds kind of lonely."

I shrugged. "Some of us have to work for a living." I said it like a joke, but it was real to me. "I've worked pretty much every day since I was fourteen. When my mom got sick, she couldn't work anymore. It was just me and her, so I didn't really have a choice. All of the rent and groceries, her medications, everything, it was suddenly all my responsibility."

"That's a lot for a kid," he said grimly. "Is she doing better now?"

I sipped my latte and shook my head. "She passed away a few years ago."

Charles touched my arm to stop me. "Elle, I'm so sorry."

His face was stricken. I sort of felt guilty dropping that on him. I had come to terms with her death long before she was gone. The unavoidable side effect of a long illness is that you watch them leave you a little bit every day. But when you tell someone, it changes them. Changes your relationship to them. They didn't ask for that responsibility and now, boom, my dead mom was his problem too.

"I usually don't tell people," I admitted. "They get weird about it, you know? Don't know what to say and—"

"I'm glad you told me," he said, before I could trail off. "I mean it, you can talk to me anytime. About anything. I really do want to be your friend."

And the strangest thing was, I did too.

Chapter 14

I hadn't expected to enjoy myself so much with Charles. I mean, I'd *enjoyed* myself plenty in our first encounter, but as company went, he was brilliant too. He had this calmness about him. An ease that lifted some of the burden I had heaped on myself these last few weeks, fretting about money, ACE, and London. Things didn't feel so insurmountable when I was with him. Still, there was that lingering hesitation that we were doing something illicit. And that if and when we got caught, I'd have hell to pay with his mother. Though it was difficult to feel guilty when we were having so much fun together. After all, there was no rule against friendship, right?

Now I was strangely looking forward to dinner. After I got back to the house with the new provisions, I jumped right back in the kitchen to get started. Tonight, I would really aim to impress, with a venison carpaccio, beet salad, saffron ravioli with wild mushrooms, and my classic mini carrot cake for dessert.

The first step was prepping my pasta dough. A tip I'd picked up from watching my favorite TV chef, Marcus Lee, was throwing a little turmeric in there for that perfect deep yellow color. Once it was prepped and resting in the fridge, I readied my carpaccio. Using a beautiful venison loin, I trimmed the fat, sinew, and silver skin, then wrapped it in plastic wrap and popped it in the freezer to harden for a couple of hours. That gave me time to roast the mushrooms, then cool them for my ravioli and roll out my dough.

The key to any dinner service was timing, knowing exactly when to start my sauce so it was working while I built my ravioli, then taking my loin out to slice. I had all the plates spinning in my head, right on time, until Ali strode into the kitchen twenty minutes before service was due to start.

"Ravioli," she said apprehensively, eyeing the stove while I dressed and composed the beet salads on each plate. "Hmm."

"What?" I said, dread growing in my gut. "What's wrong with ravioli? Does Mrs. Hawthorne not eat pasta?"

A preposterous thing to say, but people were picky and I'd long ago stopped trying to reason with their stomachs.

"No, no," Ali said, forcing some lightness in her voice in a way that wasn't easing my nerves at all.

"What?" I snapped too forcefully. "Tell me."

"There will be three more for dinner," she said, and I watched the regret form on her face. "Friends of Mr. and Mrs. Hawthorne."

"And I'm just hearing this now?" My voice was bordering on shrill while my hands hung in midair, stained red from the beets.

"I only just found out myself."

Really, it wasn't her fault. And a part of me wondered if this was intentional. Like some sick test from Mrs. Hawthorne to break me. Spring three extra guests on me at the last minute to throw my whole meal into chaos, and watch what happened.

This must've been how she'd chased off the last chef. Only I wasn't in a position to quit. Which meant now I had to make more dough, sauté more mushrooms, and build ravioli for three more people. I had plenty of ingredients, but precious little time.

"Is there anything I can do?" Ali offered, sympathetic.

"No," I snapped too harshly. "I need to work."

I'd never moved so fast in my life. Tossing mushrooms in a pan, then pivoting to combining eggs and flour. Giving my dough barely any time to rest while I started on another sauce and sliced off some more loin. What began as a perfect dinner was now a rush job. I was barely taking my hands off each plate before the waitstaff took them away. When I'd sent out the last piece of carrot cake—slicing the pieces extra thin to make it stretch—I sunk to the floor and gulped down an entire bottle of water.

"Anything?" I asked Ali when she came to check on me.

"Mrs. Hawthorne remarked that the portions of cake seemed 'on the stingy side'," she said tightly.

I sensed she was reluctant to admit as much. Knowing it only drove the knife in further.

"Great." Maybe if I'd had some warning, I could have made more.

"And she reiterated that she told you this job would require flexibility, and you should expect to be on your toes."

Wonderful. This service just kept getting better.

Like Ali read the defeat on my face, she offered me a

sympathetic smile. "Really, don't take it to heart. Mrs. Hawthorne can be far more forgiving than she lets on."

I chuckled, grabbing us another couple of water bottles from the fridge. "I find that hard to believe."

"No, really." She took the bottle I offered her and leaned against the island. "When I started, I almost didn't last the month."

I gulped down half the bottle, sweating from all sorts of uncomfortable places. "What happened?"

Ali cringed with embarrassment. "It was Independence Day weekend and I'd driven six hours in holiday traffic to open the beach house in the Hamptons for their arrival. Stocked the kitchen, made the beds. Everything they'd require. Then I waited at the airport for their plane to land, until I got an angry phone call demanding to know why I was late."

I stared at her, puzzled and waiting for the punchline.

"They had touched down in Martha's Vineyard an hour ago!"

"No!" I gasped.

"Trust me, I got an earful. I thought she'd fire me on the spot."

"But you're still here."

She nodded, tucking a few loose strands of hair behind her ear. "She simply told me to get on a flight to the island and we proceeded on. There were a few difficult days, but ultimately, Mrs. Hawthorne gave me the opportunity to prove myself."

"Teachable moment, huh?"

"Exactly." Ali straightened and tucked the loose ends of her shirt into her waistband. "In good news, the family will be out again tomorrow. You'll have the day off."

Then she left me to sulk.

I was utterly defeated as I cleaned the kitchen and washed the dishes. Part of me expected to get a termination letter under my door the next morning. Be out by noon. But the order to pack up my stuff never came.

As I lay in bed well after ten the next morning, without even showering or brushing my teeth yet, full-on wallowing, there was a sudden knock at my door. I thought about ignoring it. Pretending I wasn't home. But they kept knocking.

"Yeah, okay," I called. "I'm coming."

I glanced out the front window and saw Charles standing on the other side.

Holy shit.

I hid behind the door. Hair greasy. Breath atrocious. In my very least attractive pajamas.

"What do you want?" I shouted through the door.

He was supposed to be gone all day. What the hell was he doing outside my cottage?

"Aren't you going to open the door?" he answered.

"No."

"No?"

"No!"

Again, he knocked. Louder. "Elle, come on. Open up."

"What do you want?"

"I wanted to invite you on a little excursion," he said. "Come on, at least open the door."

Ugh, this was stupid. Yelling at each other through the door. I felt like an idiot.

"I'm not decent, so I'm going to unlock the door, but you have to promise to wait ten seconds before you come in."

"I mean, it's not really anything I haven't seen," he teased.

"Ten seconds!" I shouted back. "Promise!"

I pictured that crooked smirk he made when he found me difficult. "Fine. I promise."

Tentatively, I unlocked the deadbolt, then sprinted to my bedroom and slammed the door shut. I didn't wait to hear the front door open before I got in the shower to wash my hair and then out to brush my teeth and get dressed. After I'd blow-dried my hair, part of me hoped he might've gotten bored and left, but no. When I walked out of my bedroom, in a cute sweatshirt and my most flattering pair of jeans, he was still sitting on my couch, dressed in only a casual pair of house sweats, like he'd just woken up himself.

"So," he said, totally undeterred. "Got any plans today?"

Only if sulking counted as plans. "Not really."

"Great." He jumped to his feet. "Then we're hitting the slopes. I've got a whole day planned. It's time to introduce you to what we call fun around here."

"A whole day, huh? That seems like a big step."

"What's wrong? Don't think I can hold your interest?"

I shrugged.

Charles flashed a crooked smile. "Is that a dare?"

"Yeah, sorry, I'm going to have to pass."

His face creased with concern. "What's wrong? You're giving me less shit than usual."

I debated how honest I wanted to be with him. In the end,

I suppose I felt we had built a certain level of trust. I mean, if he'd wanted to rat me out to his mom, he would've done so by now.

"Your mom's not too impressed with me," I said, crossing the room to sink into the couch beside him. "I kind of botched brunch the other day, and I guess she wasn't thrilled with dinner last night, either."

"Seriously? I thought dinner was fantastic. That ravioli was unreal."

"Yeah?" My little culinary heart went pitter-patter at the compliment. "Well, your mom definitely didn't think so."

"She's just enjoying torturing you. Plus, she has impossible standards. Don't take it personally," he said, turning on the couch to face me.

"Kind of hard not to."

My food was an extension of myself. Every plate I sent out was like a chunk of me I passed around for praise or ridicule. Which more than once made me wonder why I chose this life for myself. And the answer was always that I just wouldn't be happy doing anything else.

"I think it was growing up a pro athlete," Charles said, leaning his head on the hand he had propped up on the couch cushion. "My grandparents had her on ski teams from the time she was five years old. They were relentless. Always training and pushing her to be better. Nothing was ever good enough."

"Sounds rough," I agreed.

Pressure could really mess with a person, turn them into something ugly. It was a defense mechanism. I'd seen plenty of it in kitchens. Maybe even succumbed myself once or twice. Where we didn't bend, we broke.

"Don't get me wrong. My grandparents are great people. But as parents, I think they did a number on her. Got wrapped up in it, you know? My mom, she really doesn't mean it, I think, but she tends to take it out on everyone else. Like, she never pushed Amelia and me into sports or whatever when we were kids, but it's always been next to impossible to get a compliment out of her. Trust me, I know how tough it is feeling like nothing you can ever do is good enough."

Much as he smiled through the words, the pain in them was evident. I sensed he'd spent a life searching for her approval, and always falling just short. Still, I knew how much she cared for him. Mrs. Hawthorne wouldn't be so adamant about these upcoming events being perfect if it didn't mean a lot to her to honor her son.

"So . . ." I said, my resistance faltering. I guess I just wanted to make Charles smile. "Hitting the slopes, huh?"

It worked.

Chapter 15

The mountain was slammed with skiers and snowboarders zipping around like bees over wildflowers. Long lines to the lift snaked the distance of a football field, past the pro shop and snack stand. The bunny slope stretched out in front of me, ostensibly gentle, but to my untrained eyes, it looked more like the end of the world. I tugged at the mismatched ski jacket and snow pants that I'd rented. Every time a kid whizzed past me on tiny skis, my confidence took another hit.

"You're doing fine," Charles said, his voice smooth and reassuring.

Standing beside me at the top of the small hill, he looked effortlessly perfect, of course, in his sleek black ski jacket and expensive goggles perched on his head. He might as well have walked out of a catalog. Meanwhile, I looked like a walking thrift store.

I scowled at him. "Fine? I haven't even moved yet. When do my legs stop shaking? Is it time for a break now?"

He grinned. "You're already better than half the people who crash before they even start."

"Very funny," I muttered, gripping the poles like they were lifelines. I guess, to a degree, they were.

Charles moved closer, his gloved hand resting lightly on mine. "Relax. You're overthinking it. Bend your knees, lean forward a little, and let gravity do the work."

I glanced at him, skeptical. "Let gravity do the work? Sounds like a fast track to a face-plant. Why did I agree to this again?"

"Trust me," he said, his tone dropping into something softer, more coaxing. "I've got you."

And I found that I believed him. He wouldn't let me crash if he could help it.

"And you agreed because I said that I'd warm you up afterward." He waggled his eyebrows.

With a deep breath, I pushed off, my skis sliding forward in a wobbly line. For a few glorious seconds, I was moving—until a kid about eight years old sliced by me, causing me to lose my balance and topple sideways into the snow. Charles was there in an instant, laughing as he helped me up.

"Okay, see? You've had your first fall. The scary part is out of the way. Now you're ready to go again."

"Again?"

"Come on," he said, dusting the snow off my shoulders. "Four-year-olds can do this. You're at least as brave as a four-year-old, right?"

I glared at him. "You think getting me angry will work?"

"Yes," he said, grinning. "Absolutely."

Maybe he was right.

I couldn't help the laugh that bubbled up inside me. "This is mortifying."

"Nah," he said, picking up one of my discarded poles. "You're adorable."

My cheeks burned, and not from the cold.

So, once we had my skis pointed the right direction again, I gave it another try. I leaned forward and pushed off gently.

"Remember," he called from behind me. Probably because it was safer back there. "Pizza to slow down. French fry to go faster."

It felt infantile, but it worked. As I very slowly sailed down the small slope, I kept my toes mostly pointed inward, getting used to the feeling of a controlled descent.

"There," he said. "You're doing it. Piece of cake, right?"

"Don't throw any more foods at me!" I shouted back. "I'm concentrating!"

With my eyes firmly trained on the end of my skis and my full attention dedicated to keeping my balance, I felt like I was starting to get the hang of it. Until I saw the cluster of people at the bottom of the hill getting ever closer, and the bright orange plastic fencing that marked the dead end. Panic set in.

"Hey!" I shouted at Charles. "Hey! How do I stop these things?"

"Pizza!" he shouted back.

"I am pizza. I'm doing pizza!"

I pointed my toes inward but I kept sliding. Just as I was about to take the emergency escape route and simply fall over, Charles grabbed me from behind and brought us to an abrupt halt. Not a moment too soon, as a corral of unsuspecting children almost became my crash barrels.

"See?" he said, coming to stand in front of me with a silly grin overwhelming his face. "You did it. Fun, right?"

We weren't quite at fun yet, but I was starting to get a taste for it.

"Again," I told him.

So once more, we trekked up to the top of the bunny slope with the children. I felt like a giant standing up there, the munchkins scooting around me at knee height like they were born on skis while I clumsily waddled about. At the daunting peak, I took a moment to adjust my goggles and gloves again. Nothing quite fit right and none of it was exactly comfortable.

"Come on! Let's go already!"

The rude exclamation came from a freckled child in a bright blue snowsuit with a red fringe mohawk helmet.

"Excuse me?" I answered back, glancing at Charles to laugh, a bit perplexed.

"You're hogging the powder," the little snot whined. "Move it or lose it!"

I scoffed, aghast at this kid. "Oh, I'm sorry. I didn't know this hill belonged to His Majesty."

"Aren't you a little old for the bunny slope?" he shot back in a nasal voice.

"Incredible," I said to Charles. "There's a toddler giving me the business."

"Smell you later, old farts!" The kid blew a raspberry at us and slipped down the slope backwards while throwing up two peace signs.

"Congratulations," Charles laughed, shaking his head. "You just met your first ski bully."

I pulled my goggles down over my eyes and planted my poles. "I'm going to end that kid."

With a renewed motivation to not be shown up by a first-grader, I pushed off down the slope, albeit at an extremely responsible speed. This time, my knees were more confident. My balance was sure. I opened my hips and pointed my toes straight ahead.

Yeah, French-fry mode.

I began to pick up speed. Maybe a little too much. But I hadn't fallen yet and my size meant the other kids were staying out of my lane, so I had a clear path. It gave me perhaps an undeserved confidence. So, like I'd seen on TV, I bent my knees a little and leaned forward. Tucked my poles under my arms, and zipped right past the twerp in the bright blue suit.

Only I'd forgotten about stopping in my triumph, and suddenly was faced with another bail-out situation until I again felt the deft, steady hand of Charles at my back, tugging on the hood of my jacket to slow me to a gentle halt.

"We've really got to work on your braking maneuver," he quipped.

"Yeah, but did you see how I smoked that kid?"

Charles smirked, picking an errant snowflake from my cheek. "I did. You showed him."

"Damn right!"

After a few more turns down the bunny slope, I was feeling pretty good about myself and let Charles convince me I was ready to take it up a notch. Only I forgot that meant a ride on the ski lift. An apparatus I'd avoided my whole life, because the idea of dangling a few dozen feet over a mountain by little more than a steel cable was not my idea of dependable transportation.

"How do I do this?" I asked nervously as we waited in line for our turn.

I watched each group in front of us be scooped off their feet by the jerky, swinging chair that did not inspire a great deal of confidence.

"Just let it pick you up," he said. "Nothing to it."

"It won't, like, knock me over?"

"Don't let it knock you over."

"Great. That's helpful."

As we inched closer to the front of the line, a queasy feeling rumbled in my gut.

"I don't know," I said. "Maybe I'm not ready for the real thing yet."

Then Charles took my hand in his and squeezed. I looked up, meeting his eyes.

"I've got you," he said. "Trust me."

The conviction in his voice sort of bowled me over. He was so sincere, so encouraging. I felt lighter. Whatever kind of Jedi mind trick he pulled on me, he needed to bottle that stuff. It was potent.

Before I knew it, I was off my feet and the ground was quickly getting farther away.

"Whoa!" I said, latching on to his arm for dear life as the lift carried us upward.

"See? Easy."

"Uh-huh."

Charles chuckled softly into my hair. "I love it up here. It's the best view in town."

He had that part right. As we were carried above the trees,

the whole mountain range spread out before us, surrounded by bright blue sky and snowy lanes of swerving skiers.

"I suppose your mom taught you how to ski," I said.

"My grandfather, actually. By the time I was old enough to get up on skis, she'd already given it up."

"What were they like, your grandparents?"

A warm smile of reminiscence grew across his face. "The best. The kind of people that made everyone they met feel like family. They believed in community and helping people." His expression turned wistful as he stared out at the scenery. "I don't know. I think somewhere along the way we lost that. Nothing feels like it did when they were around."

"You really miss them."

"I do. Grandad was my best friend growing up."

I loosened my death grip on his arm, which he then placed over my shoulder to hug me closer. It was a sweet, innocent gesture that still somehow felt intimate. Until the lift suddenly jerked to a halt. The chair swayed back and forth, dangling from the cable overhead.

"It's not supposed to do that, is it?" I said, looking up at Charles with panic bubbling in my chest.

His brow furrowed. "Give it a second."

A second turned into several, while we both peered toward the platform that was still several hundred yards up the mountain.

"I'm sure it's nothing," Charles assured me, obviously sensing my growing unease.

A gust of wind rattled the chair and a metal groan echoed above our heads.

"Well, that can't be good," I said, trying to cover the

creeping alarm rising in my gut. "Is this a bad time to say I'm sort of mortally terrified of heights? Well, less heights than falling to my gruesome death."

"Oh," he said. "So, this was basically your nightmare idea of a second date?"

"Yeah, pretty much. But you were so excited, I put on a brave face."

This hadn't been my first choice of leisure activity, but I was grateful to have gotten out of my comfort zone a little. Less so now, however.

"Awesome," he laughed, smothering his face in his hands. "I am really batting a thousand here."

"I have had fun," I told him, taking his hand. Because I didn't want him to think the day so far was a total loss. "Now, as far as second date . . ."

"Well, I don't count making croissants as a date," he quipped.

"What about being friends?"

"We can do both." He turned slightly to face me more directly. "I'm great at multitasking."

"Yeah, I bet."

But as time ticked by, my humor faltered. And without the trees to shelter us from the wind, the temperature seemed to plummet.

"Here," Charles said, shrugging out of his jacket. He placed it over my shoulders and zipped me up inside, then pulled me closer into his arms.

"Aren't you freezing?" I said, starting to shiver as I tried to look anywhere but down.

"I've got a lot more mass to keep me warm. You need it."

Charles rubbed my upper arms to generate some heat as I curled up against his chest. He was surprisingly warm, given the temperature up here must've been well below freezing.

"You know what we need?" he said. "S'mores."

"Afraid I forgot to pack my emergency s'mores kit," I said, teeth chattering.

"When we get back to the house later, we'll roast marshmallows by the fire. Have some hot cocoa. Get all bundled up in our sweats and thick wool socks."

"I'm going to eat every marshmallow in sight, then take the longest, hottest shower of my life," I answered, tucking myself deeper under his chin.

"I'll join you," he laughed.

"Nice try."

"Tell me," Charles said, furiously rubbing the outside of my thigh to keep me from losing feeling in my limbs, "what are your plans after the season ends?"

"London. I've been accepted to culinary school."

"Hey, that's terrific. Ever been?"

"I've never even left the country."

"Maybe I can come visit," he said. "Show you around a bit."

"Let me guess, you have a flat."

He chuckled softly and it warmed my face against his chest. "Let's just say I have a few favorite neighborhood spots I'd love to show you."

I knew what he was doing. Like a nurse distracting you with conversation while they jammed the needle in your arm. Keep me talking and my mind off freezing to death while we dangled above the chasm below.

"You don't have to do that, you know. Make promises. I

don't have any delusions that we'll still be hanging out after my job with your family is over."

He stopped rubbing my leg and ducked his head to seek my eyes. "Why would you say that?" he asked, a wounded note in his voice.

"Just being realistic."

It was nothing personal, but I knew the score here. I was a one-night stand that got stuck here and now we were both making the best of a strange situation. I gave him all the credit in the world for not being a dick about it. Still, I didn't expect to get a Christmas card next year.

"You know, you should give people a little more credit," he said flatly. "They might surprise you."

"What would make you fly halfway around the world to take me to dinner?" I said, teasing.

"Maybe I just like your company."

The lift gave another metal groan and jerked forward. The chair swung again, testing the strength of my stomach as I once again held on to Charles for dear life. I took several deep breaths, and when I looked up at him, Charles was watching me, his arms still tight around my body.

"We're moving again," he said, as the lift creaked and resumed its slow progression upward.

"Just in time. For a second there, you looked like you were going to kiss me."

"Well, now that you mention it . . ."

He ducked his chin and I closed my eyes. Our lips met. Soft, gentle. Though there was nothing subtle about the thrill of excitement that fluttered through my belly at the familiar sensation. Whistles erupted from the chair behind ours and I pulled away, smothering a laugh and sinking down slightly in the chair.

"See," he said, that easy smile once more in place. "You survived. Nothing to it."

"The kiss or the ride?"

His only answer was a self-satisfied smirk.

Unfortunately, my euphoria was dashed the second we arrived at the slope. I didn't have time to fret about distractions, or how that kiss would complicate our delicate professional relationship. I glanced down the seemingly infinite runway of snow and the experienced skiers shredding powder at breakneck speeds, and swallowed past the lump in my throat.

"You know what?" I said, lifting the goggles off my face. "I think I'd rather take my chances with the ski lift again."

"No can do," he said beside me. "The only way down is right there."

"Uh-uh."

"Uh-uh?"

"Yeah. Uh-uh. Carry me. I'll hop on your back."

Charles smothered a laugh. "You conquered your ski bully, remember? You can do anything. This isn't much harder than what you've already done. Just a little longer of a trip down."

But my knees began to shudder and my breath became a little ragged. As Charles appraised me, his expression sobered and he lifted the goggles off his face to meet my eyes.

"Hey, hey. You've got this, okay? Think of it like cooking."

"This is nothing like cooking," I shot back.

"Sure it is. When you're in the kitchen, you're not panicking, right?"

"Only when I'm cooking for your mom."

Charles coughed out a laugh. "Fair. But otherwise, you're in your element, right? You've got control. What does it feel like?"

"I don't know." I'd never really asked myself the question in those words. "I suppose I just sort of get into a rhythm, you know? A flow. Sort of space out and just let the muscle memory take over."

"There," he said. "Exactly. Skiing is the same way. Don't overthink it. Just trust your body and let go. Relax into it. Tensing up is the worst thing you can do."

I took a deep breath, steadying myself.

"Good?" he said. "Ready to give it a try? I'll be right here beside you the whole way. I promise."

"Don't let me face-plant."

Charles kissed my forehead, smirking against my skin. "I won't let you face-plant."

So, I put on a brave face and crept up to the precipice, saying a silent prayer to the ski gods not to let me slam into a tree or go tumbling off a cliff. Then I mustered up all my nerve, leaned forward, and pushed off.

I started slow. Ignored the other skiers breezing past me and concentrated only on myself and the snow ahead. And I kept telling myself to relax. Don't think. Go with the flow. Then, somewhere along the way, I became aware of the sweet, woodsy scent of fresh pine. The elegant way the tree limbs bowed under the weight of snow piled on their branches. That lovely sound of skis slicing through the powder. The luxurious warmth of the sun on my face and the wind in my hair.

Until suddenly, it was over. I was at the bottom and I'd stopped all on my own, without crashing or falling over or causing a ten-person pile-up.

"Hey, look at you!" Charles exclaimed, almost slamming into me to give me a huge hug. "That was terrific. Didn't it feel great!"

It was exhilarating. And calming. Sort of like a trance.

"I can't wait to do that again!"

Chapter 16

After my successful mastery of the mountain, I was desperate to put my feet up and relax. Charles said he had the perfect place in mind. The cryptic declaration gave me pause as we got in his Land Rover and took to the winding roads away from the crowded ski village.

"Do I get to know where you're taking me?" I asked, warming my hands in the heat blasting from the air vents as he drove.

"I want to show you my favorite spot in Maplewood Creek."

"The less you tell me, the more worried I get."

He flashed me a devastating grin. "Trust me. This surprise, you'll like."

Ten minutes later, we pulled up to a nondescript patch of dirt along the road's shoulder.

"Up for a quick hike?" he said, parking the Land Rover beside a wooden stake with a simple arrow pointing toward a trail into the forest.

"Not sure I'm wearing the right shoes for this."

I'd thrown on a pair of duck boots that were perfect for navigating slippery sidewalks, but maybe not trudging through snow and foliage.

Charles shot me a wink. "I've got you."

My heart sort of leaped into my throat at the way his eyes shimmered when he said it. He got out of the SUV and came around to open my door, offering me his hand to climb out.

"It isn't far," he said, taking my hand. "Just hang on to me. I won't let you fall."

As we started up the trail, he kept my arm tucked under his, supporting my weight over protruding tree roots and slippery rocks. He led us with sure-footed purpose, never hesitating as the path periodically diverged or became less distinct. He knew it by heart.

"You've been here a lot?" I asked, marveling at the occasional evidence of a critter's footprints in the snow.

"Since I was a kid. It's sort of a local secret. A spot you don't tell tourists about."

"Aren't you breaking the code of silence by taking me here?"

He smirked, squeezing my hand as he held back a branch. "I think you can keep a secret."

It did feel a little like being in a very exclusive club. This secret we shared. The only two people in the world who knew. Hiding from his family. I guess it made me feel like this Charles belonged only to me.

About ten minutes into our trek, the trees opened to reveal a small, rocky pool, with rising steam that'd melted the snow around it. And at just the right angle, you could peer through the tall pines to see the vista of the Rockies climbing into the clear blue sky in the distance.

"Oh, wow," I hummed.

"Worth the hike?" he asked proudly.

"Definitely. But, uh, I didn't bring a bathing suit."

I watched a slow, mischievous smile widen across his face.

"I don't mind if you don't," he said.

Charles unzipped his coat and began peeling off layers of clothing to hang on a low branch. Then he dropped his boxers, facing away from me, and carefully stepped into the warm pool of crystal water.

"Feels great," he said, submerged to his chest and encouraging me to follow. "Come on."

Without several mulled ciders to give my confidence a boost, I felt a bit self-conscious undressing in front of him. Maybe Charles sensed that, because he casually turned around to sink deeper into the water, then gaze at the view, while I kicked off my shoes and stripped down. A few freezing, shivering steps later, I clambered into the water and hugged my arms to my chest.

"Oh, that was cold," I said with a slight shiver, submerging my shoulders.

"Yeah, that first step's a doozy, huh?" Charles approached me, tentative. Then when I didn't scurry away, he wrapped his arms around me to rub the goosebumps away, bringing me against his firm, slick chest. "Getting warmer, right?"

"Uh-huh," I muttered, nuzzling into him just a little. Because he was warm. Not because I really liked the way he smelled. "Yeah."

Charles chuckled softly against my face. "Beats hanging around your cottage all afternoon."

"Honestly, yeah," I said, pulling away when I started to feel silly letting him keep holding me like an injured bird. "I wasn't in a great headspace this morning, so thanks for coming to cheer me up."

His face knitted with concern as we both came to sit along a natural rock ledge in the water. "Any time. I know my family can be a lot. Promise you'll give me a chance to fix it before you think about running for the hills?"

"Yeah, okay."

"I mean it," he insisted at my noncommittal answer. "You can talk to me about anything."

I dragged my arms through the water, making little swirls between us with the motion while I told myself not to gawk at the distorted view of his naked body beneath the water. "It probably wouldn't even get to me so much, except that my whole future is riding on not getting fired from this job."

"Because of London?" he said.

"I already have a diploma in pastry, but this program at ACE will give me the broader education I need to work anywhere I want. I need this job to pay for it."

"And what's your dream job?" Water dripped down his shoulders, traveling the smooth ridges of his muscles. It was more than a little distracting. "If you could do anything at all?"

"I've got a whole plan that starts with ACE. That will open doors to working in the best restaurants in the world. Training under Michelin star chefs. Really learning how to run a top-notch kitchen. But the ultimate dream is to have my own restaurant. Once I've established a brand. Sort of a chef's table, prix fixe situation. Or like a traveling supper club doing pop-ups. I'm just not sure I could be content with cooking the same menu every night for the rest of my life. I need variety. A little adventure. I hate standing still, you know?"

"I know exactly what you mean."

I suppose that was partly why I spent the night with Charles in the first place. My whole life to date had been schedules and responsibility. Predictable. Stable. And every now and then, I got the irresistible urge to break out of that mold. Shatter the status quo and damn the consequences. If just for a night. Or a season.

Charles slid closer. "For me, it's like I appreciate having a role in the family business, sort of bouncing around behind the scenes wherever I can be useful, but I think about the next thirty years of my life and I'm not sure if I want to be sitting in the big chair."

"Right, your mom hinted at a big announcement soon."

He sighed, rubbing his hands over his face. He suddenly looked tired, overwhelmed. "I've been raised my whole life to take over for my dad one day. And for a long time there, I was excited about it. I'm sure it makes me a miserable bore, but I did enjoy business school. That stuff just makes sense to me. It's in the genes, I suppose. Only now that I'm in touching distance, I worry that I've never really considered doing anything else. What if I wake up and realize my heart's not in it? I let my family down. I let the company down. That's people's livelihoods, you know? It just feels like maybe I've wasted the chance to figure out if I would've been happier doing something else."

"What about your sister?" I said. "Has Amelia ever wanted the big chair?"

He paused, thinking about that a moment. "Amelia's chief ambition has always been pleasing our mom. She wants her approval more than anything."

I laughed gently. "I can relate."

"But I'm not sure business is her first love, you know? She's more into the public side of things. Marketing, PR. She's got a great head for that stuff. She's good at making people like her."

"Well, take it from me," I said, absently touching his arm. "You're not so bad at that either."

A bright toothy grin overtook his face, those dimples forming on both cheeks. "Yeah?"

I rolled my eyes, smothering a smile. "Try not to let it go to your head."

"Nope. Too late. You like me."

"Barely."

"No, you really like me. I'm basically your favorite person."

"Oh, please."

He reached out to grab me off the ledge and instead I splashed an armful of water in his face. Charles sputtered, wiping his eyes.

"Seriously?" he grimaced playfully. "That's how it's going to be?"

I splashed him again.

"I have a little sister, remember. You're not going to win this game."

And just for that, I splashed him a third time. Which turned into an all-out splash war, the two of us chasing each other around inside the tiny pool until he wrapped me up in his arms to tickle me. And when he pulled me tight against his chest to stop my assault, our faces came just inches apart. My pulse raced. He stared at my lips. This time, I went to him, rising up to press my mouth to his.

This was a terrible idea. Every time I let this man wiggle a little further under my skin, I was setting myself up for even more of a disaster. Because there was no way this could end well. It was tempting fate. But then, the heart was irrational. And our attraction was undeniable. That damn boy-crazy girl in all of us that swooned at a square jaw and dimples.

Charles grabbed the backs of my thighs to hoist my legs around his hips. I tangled my arms behind his neck and held on, breathing him in with the fresh scent of pine and cold mountain air, the subtle fragrance of his skin and the taste of his tongue on mine. His fingers squeezed, pressing against my flesh while flashes of our night at The Snowdrift danced behind my eyes.

I wanted more. As I deepened our kiss and lightly dragged my nails through his hair, I wanted to forget all the reasons I'd regret him and just give in. Give myself over to our instincts. And when Charles pressed my back against the hot, smooth rocks that surrounded the pool, I was sure he felt the same. Both of us were desperate to relive that release.

Like he could hear my thoughts, Charles exhaled and pressed his forehead against mine.

"You're seriously trouble, you know that?" he said.

"Me? You're the one who lured me into the woods to go skinny-dipping."

"I don't know." He teased his fingers up and down my rib-cage while I held myself to him with my legs locked around his hips. "Lure is a strong word. Tempted, maybe."

"Right. Because you're just that irresistible, girls will follow you anywhere."

He shrugged, playfully impressed with himself. "Your words, not mine."

The arrogance won him another face full of water as I ripped myself away to splash him again.

"Now you're in for it," he growled, before launching a wave of water at me.

I quickly scrambled out of the spring.

"Come on," he chided. "Don't run away just because you're losing."

"And just for that," I said, quickly tugging on my clothes and shoving my feet into my boots, "I'm taking your pants."

Chapter 17

"You play dirty," Charles said, climbing into the Land Rover and cranking up the heat after putting his pants on at the side of the road. "Not cool."

I hadn't stopped laughing since he came sprinting out of the forest in his coat and boots, bare legs hanging out.

"Worth it," I said, giggling. "You should've seen yourself."

"Just for that, you owe me dinner."

"Sort of a hollow threat. It's literally my job to make you dinner."

"Good point," he said, putting the SUV in gear and pulling back out onto the road. "In that case, let me buy *you* dinner. I know just the place."

The sun was just dipping behind the tallest peaks when we arrived at the mountaintop bistro by gondola. I'd read about this place but never considered dining here, because its menu was famously exorbitant and reservations were basically impossible.

"The owner of the restaurant group is a friend of the family," Charles told me as we were escorted by a waiter in a black vest and bowtie to a window-side table with stunning views of the snowcapped landscape. The lights of the town twinkled in the distance below. "You have to try the elk. It'll change your life."

Exposed beams were juxtaposed with white plaster walls, white linen on the tables, and centerpieces of pine cones, magnolia leaves, and votive candles. One end of the dining room featured a fireplace large enough to stand up inside. At the other, the stainless-steel open kitchen with white subway tile walls framed a large wood-burning oven.

"I feel incredibly underdressed," I whispered as the waiter placed a white linen napkin in my lap. "And my butt's still wet."

Charles smirked, ordering us a bottle of wine. "Mine too."

Yet it was easy to feel completely comfortable around Charles. He made the slight embarrassment entirely melt away. His smile, his effortless confidence. I guess they sort of rubbed off. Or else enveloped everyone around him, creating a shield of self-assuredness that kept the bad thoughts away. About how that one bottle of wine cost more than my entire electric bill. And how he'd traipsed through the forest in an outfit that probably cost more than my rent.

Those things didn't matter when Charles looked at me, because he saw *me*. Not our differences.

"Oh, God," I mumbled around a bite of wood-fired elk when our plates arrived. "Oh my God."

"Right?" he smiled, eyeing me over his wine glass. "Told you."

The meat was perfectly seared on all sides with a simple crust of salt, pepper, paprika, garlic, onion, and thyme. It was finished in the wood oven to keep the inside moist and tender, at a perfect mid-rare temperature with a generous basting of butter and aromatics. They served it with a berry balsamic reduction for a touch of sweetness to balance the gaminess of the meat. Not to mention the exquisitely buttery potato purée artfully infused with rosemary.

"This is incredible," I moaned around another bite. "Nothing I've ever cooked has been this good. You think they'd give me the recipe?"

I meant it as a joke, but of course Charles had never met a challenge he wouldn't take on.

"I'll have a word with the owner."

"Thank you for bringing me here. A meal like this reminds me why I want to cook for a living." And why I would stick it out in this job, no matter how tricky at times. London would be worth it.

"My pleasure." Charles held up his wine glass to clink with me. "To us."

"To . . . friendship."

He sipped his drink. "For now."

I didn't want the day to end. I thought about the tomorrow version of me, and whether she'd be kicking herself when the spell wore off, for the entire ride back to the chalet. While we talked about movies and random things, I wondered what might've happened if the night forked in a different direction that first night after The Foggy Goggle. Where were alternate Elle and Charles now?

"Uh-oh," he said, stopping at the door to my cottage. "You look deep in thought. What's up?"

I put on a smile. "Nothing. Just, you know, menu planning in my head."

"I had fun today. Pant-stealing notwithstanding."

"Yeah, me too. Thanks for inviting me."

"Actually," he said, leaning against the door, "If I'm honest, I even enjoyed getting stuck and nearly freezing to death with you. Is that weird?"

"No, not really," I admitted. "It wasn't so bad."

The space between us got smaller. I wasn't sure which one of us was doing it first, but his hands found my waist and my lips touched his. I rose up on my toes, winding my arms behind his neck.

So much for tomorrow me. Turned out I wasn't capable of enjoying this man in moderation. I wanted all of him. All the time. Damn the consequences, and the morning-after regrets.

The soft, gentle kiss became deeper. He pressed my back against the door, fingers digging into my hips. I exhaled, feeling him reach behind me for the doorknob.

"This is a very bad idea," I whispered against his chest. "Someone could see us."

"So, let's go inside."

Then a sudden noise yanked us apart. A light briefly flashed across the cottage and disappeared again. Like someone had opened the door to the main house across the small courtyard.

I just had to jinx us.

"It was probably just Ali," he whispered.

"And that's better how?"

At any rate, the moment was lost. Anxiety began to crawl

through my head, imagining Amelia hunting for a snack. Or worse, his mother coming to summon me and finding me snacking on her son instead.

"Good night, Charles," I said, opening the door and leaving him standing at the threshold.

He grabbed my hand and left a sweet kiss on my knuckles. "Good night, Elle."

How the hell was I going to make it three months living here with this man? He was the very definition of a distraction.

Chapter 18

I left my cottage the next morning feeling inspired. Rejuvenated, even. Maybe it was the restorative power of nature, or the handsome man who saved me from becoming a Popsicle last night, but I dare say I had a little pep to my step as I made my way to the kitchen to start breakfast. And when I walked in, there in the center of the marble island, was one single marshmallow waiting for me. The small token sent a giddy shiver all the way to my toes.

I knew I shouldn't encourage this behavior. It was thoroughly against the pact I'd made with myself. And yet as I popped the sweet, chewy morsel into my mouth, I couldn't deny I'd fallen hard for this guy. Sure, the situation was less than ideal, but sometimes perfection was the enemy of good.

Charles was a funny, kind, handsome, and charming man, who for some strange reason seemed to want nothing more than to make me like him. Well, mission accomplished. Now I just had to keep my wits about me and not let . . . whatever this was . . . get in the way of my job. No matter what else happened, work came first.

Which meant today I was making crepes. They were always a crowd-pleaser and a genuine demonstration of skill, from the perfect silky batter to the delicate sweetness that melted like fluffy air in your mouth. Plus, Charles might have let slip they were his mother's favorite.

First, I got to work preparing a grazing tray of fresh fruit. Next, I whipped up batches of banana bread and oatmeal-raisin muffins for Mr. Hawthorne. Ali strode into the kitchen just as I was popping them in the oven.

"I'm doing table-side orange ricotta crepes," I told her.

Ali's eyes widened.

"Let's set up a convention burner on a cart with a crepe pan. I'll bring the rest."

"Crepes are Mrs. Hawthorne's favorite," she said with a slight note of trepidation.

"Perfect."

The batter was the easy part. I beat eggs in a bowl, then whisked in milk, flour, butter, and salt. All that was then strained through a fine-mesh sieve into another bowl, to get a texture like heavy cream. While that rested in the fridge, I got to work on my ricotta, which wasn't nearly as complicated as it sounded.

In a Dutch oven, I combined milk, cream, and salt and brought it to a rolling boil. I stirred in fresh-squeezed lemon juice, then turned off the heat and let it sit for about ten minutes while curds began to float to the surface. I transferred those curds to a cheesecloth-lined strainer to drain the excess liquid for another ten minutes. To that, I added orange zest and another pinch of salt, stirring until creamy, and set it aside.

For my orange marmalade, I added the flesh and thin-sliced rind of several oranges to a small saucepan with sugar and a splash of champagne to cook down. By then, Ali was back to tell me the family was just sitting down to start on the fruit and muffins.

A brief wave of apprehension flooded through me as I assembled the portable cooktop and ingredients on the cart, but it was too late to back out now. Mrs. Hawthorne wanted to be wowed. This was the best I could come up with.

So, in my ironed white chef's coat and with my hair pulled up tightly in a bun, I entered the formal dining room with my cart. Charles smothered a smile but gave me a meaningful nod as my eyes flicked to his for just a moment before greeting the family.

"Good morning," I said. "I've readied a special tableside preparation for you today."

I got the impression Charles might've kicked Amelia under the table, because she suddenly dropped her phone in her lap and glared at him before her startled attention landed on me.

"I learned the technique to a proper crepe from a French chef who was staging at a restaurant where I used to work," I began.

Another thing he taught me was that the trick to a successful tableside service was talking. Building a rapport with the guest. It should be a show, so give them a little showmanship. A story.

"How fun," Mr. Hawthorne mused, smiling at his wife, who flatly sipped her mimosa.

"He said more important than the batter or the seasoning

was the cook." I smeared my heated pan with a pre-cut cube of butter, letting it sizzle and coat the entire surface.

The Hawthorne family looked on with rapt anticipation.

"Crepes require patience and attention." I poured the first batch of batter into the pan and used a wooden crepe spreader to evenly distribute the liquid across the entire surface. "People have a tendency to rush the batter. Because they're so thin. But he said you have to trust the process. Trust yourself."

Mrs. Hawthorne watched me closely, her icy gaze revealing nothing. And again, I stole a glance at Charles, whose nod of encouragement helped tamp down the butterflies.

With a spoon, I spread a thin layer of ricotta in the center of the crepe, then drizzled my orange marmalade on top. I used a silicone spatula to fold the crepe in half, and in half again, to form a perfect pie wedge, and slid it off onto a plate that Ali placed in front of Mrs. Hawthorne.

"That, he told me, was the lesson of cooking." I repeated the process again for the rest of the family, each crepe sliding perfectly off the pan.

"Wonderful," Mr. Hawthorne said, appreciatively inhaling as his plate hit the table. "Don't these look great?"

"Delicious," Amelia hummed around her first bite. "Compliments to the chef."

Charles beamed at me while I ducked my eyes to keep from blushing. I felt like they could all see the silent messages passing between us, clear as writing in the air over the table.

"You could practice and perfect a recipe," I continued, "but its execution was always entirely dependent on trust. The confidence of the cook. That confidence would always shine through in the food. Please enjoy."

"Thank you, Eleanor," was Mrs. Hawthorne's only response.

As I watched the tiny hint of a smile tug her lips at her first bite, I thought to myself that my plan had gone well.

"My pleasure."

I rushed back into the kitchen with my cart to breathe a huge sigh of relief and start washing dishes. Not before setting a crepe aside for Ali, of course. Even if Mrs. Hawthorne hated me, I'd keep the house manager on my side.

"Well . . ." Ali said when she returned, standing over her breakfast at the island. "She ate every bite."

"Really?" I nearly fell over with excitement.

Ali smiled and gave me a thumbs up. Which was downright giddy for her.

Yes. I could do this, I told myself. Confidence. Project confidence and I could win over Mrs. Hawthorne. Manifest that shit.

I was going through provisions at the house pretty fast, so while the family would be out of the house for the day, I took the opportunity for another trip into town. My primary mission was another trip to the marketplace, but I really wasn't in any rush, so I decided a little sightseeing couldn't hurt.

The first spot that caught my eye as I meandered the crowded sidewalk was a blue storefront with white trim and a festive model of Santa's Village in the window. A working train set chugged around the tiny town of gingerbread houses, elves, and a Christmas tree centerpiece. Stories & Sips bookstore and coffee shop was bustling with ski moms chatting over lattes, while their rambunctious children darted around bookshelves themed and decorated to their genre. Two employees stood on ladders near the front windows hanging lighted garlands over posters for the latest bestsellers and new releases.

"This town really goes all out on decorating," I said to the young woman behind the register with a ski goggle tan around her eyes, who took my order for a cappuccino and chocolate muffin.

"Oh, yeah," she said, pulling a muffin from the display case to put on a porcelain plate. "The annual holiday decor contest is basically our World Series. We take bragging rights pretty seriously."

After I took my snack to a cozy corner and tucked myself into a worn leather chair, I snapped a few pictures for the Instagram account. This shop was a charming small-town treasure. The place to be for people watching when snow was falling gently outside. My coffee mug was perched on one side with a mis-matched saucer beneath it while I scrolled the time-line, saving and un-saving recipes to try.

"Elle, hey!"

I glanced up from my phone to spot Bea, her nose ring tipping me off, striding over before she dumped herself into the chair beside mine.

"Hey," I said, excited to see a familiar face. "How's it going?"

"Yeah, good." She shrugged out of her jacket, a blue plaid flannel shirt tied in a knot underneath, and draped her legs over the arm of the chair. "Haven't seen you around in a few days."

"I basically live in the Hawthornes' kitchen."

"How's that going?" Her hair was slightly different than the last time I saw her, smaller braids arranged in one larger

166

French braid and worn to the side over her shoulder. "Regret your whole life yet?"

I choked back a laugh, shaking my head. "No, not yet. Really, it could be a lot worse."

She arched a curious eyebrow. "That right?"

"What?" I asked nervously.

"Nothing. Charles Hawthorne tends to have that effect on people."

I was immediately defensive, smiling too much like it made me look innocent. "What? No. Nothing like that."

It was exactly like that.

"Okay," she said, putting her hands up. "Whatever you say."

"Really."

Amelia's warning about gossip rang in my ears.

"None of my business," Bea insisted, although her conspiratorial smirk said she wasn't buying it.

"Anyway . . ." I said, begging to talk about anything else. "How's Pops? Looks like the town's decorating wars are in full swing."

"It's getting brutal out there. Have you seen the two-story yeti outside Grover's Hardware yet?"

"I can't believe I missed it."

"Just went up this morning," she said. "Last year it was a twelve-foot nutcracker. I keep telling the town commerce committee we need a height limit. They're completely out of control."

"Next it'll be a dozen sugar plum fairies casting a shadow down Main Street."

Her face turned severe. "Don't even joke. They'll hear you."

By Christmas, this place would put the Macy's Parade to

shame. I couldn't wait to walk the streets once the official voting period for the contest opened.

"So, what brings you around today?" I asked Bea, who didn't seem in any particular hurry.

"Refreshing The Snowdrift's library. A couple of times a year we like to turn over the selection. Want to help me pick out some new titles? We don't let Delilah do it anymore because she only picks the smuttiest rom-coms and the most gruesome murder mysteries. Lots of snowed-in motel stuff. Scares the guests."

"I can see why."

After I deposited my dishes at the counter, we first took a glance at the Featured Release display. There were little handwritten cards under several titles with quotes and recommendations from various town personalities and business owners.

"Hey, that's you," I pointed out.

Delilah and Bea's names were side by side and I chuckled at how different they were, even in reading preferences. Bea had recommended a memoir I'd heard about on the daytime radio that played in The Denver Drip every morning. Delilah's choice was a psychological thriller by a Colorado author. She described it as visceral, gripping and unputdownable, about a twin who gets murdered, and her sibling is the number one suspect.

"See what I mean?" Bea grimaced at the book as I picked it up to glance at the inside flap and the fittingly moody author portrait. "She's a little scary sometimes."

"Let's see what else we can find," I laughed, setting the book back on the shelf.

"So, what about you?" she asked, leading us toward the non-fiction section. "I see the Hawthornes do let you have some time off?"

"Sure. More than I expected, actually. They're out of the house a lot, which occasionally leaves me with not much to do. Made my first attempt at skiing yesterday."

"How did that go?"

"I didn't die." Which felt like a significant accomplishment. "But I think maybe I'm better suited to the après lifestyle than the slopes."

"Speaking of which . . ." Bea paused at a shelf to scan several covers from a selection of coffee table books about wildlife and travel. "Have you seen that Après Brie account on Instagram?"

My face flushed pink while I quickly grabbed a random photography memoir off a shelf. "Um . . ."

"They mostly post incredible-looking food. But also, a ton about Maplewood Creek. Shops, cafes, and whatnot."

"Sounds neat," I said anxiously.

I had picked up quite a few new followers recently, but the whole idea of a pseudonym was to remain anonymous. Not that I was posting anything private or salacious. The content was strictly food and fluff. Still, I was walking on eggshells where Mrs. Hawthorne was concerned. I didn't want to give her any reason to look at me sideways.

Well. Other than making out with her son. But that was beside the point.

"Everyone in town is talking about it. Business owners are starting to get jealous about who's showing up in posts and who isn't. One more competition for everyone to fight over."

Oh, great. I'd just gotten here and already I'd started a new Cold War.

"We're all trying to figure out who's behind it," she said. "My money is on some influencer paid to stay at one of the absurdly expensive Airbnbs. Any day now, they're going to be posting promo codes and referral links. Watch."

"Yeah," I said, relieved. "I'll have to check it out."

"Oh! That reminds me. Have you heard about the Thanksgiving Throwdown?"

"No, I don't think so." I found a shelf of cookbooks and flipped through a new one from Marcus Lee. "Let me guess, it's a giant town-wide snowball fight?"

"No," she said, cocking her head. "That's a great idea, though. I might have to mention it at the next chamber of commerce meeting. The Thanksgiving Throwdown is an annual baking competition held over the course of a day. This year's theme is gingerbread. You should enter."

"I'd love to." My pulse jumped at the thought and crashed back down just as quickly. "But my schedule's sort of unpredictable. And I'm not sure it's a great idea to ask for time off when I just started a new job. Something tells me Mrs. Hawthorne isn't the accommodating type."

"Maybe they don't need to know," she suggested with a coy smirk. "Like you said, they're out of the house a lot. They probably wouldn't even notice you're gone."

She had a point. My off hours were my own. As long as the family didn't need me, I was free to roam around. The caveat being, I was always at their beck and call, ready to jump into action at a moment's notice. But with a little clever coordination, I suppose it was possible.

"I'll think about it," I told her.

"Terrific. There's an entry fee, and of course materials . . ."

Materials. That sounded ominous.

"But The Snowdrift will sponsor you. Plus, there's a thousand-dollar prize to the winner."

"Well, shoot. You should have led with that," I laughed. 'But thank you, that's very generous.'

"Anyway, think it over. And when the Hawthornes don't have you chained to the chalet, don't be a stranger. Swing by the inn or come find us at The Foggy Goggle. I can introduce you to some people. If you're going to be here a while, you might as well make some friends."

"Thanks, I'd love that."

A big part of me was missing home. I didn't have a big social circle in Denver either, and maybe I was better known for canceling on plans than being the life of the party, but still, it could get a little lonely in the cottage all by myself. And I didn't want to cling to Charles as my only source of entertainment. Wonderfully distracting as he was.

So, after leaving Bea at the bookstore, I called Hannah on my way to start my provision shopping.

"Elle, finally!" she answered.

"Hey there." I strolled toward the looming white yeti peering above the rooftops in the distance. "You still at work?"

"Nope. Just got home. It's about time you called. Feels like I haven't heard from you in forever. Forget about me already?"

"Never. Calling to give you the full update now."

"Hang on." I heard the refrigerator open and close in the background and the sound of a soda can popping. "Okay, go. What's it like so far?"

Children in ski suits ran up a hill across the street beside the post office, carrying their sleds and getting a running start before shooting down the snow-covered slope.

"I had the most amazing meal of my life at this incredible mountaintop restaurant," I told her. "I'm going to send you the link. You'd absolutely die for the elk."

"Oh, I'm so jealous. What else? Hook up with any hot ski instructors yet?"

Hannah always did get right to the point.

"Not quite. Though I did almost have to punt a first grader off a mountain."

She barked out a sharp laugh. "I'd have paid to see that."

"And I got on a ski lift."

Christmas songs played like a radio changing channels every time a shop door opened. Tourists were pouring out of the storefronts with arms full of bags.

"Wow. You've changed. Where's the girl I knew who hated getting up on the ladder to change the special on the menu board?"

"I killed her. Buried her in the snow behind the woodshed."

Hannah giggled down the phone.

"Oh, and I'm thinking about entering a pastry competition. Winner gets a thousand bucks."

"You'd kill it. Those poor, unsuspecting townsfolk wouldn't know what hit them."

"Only trouble is, gingerbread is the theme and that's not exactly my strong suit."

"Pfft," she scoffed. "You can rock any pastry. I say go for it."

"We'll see. If the way this town decorates is any indication, I might be getting in over my head. Somehow, I don't think a simple gingerbread man is going to cut it."

More like the Terracotta Army of gingerbread.

"Okay, but here's the really important question: What's the forecast out there?" she demanded. "Hunky with a chance of flirting? I need the scoop."

"The scoop is I'm here to work, not flirt."

"Oh my God, that's a yes," she insisted.

"What? No, it isn't."

"Please. I know you. Who is he? Is he tall? Rich? More importantly, does he have a younger brother?"

Her powers of deduction were uncanny and a little annoying.

"If there *was* a guy . . . we would just be friends."

"Uh-huh," she hummed. "So, you're basically in love with him."

"Well, now I'm hanging up," I threatened.

"Wait! Before you go, I'm trying to talk my mom into taking us up there for Thanksgiving. It really doesn't seem right celebrating here without you and I hate the idea of you up there all alone."

My heart swelled at the thought. "Actually, that would be amazing. I'd love to see you both. And I know the perfect place for you to stay, if Megan thinks you can swing it."

"I'll let you know. But plan on it!"

After hitting up the wine shop and finding some excellent local olive oil, I drove over to the marketplace to make another pass at Mia's produce and get her advice on some proteins.

The sprawl of holiday decor had certainly made its way to the barn as well. Everywhere there were tufts of fake snow dotted with small Christmas trees, big blue and silver menorahs, giant inflatable turkeys and papier-mâché cornucopias overflowing with fake plastic vegetables. It was a little chaotic, but I appreciated their devotion to tradition.

When I approached Mia's stall, she was cashing out a customer with a wagon full of canvas tote bags and a sleeping dachshund in a red knit sweater.

"See you for happy hour later?" the woman asked, taking her receipt.

"Race you there," Mia told her as she noticed me and nodded hello.

The woman tugged her wagon as she walked away, the pup never stirring as they left to continue their shopping.

"Welcome back," Mia greeted me, dusting off the front of her apron. "I see you survived your first week."

"Guess you can't get rid of me that easy."

"Glad to hear it," she said with an encouraging laugh. "What can I get you?"

"Load me up," I said. "I really should get one of those wagons, come to think of it."

"Grover's Hardware." Mia winked, tapping her nose.

"The one with the giant yeti out front?"

"Can't miss it."

I made a mental note to swing by there while I perused her selection of soil-spotted mushrooms and fragrant, leafy herbs. I even snapped a few surreptitious photos of Mia's stall while she briefly turned to check on another customer, then went back to squeezing waxy cucumbers.

"So, how's the chef life treating you?" she asked.

"So far so good," I admitted. All things considered, it was far from the worst gig I'd ever worked.

"Really?" She cocked her head like I'd given her a riddle to solve. "Huh."

"What?"

Mia shrugged, absently rearranging a display of carrots with long, leafy stalks. "Nothing. Just the Hawthornes are notoriously difficult clients. Folks joke that half the tourism in this town is just the turnover of their staff."

"I don't know," I said. I grabbed a paper bag from a crate on the ground and started filling it with stone fruit. "I'm new to private cheffing, but they don't seem any more difficult than most rich people, I guess."

No doubt Mrs. Hawthorne was a handful. Sometimes it felt like she made a sport out of keeping me on my toes. But it wasn't like her demands were outlandish or exceptionally malicious. She just craved perfection. I'd say she was paying me enough to deserve at least the attempt.

"Give it time," Mia groused, smile faltering. "They'll find a way to let you down."

"Speaking from personal experience?"

That was a pretty specific accusation. The tone of Mia's delivery said it was more than idle small-town chatter. Though I didn't want to take a wrong step and end up neck-deep in the gossip, I couldn't deny a growing curiosity about why Mia seemed to have a particular aversion to the family.

"I'm just saying . . ." Mia plastered on a flippant expression and shook her head, aloof. "Don't expect too much and you won't be disappointed."

The vibe had turned unavoidably awkward while I finished my shopping and Mia began to ring me up. I felt bad that I'd soured her mood.

"Hey, what can you tell me about the Thanksgiving Throwdown?" I asked, changing the subject.

Her eyes perked up. "Oh, yeah. One of my favorite holiday events. Takes place outside city hall. Last year someone made the Grand Canyon out of German chocolate cake. Year before that, there was a life-size toffee Elvis. It gets pretty intense."

I sighed inwardly. Knowing this town, I'd had a feeling.

"Ran into Bea at the bookshop earlier. She's trying to get me to enter."

"Do it," she said. "I'm not much of a baker, but I love to watch. A huge audience gathers to watch the creations come together. People get so creative. But if you're going to do it, better get planning now."

"Yeah, I guess I'll have to figure out what I can build out of gingerbread and frosting that could beat a gingerbread Taj Mahal."

Mia's face brightened suddenly. "Hey," she said, picking up several of my bags, "What are you doing tonight? A group of us are getting together. Low-key hang. Grab a few drinks and shoot some pool. We could have a brainstorming session."

She helped me carry my haul out to the Land Rover in the parking lot and I opened the lift gate of the trunk.

"I've got dinner service for the family, then I'm probably going to crash out and catch up on some sleep."

"Boo," she teased as we loaded the bags.

"Raincheck?"

"Fine. But I'm going to keep bugging you."

"Good. I want you to."

I appreciated the effort. Back home, people stopped inviting me places because I was always too tired to go out after pulling double shifts. Then I forgot how to make friends. Here, I seemed to have a little more time on my hands than I'd expected. And more importantly, great people that I genuinely wanted to spend that time with.

Chapter 19

Over the next few days, I didn't hear much from Charles, as the family was out of the house more often than not. If I was honest, there was a tiny niggling seed of paranoia in my mind that wondered if our date day had somehow given him the ick and he was done with me. Or that his mother had found out and was purposefully keeping us apart. Then I reminded myself that there was an entire genre of fiction about people who went mad while secluded in snowy mountain retreats, and that maybe I should stop overthinking it.

Instead, I browsed the Maplewood Creek town Instagram account for photos from last year's Thanksgiving Throwdown. As expected, those bakers didn't skimp on the grandeur. It was like *Holiday Wars* run amok. There were *Home Alone* houses with working booby traps, and life-size reindeer on snowboards. Every new image exploded my preconceptions of what was possible to construct from sugar and flour. Enough that I started to feel a little jealous. And a lot inspired. Even if I couldn't rig up a fully articulated Charlie Brown out of chocolate, I wanted to be part of the experience.

That evening before I started prep for dinner service, I found Ali in the dining room arranging the place settings.

"The family should be back by seven," she said, wiping spots from the wine glasses with a microfiber cloth.

"Actually, I wanted to ask about the schedule next week. There's a baking competition in town and I was thinking about entering. It's about six hours. I could leave right after breakfast service and still make it back in time for dinner. If the family planned to be out for lunch."

They usually were.

Ali paused, holding up a glass to the light to inspect for more spots or errant specks of dust. "I suppose that's alright. As long as it doesn't interfere with your event prep. I'll reconfirm the family's plans with Mrs. Hawthorne and let you know tomorrow."

"Thank you. I'd really appreciate it."

She placed the glass down on the table and moved on to polishing the next. "Of course, if the family did suddenly come home early, you'd have to accommodate them."

Meaning drop everything and haul my ass back up the mountain to push out a gourmet meal on zero notice.

"Understood," I told her, already fizzing with ideas. "Thank you, Ali. I'll get back to it."

"Okay," she said, nodding indulgently. "Off you go."

Between obsessing about the ramifications of my day with Charles, and wondering how to top a scale model of the Overlook Hotel complete with film-accurate hedge maze, I decided that after dinner service, the best cure for my rampantly accelerating imagination was a night out with the girls. So, I finally took Mia up on her invitation to hang out in town. After dinner was complete and washed up, I texted her and got a reply to meet her at The Goggle, where she was already a few drinks deep with Bea and Delilah.

Entering the bar, I shook the snow from my shoulders and shrugged out of my jacket while I scanned the room for the trio. The place was packed, with sports on the several overhead TVs mingling with the noise of conversation, glasses clinking, and the crack of pool balls in the billiards area.

I quickly spotted Mia and the twins, who waved me over to their high-top table sandwiched beside a group of ski bros playing beer pong on a purpose-built table.

"Look who made it," Mia announced, kicking out a chair for me while she downed the last of a beer and whistled to an unseen waiter for another. "Finally!"

Her wavy red hair was down and blow-dried, flowing like lava around her shoulders to compliment her V-neck sweater that put her own set of twins on full display.

"Thought we'd never get you down the mountain for a drink," Bea said, sliding over to make room for me.

"I know," I said, sitting. "Sorry. My schedule's a little unpredictable at the moment."

"What are you drinking?" Delilah said when a young waiter with shaggy hair reached our table with Mia's refill.

As usual, the sisters couldn't have been more different in their fashion choices. Bea was rocking a simple blue flannel shirt tied at the waist—clearly her signature—while Delilah wore a pink check crop top and coordinating leggings.

"Shots!" Mia exclaimed, throwing her arms up.

"Definitely not." I glanced up at the waiter. "Something cheap. Anything but the mulled cider." That stuff was dangerous.

"Bring her the Face-plant IPA," Delilah told the waiter.

"I don't know if I like the sound of that," I laughed, a little nervous.

"You'll like it. From a local brewer. Trust me."

I suppose they'd earned the benefit of the doubt.

"Hungry?" Bea asked.

"Starved, actually. I spend all day around food, but constantly forget to eat."

"Hazard of the job," Mia said, nodding. "Not easy being a boss bitch."

"Let's do two dozen hot wings, grilled, and some potato skins, please. And more waters all around," Delilah said to the waiter, who jotted down our order and scurried away.

"I noticed the decorations outside The Snowdrift are really coming along," I said to the twins. "At least twice as many since the last time I swung by."

"Pops is singlehandedly causing a national tinsel shortage," Bea chuckled. "Keeping him off ladders is becoming my new full-time job."

"Oh, no." Mia slunk down in her seat, covering her face like she could hide behind the wall of half-empty bar glasses crowding the wet, sticky table.

"What?" Delilah glanced over her shoulder, searching for the sudden cause of Mia's disappearing act.

"Tom. Two o'clock."

"Yikes." Bea cringed, slouching in her seat with nowhere to run.

"Evening, ladies." A tall, skinny guy with curly black hair, wearing an expensive wool coat and too much cologne, stood behind Bea's chair, with the sort of toothy grin you only saw in local car commercials. "Mia, always a pleasure."

Her face turned sour as she reluctantly sat up in her chair. "What do you want, Tom?"

The man held up his hands in mock defense, smile never faltering in the face of her obvious disdain. "Whoa. Cease fire. Just came to remind you about our little opening next weekend. I didn't see your name on the RSVP list."

"That's because I put the invitation through a woodchipper and turned it into mulch, Tom."

"Isn't she hilarious?" He laughed, glancing at the rest of us while we sat in awkward silence and slight fascination at their testy exchange. "You're all invited as well. The more the merrier."

Tom plopped down several business cards on the table. They immediately turned soggy in the condensation from our glasses.

"They'd rather suck a tailpipe, Tom."

Undeterred, he just laughed and shook his head as our waiter returned with four waters, my IPA, and refills for the girls.

"If you change your minds," he said. "We're having some live entertainment and an open bar. I've never known you to pass up a free drink, Mia."

She lifted her glass with a sarcastic sneer. "First time for everything."

"Pleasure as always," he answered, walking away with a nod.

"The guy seriously can't take a hint," Delilah groaned. "What a douche."

"Somebody fill me in," I said. "What was that all about?"

"Tom thinks he's John D. Rockefeller or something," Bea responded.

"Okay . . ." That didn't tell me much.

"He went to school with us," Delilah said while Mia began chugging her beer with grim-faced determination. "Just a regular local boy who lucked into business school and came back to town with delusions of grandeur. Now he's intent on replacing as many small businesses as possible with huge obnoxious chains."

Mia slammed her empty glass down and wiped her mouth on her sleeve. "Tom is the demon spawn of Ebenezer Scrooge and Hans Gruber."

"And he stole Mia's business idea," Bea added.

"Really? What was it?"

Mia slouched back in her seat, sighing. "It was stupid."

"No," Bea told her forcefully. "It was terrific. It still is."

"I want to hear it," I said eagerly.

Mia rolled her eyes. "I wanted to do, like, curated foodie vacations to Maplewood Creek that would include accommodation and seasonal activities, but mostly focused on the local farm-to-table culinary scene. Tours and demonstrations. Let people come to learn about our agriculture and local brewers, maybe take cooking classes. Wine pairings. That kind of thing."

"Sounds fantastic," I told her. "That's exactly the type of vacation I'd love to take."

"Only I made the mistake years ago of mentioning it to Tom. Back when I thought I had an investor. Then suddenly, the money guy bailed on me and Tom got super into the Airbnb boom. Buying up properties to turn into outrageously expensive rentals. Then last year, he announced he was part-nering with a new restaurant chain to do basically the exact same thing I'd told him about, except squeezing out all the locally owned businesses that were supposed to be the whole point."

"Once the new money came in from all the rich folks up the mountain," Delilah interjected, "big chain corporations got interested. They want to turn this whole place into ski-themed Disneyland and completely wreck the vibe."

"Don't get us wrong," Bea said. "Tourism is great. It keeps the lights on around here. We're not allergic to money."

"But you all were here first. It's only fair locals should reap the benefit," I said.

Mia pounded the table, rattling our glasses. "Exactly. She gets it."

"So, what happened to your investor?"

We shared a pointed glance just as our waiter arrived with our food, putting an end to the topic.

"Let's just say, never rely on a man for anything," Mia answered flatly. "They'll only let you down."

Once we had put down a few dozen wings, the four of us pulled on gloves and scarves as we prepared to brave the cold and check out the progress of the holiday decorations down Main Street, in all their lighted glory.

"I swear, the bakery better have upped its game this year," Delilah said, pulling a faux fur hat over her braids. "If their display is as uninspired as last year, I'm deducting points."

"You're brutal," Bea teased, zipping up her puffy jacket. "It's supposed to be fun, Delilah. Not the Hunger Games."

"Fun? This is serious business," Delilah shot back with a

wink. "The winner gets that big trophy and bragging rights for a year."

"Speaking of bragging rights," Mia said, "Elle, have you given any more thought to the Thanksgiving Throwdown? I heard Tom is sponsoring a contestant, too. Would be nice to shove an epic defeat in his face."

"Yeah, come on, Elle." Bea gave me a playful nudge with her elbow. "Win one for the good guys."

"I did run it by the Hawthornes' house manager. She didn't think it'd be a problem. Just so long as Mrs. Hawthorne doesn't decide to throw an impromptu twelve-course tasting lunch that day."

"So, that's a yes?" Bea asked.

"Yeah, okay. Since it's a matter of town pride. I'm in."

"Excellent." Mia clapped her hands, rubbing them together like she was already imagining the ruthless levels of gloating that would take place when Tom tasted defeat. "I can't wait to rub that bastard's stupid face in it."

Mia linked her arm through mine, her cheeks pink from the cold. Outside, the streets were alive with twinkling lights, garlands, and window displays, each shop more elaborate than the last. It felt like something out of a movie—the kind of small-town charm that was impossible not to fall in love with.

As we strolled the sidewalk, commenting on everything from the giant arch over the toy store's entrance to the elf hockey team skating on a fondant pond in the bakery window, Mia pulled out her phone to snap a few pictures. "Have you guys seen this account?" she asked, holding her phone up so we could see. "It's called Après Brie—this foodie account that's been posting about stuff from all over town. Some of the captions are hilarious."

Bea leaned closer, squinting at the screen. "We were just talking about that the other day. Didn't they post something about the caramel pecan pie at the diner last week?"

With the family constantly out of the chalet, I had more free time on my hands during the day than I'd expected. So, I had spent some of it exploring the town for content on my new account. I wasn't going to break the internet any time soon, but I was definitely starting to build a small following. Particularly among the Maplewood Creek residents, it seemed.

"Yep." Mia nodded enthusiastically. "I heard they sold out the next day. There was a mad rush for pecan pies."

Delilah laughed. "Who runs it? Do we know?"

"Definitely not a local," Bea insisted. "I told Elle I'm betting on an influencer. Some viral marketing campaign."

"That would make sense," Mia said, nodding while we continued to walk. "Sounds like the kind of thing Tom would come up with."

"I don't know about that," Delilah argued. "The posts feel a little too sincere for the usual online influencer types. And the dishes they post are chef-quality. Lots of fancy plating and whatnot."

"Well, we know a chef who's new in town," Mia joked, elbowing me in the ribs. "What do you say, Elle? Are you a secret celebrity?"

"Oh, um, yeah." I froze, the words catching me off guard. My heart thumped wildly as I tried to play it cool. "You caught me."

Mia raised an eyebrow. "Wait. I don't think you're kidding."

"What? No, of course I am."

Shit. That backfired.

"Holy shit! It is you!"

"That's crazy," I deflected.

The twins shared a glance.

"I think you're busted, Elle," Bea said.

"You kind of suck at lying," Delilah added.

My cheeks burned, and I let out a nervous laugh. "I . . . it's definitely not me."

"Uh-huh," Bea said, smirking. "Your face says otherwise."

I looked away, pretending to admire a particularly extravagant light display. I'd started Après Brie as a fun way to document my culinary journey, never imagining it would gain any real traction.

"Okay, fine," I admitted, sighing. "It's me. But please don't tell anyone."

"Why?" Delilah asked, genuinely curious.

"Because if the Hawthornes find out, they will fire me," I said, glancing around nervously. "Even if I've never said anything *mean*, I . . . some of the comments could be taken the wrong way."

Mia gave me a sympathetic look. "Don't worry, your secret's safe with us. Right, ladies?"

Bea and Delilah nodded in agreement, and I felt a wave of relief. We continued down the street, the conversation shifting to the competition again, but my mind lingered on the account. I'd have to be more careful in future.

We approached the courtyard in the center of town, where mostly couples held hands as they skated around a small ice rink or cozied up around several firepits, sipping cocoa and roasting marshmallows from a street vendor.

"I would kill for s'mores right now," Bea announced.

So, we hopped in line to procure some dessert treats and took up a few chairs around a vacant propane firepit.

"So . . ." Delilah said, blowing on her charred marshmallow. "Speaking of secrets, I heard a rumor that Charlie Hawthorne's been gallivanting around town recently with a new mystery woman." She turned her long marshmallow roasting stick toward me like a microphone. "Care to comment?"

"Absolutely not," I told her, hiding my blushing cheeks behind my cup of cocoa. "That's expressly against my NDA."

Bea snorted. "That's a yes."

"You know they shared a bathroom at the inn when she arrived," Delilah tossed out, smirking at me.

Mia almost dropped her graham crackers. "Hold on. What?"

"Well, not at the same time," I laughed.

"Strangely, they both came back that night of the blizzard at almost the same time," Delilah added.

"How do you know?" I said, outraged. "I didn't think anyone was still awake."

Bea pulled a marshmallow off her stick to build her s'more. "Sounds like an admission to me."

"We're all friends here now, right?" Delilah prodded. "So, let's have it. No more secrets, Elle. Did you bang the golden boy?"

I shoved a whole smoking marshmallow right into my mouth and felt it singe my tongue. "No comment," I mumbled around the gooey ball of molten sugar.

Guess I wasn't as under the radar as I'd thought. Still,

just the mention of Charles brought a smile to my face. And a warm feeling that hadn't gone away since the night we'd met.

"Mia . . ." Bea sent a look her way. "You're awfully quiet over there."

She shrugged, watching the flames dance around our marshmallows. "I have absolutely no opinion on the topic."

Her demeanor suggested otherwise. I didn't know her that well yet, but even I could spot that when Mia fell silent, there was a lot she wasn't saying.

"Okay, that's the second time you've clammed up about the Hawthornes. What, is there some kind of bad blood there I should know about?"

At this point, I was done being subtle. And it reminded me I really didn't know this family, or Charles, at all. Gossip clause be damned, I wanted to know what I'd gotten myself into.

"Somebody would tell me if I was accidentally working for the mob, right?"

Delilah laughed. "Nothing like that. At least, I'm pretty sure there aren't any bodies buried up at that chalet. But then, you never can tell."

"They say it's always the quiet ones," Bea quipped.

"That family is anything but quiet," Mia snarked.

"What does that mean?"

"The Hawthornes go way back in Maplewood Creek," Delilah explained. "Everybody loved the grandparents. Pillars of the community and all that. They had a lot to do with bringing some of the initial investments that turned us into a resort

190

town. Made us a ski destination. All to support Mrs. Hawthorne's career when she first got into competitions."

"Mrs. Hawthorne was practically royalty around here back in her skiing days," Bea told me. "Biggest celebrity the town had ever seen. Way before our time, of course."

"Then she got injured," Delilah added. "Ended her career. It was a real shame. They said she could've become one of the best in the world."

Which would certainly explain her penchant for perfection, and maybe even her sour disposition, but that was hardly a scandal.

"Okay, but what's that got to do with all the sideways glances every time someone mentions their name?"

"Well . . ." Bea flicked her eyes to Mia to see if she planned to interject, then said, "back in the day, Charles, for one, was kind of a hellion."

That didn't strike me as all that surprising. Young, handsome men were usually trouble.

"Him and his Ivy League buddies used to be notorious for getting kicked out of bars," she continued. "Throwing wild parties. Trashing hotel rooms."

I didn't doubt her, though it was difficult to picture that version of him. Then again, I knew very little about the guy. All things considered.

"But something must've happened," I said. "The reason he was gone for so many years?"

"There was a car accident," Bea admitted. "Some property damage. And a whole lot of embarrassment."

I sat back, a bit stunned. "Was anyone hurt?"

"No," Delilah assured me. "Not seriously. Nothing like that . . ."

"Point is, for too many years that family has chewed up this town, then spit us out," Mia snapped. "They run around doing whatever they please, and to hell with the consequences. So, forgive me if I'm not signing up for the fan club."

Chapter 20

That night with the girls had given me a lot to think about. And while I was eager to ask Charles about some of the things I'd learned, I needed to find the right moment. Today, after breakfast service, he found me brainstorming in the kitchen for the Thanksgiving Throwdown.

"Don't suppose I can tempt you back out on the slopes?" he asked, decked out in ski gear while he watched me sketch at the kitchen island.

"Not today." I hunched over my notebook. "I have to come up with an amazing gingerbread design, or else I'm going to completely embarrass myself."

He peered over my shoulder at the numerous evolving ideas jotted down in pencil. "The locals do take their pastry contests seriously. Generational feuds have been born. Blood spilled."

"Blood, huh?"

"Well, maybe it was raspberry jelly," he laughed. "Who's to say?"

"No one warned me there were so many rules and requirements," I told him, unfolding the four-page contest regulations from my notebook. "I'm starting to think I've gotten in over my head."

The contest was in just three days and already I felt behind the eight ball.

"You know, there is such a thing as too much preparation." Charles pulled the pencil from my hand. "Maybe I can help."

I reached for the pencil but he held it away from me, teasing. "I don't see how flirting is going to help me beat a guy wearing a film-accurate Storm Trooper uniform made of gingerbread."

Charles stopped short. "Wait, really?"

I shrugged. "That's the rumor."

"But what does that have to do with the town or the holidays?" he scoffed.

"I don't know. But it would be pretty impressive."

"No." He tossed my pencil at the countertop. "Unacceptable. The Thanksgiving Throwdown is about the season and celebrating Maplewood Creek. We can't let some hokey pop-culture pandering take the top prize."

"We?" I arched an eyebrow at him. "You're really bothered by this, huh?"

"Damn right," he said, face scrunched in a determined grimace. "You're going to win this thing. And you're going to do it the Maplewood Creek way."

"Yeah?" I said, skeptically amused by his sudden enthusiasm. "And how am I going to do that?"

A plan formed behind his brown eyes. "What you need is a little inspiration."

I should have known better than to trust that smirk, but

when Charles canceled his ski day to coax me out on a field trip, I couldn't say no to another afternoon in his company.

"So, you want to tell me where we're going?" I asked from the passenger seat of his Land Rover, while we bypassed the road to town and instead headed to the other side of the valley.

"If I did, you'd probably try to jump out of the car." Charles shot a mischievous glance my way.

"You know, that doesn't exactly inspire confidence. What could you possibly have planned that would make me want to do a tuck-and-roll?" I said, searching the snow-covered scenery for any hint of what he had in store for me.

"Trust me, you'll love it. It's just the thing you need to get a new perspective on your project."

There was nothing but trees and sloping rock faces all around us until a sign crept out of the ground:

Maplewood Creek Executive Airfield

I glanced over at Charles. "I'm not sure we have time to fly to Bavaria and back before I have to start dinner service."

He smiled to himself. "Don't worry. I was thinking something a little closer by."

Through a gate and inside the chain-link fence, Charles drove us past several hangars before driving right onto the tarmac.

"You can't be serious."

Looming in front of us on two skids was a blue and white helicopter.

"I never joke about flying."

Charles jumped out of the Land Rover and walked right up to the pilot standing beside the aerial death machine. He left me sitting in the SUV while they shook hands and chatted, walking around the aircraft like he was on a car lot. My eyes immediately went to the center console, but he'd taken the keys with him.

Ugh. This man was seriously annoying sometimes.

So, I took a deep breath and plastered on my best unbothered expression before I hopped out of the Rover and threw the door shut behind me. A gust of wind blew across the tarmac, whipping my hair around my face. It was a clear day, if a little blustery. Not a cloud in the sky.

"Elle, come meet Jason," Charles said, grinning cheekily. "Jason, this is my friend Elle. She's new to town and I thought we better give her the grand tour."

Jason was a stocky man in aviator sunglasses and a blue flight jumpsuit, like he'd just stepped off the set of *Top Gun*.

"I think we can handle that," Jason answered. "Hop on in and we'll get going."

While Jason disconnected the fuel line and jumped in the pilot's seat, Charles grabbed my hand to squeeze gently.

"Excited?" he asked, already knowing the answer.

"I sort of hate you right now," I told him.

"Yeah, but you sort of love me, too." He took me by the waist, threatening a kiss while Jason sat in the bird doing his pre-flight checklist.

"Pfft. I haven't totally decided not to push you out the door of this thing."

Charles pressed a brief kiss to my temple. "Like I said, you're going to love it."

The helicopter's engine whirred to life, the blades slowly rotating while Charles helped me into the rear passenger seat. He pulled the harness seatbelt over my shoulders and clicked it into place, then pulled a headset down from overhead and fit it over my ears.

"So we can talk to each other," he said.

"Yeah, I figured that part out for myself."

He just grinned, enjoying my malcontent. "Relax. It isn't scary at all."

"That's how I know you're lying."

Then, instead of climbing into the back beside me, Charles took a seat beside the pilot.

"What's the matter?" I said into the headset's microphone while the blades outside grew louder. "Afraid to sit next to me?"

"I wouldn't want to obstruct your view."

As a kid, I'd reluctantly let my best friend peer pressure me onto a rollercoaster once. I spent the entire ride looking straight down at my feet and digging my nails into his arm. I guess Charles knew better than to let me draw blood.

"Everybody comfy?" Jason asked.

"Nope," I answered.

"Alright. Then here we go."

With a little jostle, the ground suddenly fell away and that awful weightless feeling churned my stomach. Even in planes, takeoff was always the worst part. My knee bounced relentlessly, so vigorously that I thought I might shake the whole chopper as we climbed higher, over the trees and through the valley.

"Come on," Charles's voice said through my headphones. "You have to see this view. It's incredible. We're coming up on the town."

Before I knew it, we were far above the heart of Maplewood

Creek. The giant Christmas tree. The skating rink. All the people and decorations evident from above, like looking down on a huge snow globe.

"I can see The Snowdrift," I said. "And Pops's inflatable reindeer. Hey, and there's the Grover's Hardware yeti."

From up here, it looked like a tiny toy village. We soared over the ski resort and traced the curve of the slopes. The lift looked much less daunting from up here. Then we circled around toward the chalet and all the immaculate mansions nestled in the snowy pines. I pressed my face against the window to peer down at the frozen lake, the hot springs hidden deep in the forest. I was so fascinated with the landscape that I completely forgot to be scared. Until I heard Jason speak his next terrifying words.

"Ready to take the stick?"

"I've got the stick," Charles answered.

"The bird is yours."

"You're not seriously letting him fly this thing?!" I screeched.

Charles laughed. "I slipped him a little extra to let me take it for a spin."

"That's not funny!"

"Don't worry. I got my license years ago. Just keeping up with my hours to stay current."

"He's really not a half-bad pilot," Jason said.

"I don't want a pilot that's only half-good," I shot back.

The boys just laughed, thoroughly amused at my discomfort while Charles circled us smoothly around Maplewood Creek and over the mountain peaks. We watched intrepid snowboarders slalom down the fresh powder from the highest rocky ridges, and spotted backcountry skiers traipsing through secluded trails.

"Keep your eyes out for polar bears," Charles joked.

"Ha-ha."

Once Charles had had his fun, Jason thankfully took over the controls again, and brought us back to solid ground. I couldn't wait to climb out of that thing and feel the tarmac under my feet again while the boys said goodbye.

"See? You loved it a little," Charles said, after we climbed back into the Land Rover and cranked up the heat.

"Not sure I would have signed up for that if I knew I was putting my life in your hands," I said, rolling my eyes with a smirk.

Honestly, it was sort of hot he could fly a helicopter. I don't know. Maybe it appealed to the lizard part of my brain that thought it would make him useful in an apocalypse. Women dig guys who can be handy in an emergency.

"Admit it, you had fun."

"I had half-fun," I told him.

His self-assured smile pulled wider across his face. "I'll take it."

He reached over to cover my hand with his and held it the rest of the way home.

It turned out he was right. Seeing Maplewood Creek from a new perspective did give me a spark of inspiration for the contest. I spent the night after dinner service at the dining table in my cottage, furiously sketching out a plan. Now, I just had to pull it off.

Chapter 21

The night before the Thanksgiving Throwdown, I couldn't sleep at all. Too many thoughts were running through my head. Ingredient measurements and structural integrity calculations. I thought about architects building skyscrapers, and wondered how any of them didn't collapse from the overwhelming immensity of it all. And my gingerbread house wouldn't even have people in it.

I was up and in the kitchen well before the sun that morning, getting started on breakfast for the family. Which was fortunate, because it turned out Amelia had a couple of friends who flew in late last night for a brief layover before heading off for Whistler, so there were two extra places at the table today.

I had decided the best move was to fill the family up with a huge meal, so there was no possible way they could be hungry for lunch, even if they decided to stick around the chalet today. Which would hopefully leave me free to attend the contest. I had every burner on the stove going, and every rack of the ovens filled with baking sheets, churning out fresh muffins, banana bread, bagels, bacon, turkey sausage, hash browns, scrambled eggs, and cinnamon French toast with berry compote and crème fraîche. I even pre-blended half a dozen smoothies and green juices, just in case someone wanted to be a real pain in the ass.

"You've really outdone yourself this morning," Ali said, standing over the island while I plated up the pastry basket. "They might not be hungry again at all today."

"That's the idea."

I transferred maple syrup to individual ramekins and sprinkled salt flakes atop individual pats of butter for each place setting. I wouldn't give Mrs. Hawthorne the opportunity to scowl at a single missing touch. I passed a plate I'd set aside to Ali, with a little bit of everything, and she dug in gratefully.

"This turkey sausage is unbelievable," she moaned, dabbing the corner of her mouth with a paper towel. "What am I tasting?"

"Just a little bit of jalapeño and rosemary, to give some extra depth of flavor."

It was how I preferred my turkey burgers, and I figured it worked just as well for breakfast.

"Mmm," she hummed. "It's incredible. A little kick, but not too spicy."

"Charring the peppers first calms a lot of the heat."

The waitstaff entered to start taking platters and Ali quickly swallowed to accompany them back to the dining room with service, while I surveyed the messy aftermath I'd created. I glanced at my watch. If I hurried, there was just enough time to clean up and get down the mountain for the contest. Then I noticed I had a text from Mia.

> **Mia:** All set up here. We got everything on your list and your station is ready.

> **Me:** Thank you! Text you when I'm leaving.

So, while I got to work scrubbing pans, Ali returned to the kitchen to enjoy her breakfast. As the family and guests finished off various plates, the waitstaff dropped them back beside the sink. Luckily, I had the rhythm down pat now. It took hardly any time at all to get the place spotless and set up for me to jump right into dinner service this evening when I got back. Hopefully with first prize. I wasn't sure if there was a trophy involved, but it sure would look nice on the mantel above the fireplace in my cottage.

While Ali briefly went back to the dining room to check on the family, I finished up and took a minute to write myself a quick list for tonight's prep, to make sure I didn't forget anything when I was too tired to think straight later.

"Bad news," Ali said, walking back into the kitchen.

My stomach sank. "No. Don't say it."

"Mrs. Hawthorne suggested a spa day for Amelia and her guests."

I was confused. "Great. That should get them out of the house. What's the problem?"

"She wants to bring a yoga instructor and some massage

therapists up to the chalet. Said it might be nice to have some spa snacks prepared for them. Little sandwiches and the like."

I sagged against the kitchen island. I knew this would happen. It was my own fault for thinking I might be able to sneak away.

"Yeah," I said, shoving down my disappointment. "Of course. No problem. I'll get started."

"I'm sorry, Elle."

I nodded in thanks as Ali left. Astounded as I was that they could even consider folding themselves into pretzels after the meal I'd just fed them—of which they all ate nearly every bite—my first responsibility was to the chalet. If that meant cucumber sandwiches and grapefruit spritzers, the contest would have to go on without me. Whatever the entrance fee, I'd pay back Bea and Delilah if they couldn't get a refund.

I grabbed a clean cutting board and went to the fridge to see what I had to work with. I was pulling out mint and parsley when Charles burst into the kitchen.

"Ready for the big day?" he said. He looked at his watch. "Better get going if you don't want to be late."

I went to my cutting board to start chopping the herbs. "Didn't you hear? Your mom and Amelia are having a spa day. They requested snacks."

"What? When did that happen?"

I shrugged.

"They can order food from somewhere in town. I'll go talk to them."

"No," I said urgently, lifting my head from my chopping. "Please don't. That's exactly the kind of thing I've wanted to

204

avoid. I'm here to do a job. I can't have you jumping in to save me from work whenever I feel like it. Plus, it'll definitely tip them off that there's something going on between us."

Charles's face fell with disappointment. "Elle."

"I mean it. Just let me do this."

He sighed, visibly deflating. "Alright. It's your decision."

"Thank you," I told him earnestly. Because I'd much rather he respect my wishes than diminish my position by trying to leap to my rescue. "Go on then," I told him, plastering on a fake smile. "Get out of here and let me do my thing."

"I'll check on you in a while," he promised as he left.

But not a minute later, the door swung open again.

Amelia appeared in the doorway. "I couldn't help but overhear."

"I'm sorry?"

"Something about a contest?"

I was instantly mortified. "No, it was nothing. Any special requests for spa snacks this afternoon?"

She flashed a patient smile and strode over to the island where I was still chopping. "Today is the town's Thanksgiving Throwdown, isn't it?"

I was too embarrassed to answer.

"Well, then you better hurry up and get down there. Bragging rights are on the line."

A flicker of hope rose in my gut. "Your mother . . ."

Amelia waved off my concern. "We'll have a terrific spa day at the ski resort in town. Besides, what's the point of having her own wine locker at the hotel restaurant if she never uses it?"

"Really?" I asked, absolutely elated. I'd worked so hard on

my plan for the contest, it seemed a shame to let it go to waste. "You're sure?"

She smiled, shooing me away. "I'm sure. Go! Kick some gingerbread butt for me!"

"Thank you, Amelia!"

I gave her a hug, sort of surprising us both. Then I rushed out of the kitchen and back to my cottage to change and grab my backpack before texting Mia that I was on my way. I'd give Maplewood Creek a gingerbread extravaganza to remember.

Chapter 22

There was already considerable fanfare surrounding the large tent when I arrived, having jogged three blocks just to find parking. Spectators surrounded the baking stations, where folding tables and racks of portable ovens stood waiting for the frenzy of gingerbread to get underway.

"Elle, over here!" Bea called from the far station where she waited with Delilah and Mia. "You made it."

"Barely." I was still breathing heavily as I set my backpack on the ground beneath the table and pulled on an apron. "We good to go?"

"Got everything you asked for," Mia said. "Ovens are preheated."

"Everyone gets to start with one pre-boiled pot of water and four portable convection burners," Bea continued as she led me around the station, consisting of three folding tables in a horseshoe shape. "You've got two stand mixers, a handheld beater, a small blast chiller, and plenty of baking sheets."

"This all looks great," I told them. "Thanks so much for all your help."

I had brought my own knives of course, but beneath the center folding table were pots, pans, mixing bowls, and baking sheets, as well as various utensils and consumables like parchment paper. Several canvas bags behind the station contained my ingredients. Those I immediately began arranging on the station to get organized, separating structural cookie products from the decoration and tasting components.

"Five-minute warning, contestants," a voice over a loudspeaker announced. "That's five minutes until the start of the Thanksgiving Throwdown."

The crowd of spectators applauded, cheering on their favorite bakers. There were ten of us in all, a diverse group that included the owner of the local bakery, the pastry chef from the ski resort, and several local home cooks.

"You can thank us by winning," Delilah said, giving me a playful nudge for encouragement.

"We've got to get back to The Snowdrift for a bit," Bea said regretfully. "If we don't keep an eye on him, Pops will end up on the roof with more lights."

"Yeah, and I've got to get back to the marketplace," Mia said. "But you've got this. We'll swing by as much as we can to check in on you."

"No sweat," I told them. "Looks like I'm all set up."

"Ladies!" said a voice.

"Terrific." Mia's face crinkled with disgust at the sound of Tom's voice as he approached us. "Quick, hand me that pot of boiling water."

Delilah stifled a laugh, elbowing Mia.

"Lovely to see you all again. Jumping into the gingerbread fray?" Tom said with a plastic smile. He looked like he belonged on the streets of Manhattan, wearing a conspicuous Burberry scarf with black leather gloves. "I don't think I recall any of you entering the Thanksgiving Throwdown before."

"We're here supporting Elle," Mia said, lifting her chin.

He fixed me with a patronizing grin that said *aww, isn't that cute*. "You've got yourself a ringer, huh?"

"She's going to wipe the floor with the rest of them," Bea told him confidently.

"I've also decided to sponsor a contestant this year," Tom said. "My event space just happened to have a guest chef from Paris this week."

"What a coincidence," Mia groaned.

"Two minutes, contestants," the voice over the loudspeaker warned. "All non-participants, please clear the competition area."

"Why don't we make things a little more interesting?" Tom suggested. "A side wager maybe?"

"What'd you have in mind?" Mia said, taking an aggressive stance with her hands on her hips.

"How about if I win, you and your friends attend my grand opening tomorrow?" he suggested.

"And if we win, you leave town forever," Mia shot back.

"Or, you all have dinner on me. Anywhere you like. My treat."

Bea and Delilah shrugged. I knew from experience the chef's tasting menu at the mountaintop restaurant where Charles took me ran upwards of two hundred dollars per person. We could certainly do some damage there.

"Deal," I said. Because maybe I was selfishly looking forward to going back. And because I knew it meant everything to Mia to put this guy in his place.

"Final warning," the voice announced. "We are about to begin. Please clear the competition area."

Mia and Tom shook on it.

"Good luck," he said, striding away like he'd just swindled us out of our life savings.

"Now you really have to win," Mia told me, hands on my shoulders. "I can't spend a whole night around that guy. Don't let me down."

"I've got this."

Pastry was my safe space. I could bake with my eyes closed. If you ignored that little altitude hiccup with the croissants. The challenge here would be in the construction. I hadn't been able to make any test batches before the competition, so I was operating on gut instinct and some online research. The display portion of the gingerbread wouldn't be eaten, so we were free to make it more functional than delicious. Instead, only certain tasting elements incorporated into the final design would be sampled. Plus, a plated dessert piece that had to be made mostly of gingerbread, but was open to interpretation.

When the horn blew for the start of the six-hour cook, I waved goodbye to the girls and got to work. I started by mixing up several large batches of my gingerbread base. In my stand mixers, I creamed together butter and sugar until fluffy. While those worked, I sifted together my dry ingredients: flour, ginger, cinnamon, baking soda, baking powder, and salt. Then, to the mixers, I dropped in my eggs and molasses.

"The annual Maplewood Creek Thanksgiving Throwdown

is now officially underway, as our ten bakers start whipping up their gingerbread masterpieces. It'll be a long day of pastry and perspiration here, folks. So, settle in. Grab some cocoa. Get a snack. And cheer on our intrepid contestants."

I mostly tuned out the announcer's voice as they periodically bantered with the audience.

Next came the dry ingredients. At several stations I saw explosions of flour shoot into the air in great puffs of white. The audience hollered, reacting to the sudden chaos. I chuckled to myself at their rookie mistake, stopping my mixers before I added the dry ingredients, then starting again on a low setting and placing a towel over the bowls to prevent all the flour from leaping out.

I transferred the first two batches of dough from the mixers to plastic wrap, and formed them into large balls that I put in the blast chiller, while I repeated the process several more times. Once those were cooled, I cleared off some workspace and laid out a large roll of parchment paper sprinkled with flour. There, I rolled out my batter in several cookie sheet-sized slabs, meticulously measuring for identical thickness, and popped them into the preheated ovens at 350 degrees.

As I worked, I glanced down the line at the other contestants. We were all at roughly the same stage in our bake, each of us following a nearly identical game plan to get our construction batches churned out as quickly as possible, with little variation from the classic recipe.

Until I brought out my ring molds.

"Contestant number ten seems to have taken an unusual approach here on the end, folks," the unseen announcer said.

"Doesn't look like we should expect the typical little brown box from this chef."

Spectators began to gather around my station, whispering in curiosity as they watched me cut my rolled batter into long, tall strips, then form those around the outside of the upright ring molds. Several of those went on another set of cookie sheets and into the oven, molds included.

"Five hours remain of this baking battle, and we are still just getting started," the announcer's voice noted.

That was the first hour gone.

While my initial batches of baked gingerbread slabs cooled, I began on a few augmented batches. My plan was to play with different ingredients to produce a batter in varying shades, from blond to a deep chocolate brown. These would be accent pieces and didn't need to be as sturdy, so I was less concerned about how the differing formulations would affect the stability.

After yet more batches of gingerbread went into the ovens, I shifted my focus to the fun bit—the decor. That meant getting saucepans heated on the convection burners to prepare my glass candy. I added white granulated sugar to water, along with corn syrup, a pinch of cream of tartar, and food coloring to produce various beautiful shades of blue, red, green, and yellow. When the mixtures were heated to 300 degrees and had a liquid consistency, I poured each color into various molds positioned on silicone mats that were then set aside to cool and harden.

"And just like that, two hours have flown by," the announcer roared. "If you've been with us from the start, it's probably time to stroll on over to some of our sponsor booths for some holiday giveaways. There are games for the kids and lots of fun holiday swag, too. And if you're just joining us, I'd love if someone could scrounge me up one of those funnel cakes I see everyone eating."

Things started to feel a bit hectic under the big tent. The crowd of onlookers ebbed and surged at various points, while us bakers darted around our stations, checking ovens and jostling the ever-growing supply of baking sheets and gingerbread slabs. It seemed like we were all quickly running out of space to breathe, much less work. I referred to my notebook for my check list. Every step of this process was meticulously planned and plotted, to make sure I could get everything done in the time allotted, while giving each component the time they needed to bake, set, and cool.

Next up on the list were my copious ornaments that would accompany the primary structure: dozens of green rock candy trees, fondant snowmen dusted in shaved coconut, and an absurd amount of tiny sugar furniture. Just thinking about constructing them nearly made me regret this whole idea.

"Looking good, chef." Charles approached my station just as I began mixing up a batch of white fondant. "I see you managed to escape after all, huh?"

My exhaustion all but evaporated at the sight of him carrying a brown paper takeout bag and two smoothies.

"Thanks to your sister. Amelia was gracious enough to run interference with your mom. Please thank her again for me."

"Sure," he laughed. "When I offer, it's a conflict of interest. When she does, Amelia's a hero."

I rolled my eyes, smiling to myself as I concentrated on

rolling out my sugar sheets. "It's not the same thing, and you know it."

"Is there anything in the rules that says I can't bring you lunch?" he asked.

"I don't think so," I said, gratefully putting aside my rolling pin. I was starving. "What'd you bring me?"

"A berry smoothie and a BLT. Would you prefer honey mustard or spicy?"

"Spicy."

I dragged the large, long cooler over from the back of my station and positioned it under the front table, so it was long enough to give us each a place to sit.

"You sure you have time?" he asked, handing me a sandwich and unwrapping his own. "I don't want to throw you off your schedule."

I took a big bite, digging in. "I can spare a couple of minutes."

Glancing down the line, I could see several bakers step away from their stations for bathroom breaks, or to scarf down some quick food.

"So, who's our competition?" Charles asked.

"Hard to tell so far." No one had begun building yet. We were all still in the preliminary stages of baking and just getting our odds and ends sorted. "Mia from the marketplace kind of got goaded into a side bet with this guy, Tom—"

Charles laughed, nodding. "Oh, yeah. I know Tom. We all go way back. He's a pretentious try-hard, who likes to remind everyone how successful he is."

"Yeah, well, Mia hates his guts. And apparently, he's brought in some fancy French pastry chef, so the mission today is to just finish better than that guy."

Honestly, Mia seemed to have beef against all rich business-men in general. But at least Charles had the good sense to leave her alone. It seemed like Tom was a glutton for punishment. Or else he had some masochistic crush on her.

"Can I see what you're planning to build?" Charles asked.

"Uh-uh," I mumbled, my mouth full. "It's a secret."

"Come on. Just a little peek. I promise I won't tell."

I sighed. Those puppy-dog eyes were awfully potent. And he did bring me lunch. Suppose that earned him a reward.

"Okay, but don't laugh at my drawing." I pulled out my notebook and flipped to the sketch page. "I promise I'm better with cookie than pencil."

He glanced down at the sketch and back up at me, eyes widening. "Woah. Really?" Charles flipped to the next page. "Holy shit, Elle."

I quickly closed the notebook and tucked it away again to hide it from prying eyes.

"That's incredible," he said.

"If I can pull it off. I have no idea how much time it will actually take to put together. I might've sabotaged myself from the get-go. But I thought about what you said, about reflecting the town and the holiday spirit."

"This is a winning design for sure," he told me, emphatic. "I know you can do it."

"We have now officially passed the halfway mark of the Thanksgiving Throwdown," the announcer declared to a smat-tering of applause from the crowd still mingling around the tent. "That's three hours to go, and probably six more cups of coffee for me. If anyone would be so kind, I'd love a double espresso with extra whip."

"I should really get back to it," I told Charles as I finished my sandwich and balled up the paper wrapper. "Thanks for stopping by. I really needed the second wind."

"My pleasure."

He gathered up our trash and stood, letting me shove the cooler back behind my station.

"Come back for the judging?" I asked shyly.

"Wouldn't miss it." He flashed that charming smirk that reminded me why I'd found him so irresistible when he'd first sauntered up to me at The Foggy Goggle. "You know, you're awfully cute all covered in flour. I should really spend more time in the kitchen."

Blush immediately bloomed across my cheeks as I shoved him away from the station and wiped at my face with a rag.

"Get out of here," I ordered. "You're too distracting."

"Right," he said, snapping his fingers. "I'm supposed to be working on that. Sorry."

Half my time was gone, and I really did need to kick it into high gear. Because it wasn't only my gingerbread butt on the line.

Chapter 23

My shoulders were burning, my vision blurred. A solid hour hunched over this table constructing tiny sugar furniture had become an exercise in torture. My hands began to ache from so much small, intricate work. It reminded me why I'd been eager to evolve beyond pastry in the first place. The results were beautiful, but the labor was intensive.

Around me, the other contestants' designs were beginning to take shape. There was the predictable Griswold house from *National Lampoon's Christmas Vacation*, and a Nakatomi Plaza from *Die Hard*. Some more unorthodox entries too, like a gingerbread man brass band, and a parachuting turkey.

"There are just two hours left," the announcer said. "If you can believe it, we've been here four hours already, and absolutely no one has offered me a gingerbread sample yet. Not sure how I feel about that. But I'm on my second mulled cider, thanks to the fine folks at The Foggy Goggle, so it's not all bad."

That was my cue to get my tasting elements on the go. In one stand mixer, I combined gingersnap crumbs, brown sugar, ground ginger, and a pinch of salt with melted butter to form my pie crust. Once that was in the oven, I filled my second mixer with cream cheese, brown sugar, and lots of warming spices to combine, then added my eggs a little bit at a time. Next in was sour cream, molasses, rum, fresh ginger, and lemon zest, to create a fragrant and delectable gingerbread cheesecake. The baking of which was just a little trickier because it required a water bath.

Once my crust was done, I poured my filling over it and wrapped the bottom of my pan with tinfoil. That went into a larger, deeper pan filled with a couple of inches of boiling water. Then, the whole thing went into the oven for one hour. During which I absolutely could not open the door, or it would release all the steam and ruin my filling. It was a ridiculous choice to make in a baking competition, but would hopefully earn me points for bravery.

Then it was time to start construction. I made up a huge batch of royal icing—perfect for its sturdiness and stickiness—which would be my primary adhesive. First, I cut my gingerbread into precise slabs, according to numerous paper templates I'd printed and cut out last night. Then, on a piece of plywood I placed on the center table of my station, I plotted the foundation of my primary structure in icing, and began setting up the first gingerbread slabs, propping them up with small ramekins, bowls, cans, anything heavy enough to keep the walls upright while I worked.

I realized very quickly that I might've underestimated how long this design would take to construct. Minutes seemed to tick by at an increasingly rapid pace while I tediously lined my board and slabs with icing and stuck each piece in place with a wish and a prayer. The size of the whole thing seemed to balloon exponentially larger than I'd imagined in my head. My measurements were all exact, but as the structure grew higher, I faced the growing difficulty of how to access the upper portions without toppling the whole thing. I climbed up on the cooler. Then up on top on the table.

"Whoa. Looks like we might have to punch a hole in the tent soon," the announcer commented, to laughter from the audience. "Contestant number ten is certainly taking the Thanksgiving Throwdown to new heights this year. Right, folks? What do you say? Let's give our bakers some encouragement as we come down to the home stretch."

I had exactly enough materials to accomplish this design, so there was no room for error. I couldn't risk crumbling one gingerbread slab or it would endanger the whole structure. Which meant I had to work slowly. I was sweating bullets as I lathered on colored icing and glued down decorations. Inserted dozens of tiny pieces of furniture. Planted candy trees and dusted gingerbread rum ball snowmen in coconut. Installed candy glass windows and put little skating sugar people on a candy glass pond.

"This is incredible!" Mia appeared in front of my station just as I was hanging a gingerbread blondie helicopter from a hooked wire that dipped over the main structure. "Elle, I can't believe you built this by yourself."

"Don't celebrate yet," I warned her. "I've almost fallen on this thing like three times already."

"I brought you some coffee," she said, setting a cup down on one of the side tables near my mixers.

"We are down to the final hour, bakers. One hour left," the

announcer told us. "This is really getting exciting now, folks. You'll want to grab a good spot for the final judging."

"Any sign of Bea or Delilah yet?" I asked, teetering over my gingerbread monstrosity with a piping bag as I layered on the snow-covered roof.

"Not yet. But I'm sure they'll be here any minute."

"Oh, shit!" I almost forgot. I jumped down from my perch and dropped my piping bag to check on my cheesecake.

But when I got to the oven, something wasn't right. The little orange light above the temperature dial was off. Inside, the oven was dark and the water bath wasn't bubbling.

No.

No, no, no.

I opened the door and felt the inside. It wasn't nearly hot enough. I shook the pan and watched my cream cheese filling jiggle back at me.

"Shit!" I hissed under my breath.

"What's wrong?" Mia whispered, leaning across the near table.

"My oven wasn't on. How did that happen? I was pretty sure it was warm when I put the pie in."

Mia came around to the back of the station and traced the power cord to the surge protector, where two red lights indicated that the breaker had tripped.

"It shut off," she said. "What now?"

"I don't have enough time to preheat the oven again and get it baked. It needs every bit of the hour to cool and set up."

I didn't have a backup plan for my plated dessert element. It was gingerbread cheesecake or bust.

"I don't suppose you have any ideas for a dessert you don't have to bake," she said.

"Wait!" I laughed to myself. "Duh! That's exactly it."

Mia stared at me, confused. "What did I miss?"

"No-bake cheesecake."

"What's the difference?" she asked, watching me scurry around my station to see if I had enough remaining ingredients to make a go at another batch.

"Eggs, basically. Take out the eggs and you don't have to heat any part of it."

The trick was giving it enough time to set up in the blast chiller instead.

I'd used all my gingersnap cookies in the first crust, but I did have the gingerbread scraps from my construction slabs. Adding some extra sugar, butter, and warming spices, with a bit of orange zest and lemon juice, would revive the crumb into something delicious. Then it was just a matter of mixing up another batch of filling, this time minus the eggs. I'd also need to burn off the alcohol from the rum first.

Mia could only watch as I poured the last of my rum into a pan and lit it on fire. The audience reacted with shouts of awe as they suddenly leaned away from my station.

"Watch out, folks," the announcer cautioned. "We better keep those fire extinguishers standing by. Things are really heating up in here, huh?"

I popped the rum into the blast chiller for a few minutes while I mixed up the components for my second cheesecake attempt. I then added the rum, mixed the filling a bit more to combine, and applied both my crust and filling to a spring-form pan. That went into the blast chiller, with a fervent, desperate wish for things to work this time.

"How are we doing?" Charles had reappeared at the station.

"Only slightly panicking." I didn't have a moment to glance up at him while I rushed to get the final components on the plywood base.

"Where are Bea and Delilah?" he asked.

"No idea."

Even running around my station, I could sense the palpable tension on the other side of the tables, where Charles and Mia were standing conspicuously far apart.

"Hi, Mia," he said at one point while I placed a hat on Santa and put little fondant candles in the windows. "Long time no see."

"Uh-huh," was her only response.

"This is it, bakers. Get those final touches on there." The announcer's voice again broke through the commotion of the crowd. "Make it festive. Make it delicious. This is the final countdown to the end of the Thanksgiving Throwdown."

In the last few minutes, I didn't have time to think, only react. This was the most delicate part of the construction so far. I pulled out all of the stabilizing supports to let the structure stand on its own. There were audible gasps and exhales as each of us, every baker down the line, began to pull the training wheels away. I heard more than a few groans and yelps of disaster, which meant someone had just seen their gingerbread dreams dashed, but I couldn't spare so much as a peek. There was only time enough to stage my showpiece and . . .

"The cheesecake!" Mia yelled frantically.

I grabbed my dessert and tested it with a toothpick. The texture seemed right. Not too firm, but not too soft. I decorated it with piped whipped cream, cranberries, and caramelized orange slices. I set out three plates for the judges, where I would serve the slices when they arrived.

"Okay, folks. Here we go. Count down with me," the announcer called. "Five, four, three, two, one! That's it. Hands up, contestants. The baking portion of the Thanksgiving Throwdown is officially complete. Let's give them all a round of applause!"

Mia gave me a high five over the table. "You were amazing!"

"Well done," Charles said, leaning over to kiss my cheek. "Incredible work."

The wait now was excruciating. I was the last baker in line for judging, which meant I could only stand there and obsess over all the things I would have done differently. I watched as each contestant in turn demonstrated their incredible ingenuity. There was a rotating carousel and a pop-up jack in the box. Plenty of lights and even confetti poppers. Until finally, it was my turn.

Three judges stepped up to my table. While they scribbled initial impressions on their notecards, I plated their desserts.

"Alright, judges. Last but definitely not least, is contestant number ten, Eleanor Evans. Her entry, as you can see, is a scale model of Maplewood Creek's Main Street, complete with ice rink, Christmas tree, and the focal point, The Snowdrift Inn. Her tasting element is a gingerbread cheesecake. Now, go ahead and show us your special element," the announcer told me.

Every entry included some kind of surprise. Something that

moved or lit up. I'd agonized for days about how I would make this design special. I only hoped I hadn't missed the mark.

First, I flipped the switch to a tiny motor that made the blades of the helicopter spin, giving the impression that it was flying overhead.

"That's a nice touch," one judge commented to herself.

But that wasn't the real trick.

The audience gasped and applauded as my entire Snowdrift Inn opened up to reveal a fully rendered interior like an old Victorian dollhouse. Complete with furniture, guests, Pops behind the front desk, and the twins hanging decorations. Maybe mine didn't explode or shoot lasers, but it was beautiful, and a hell of a lot of work.

"That is remarkably accurate," another judge marveled. "I was just there a few days ago. You even got the umbrellas by the door."

Finally, I handed each judge their gingerbread cheesecake. I thought I saw a few smiles and nods, but I couldn't be sure their reactions weren't just polite enthusiasm. They sampled my gingerbread rum ball snowmen and gingerbread brownie cars while I obsessed over their every hum or shared glance.

"Judges, do you have everything you need?" the announcer asked. "Alright, I think that's a yes. And so, we'll be right back once the judges have had a chance to deliberate. And please, remember to come up and drop in your vote for audience favorite as well."

"You did it, Elle!" Mia shouted. "I know you won. They loved it."

"Don't jinx it," I said, collapsing to sit on top of the

large cooler. I could barely feel my feet anymore. "Hey, whatever happened to Bea and Delilah? Has anyone heard from them?"

I watched Mia and Charles reach for their phones to check, and saw both of their faces fall, a grim darkness overwhelming their expressions.

"What?" I said, anxiety rising in my gut. "What's wrong?"

"It's a message from Bea. Pops had an accident. He's in the emergency room."

Chapter 24

We all left the contest immediately, without waiting to hear the result. Mia went straight to The Snowdrift. Someone had to cover for the twins so they could stay with Pops, and she was the only one who knew what to do. I rode with Charles to the hospital, where we found the sisters pacing among the chairs in the ER waiting room.

"Charlie!" Bea called. "Over here."

"What happened?" Charles asked when we approached them.

"He was on that damn ladder again," Delilah told us. "I told him a hundred times."

"We were in the dining room when we heard a loud thud," Bea said. "We ran outside to the porch, and found him lying at the bottom of the stairs."

"How bad is it?" I asked, imagining that fall on icy steps.

"Not sure yet. The doctor hasn't come out to talk to us," Bea said.

"Pops of course said he didn't feel a thing, but I know he's lying," Delilah added. "Doesn't want to scare us. His wrist was pretty swollen, and he wasn't able to stand on his own when the ambulance got there. I just hope it isn't his hip."

"What can we do?" I offered. "Mia went to the inn to take care of the guests. Can I bring you some coffee? Snacks?"

"I am sort of starving," Bea admitted tiredly.

"I'm on it."

While Charles stayed with the twins, I found my way to the hospital cafeteria to load up on coffee, chips, some apples and bananas, and a few pre-packaged sandwiches. I had no idea how long we'd be waiting, but it was always better to over-prepare where food was concerned.

When I returned to the waiting area, they were all seated against the wall facing the double doors that led to the exam rooms, so they could leap up at the first sign of Pops's doctor.

"Thank you, Elle. You're a lifesaver." Bea took one of the coffee cups and a sandwich.

"Oh, hey," Delilah said, grabbing some chips from my arms. "What about the contest? Who won?"

"We dipped out early, so not sure," Charles told her, stretching out his long legs while accepting a coffee cup with an appreciative smile.

"Oh, no. I'm sorry we made you miss the results," Bea said, unwrapping the chicken salad sandwich.

"Forget about it." I placed the rest of the snacks on a table beside us. "This is more important."

"I called Amelia," Charles told me. "She's taking my parents out to dinner, so you won't have to do dinner service at the chalet."

"Are you sure she's okay with that? Your sister already bailed me out once today."

I felt guilty that one favor was now two. It seemed like shirking my responsibilities. But the bigger part of me wanted to be here for the twins. Pops was sort of the first friend I had made in Maplewood Creek. He quite literally saved me from the blizzard. Without him, I would have spent that first night sleeping in my car.

"Amelia's always thrilled with any excuse to dress up, and Dad never says no to her."

"What about your mom?" I asked.

Because she was the one I was really trying to impress. And I didn't think a full day's absence would reflect well on me if she found out.

Charles shrugged. "I told Amelia to order a very expensive bottle of champagne. That usually wipes the slate clean, if you know what I mean."

When all else fails.

So, the four of us settled in for a long wait. I passed out on Charles's shoulder almost immediately, the exhaustion of the day catching up with me all at once. Sometime later, he gave me a little nudge.

"Elle," he whispered. "Hey. Wake up."

"Hmm?" Wiping my eyes, I blinked against the bright fluorescents. I lifted my head from his shoulder and felt the dampness of drool pooled in the corner of my mouth. "Oh, great. That's embarrassing."

He chuckled softly. "You were really conked out."

It took a few seconds to remember why I smelled like ginger

229

and cinnamon, my brain groggy and sputtering. Then all at once it hit me and I bolted upright.

"How's Pops? Has there been an update?"

"The girls just went back to see him. You ready to go say hi?"

"Yeah." I lumbered to my swollen, aching feet. "Let's go."

Charles nodded at the receptionist behind the front desk, who hit a buzzer that opened the double doors for the hallway that led to the exam rooms. About halfway down the hall, past the nurses' station, I heard Pops's voice.

"It doesn't even hurt that bad," he was saying, as Charles pulled back the curtain to reveal Pops in a hospital bed surrounded by his granddaughters. "Looks worse than it is."

"That's because they've got you on painkillers," Bea told him, with no small hint of frustration. "Doesn't mean you need to be juggling flaming swords any time soon."

"How's the patient?" Charles said.

"Hey, you two." Pops glanced up with a jolly grin, waving a hand that was wrapped in a red- and white-striped cast up to his elbow, like a giant candy cane. "I'm quite the popular fella today."

"If you wanted to see me again, you could have just called," I teased. "You didn't have to go through all this trouble."

Pops chuckled. "What can I say? The nurses love me here."

There was a slight hint of a wince on his face that meant he wasn't so impervious to pain as he liked to pretend. He wore a hospital gown and there were wires running to his chest and an IV in his other arm.

"So, what's the verdict?" Charles asked.

"Just a broken wrist," Pops said. "No biggie."

"You got lucky," Delilah chided at his side. "It could have

been much worse. Imagine if you'd hit your head or broken a rib."

"Eh." He waved away her concern, showing a brave face to his girls. "I'm tough."

"You know it's okay not to prove it, though," I told him with a relieved grin. "You gave us all quite the scare."

My phone buzzed in my pocket and I glanced down to read the screen.

"Hey, that reminds me," Pops said. "How did the Thanksgiving Throwdown turn out? Worst part of all this was missing your entry. I hope you all took lots of pictures."

"Who is it?" Charles asked, peering over at me.

"It's Mia," I told them. "She just got the results."

"Well?" Pops urged me. "Don't leave us hanging."

A huge smile overtook my face. "We won!"

Chapter 25

With all the chaos of the Thanksgiving Throwdown and Pops's accident, the next couple of days passed in a blur. Before I knew it, the Thanksgiving event at the Hawthorne chalet was right around the corner. They'd be entertaining friends, family, and clients flying in from all around the country, so I spent the afternoon gathering the final provisions. When I called Megan to see about hiring extra help, she was excited to lend a hand, and even agreed to come up for that visit with Hannah, to make sure everything went off without a hitch. If this event was a success, it would cement her relationship with the Hawthornes and mean future referrals for new business.

Now, I lumbered back to the Land Rover with my cart full of bags. I had finally picked up my own from Grover's Hardware, one of those all-terrain wagons the nannies used to tow around the fancy dogs and exhausted children of the rich families on the mountain.

As I approached the SUV parked along the curb, I glanced over at The Snowdrift, where Charles was teetering on top of a ladder while putting up Christmas lights above the porch. After I got everything in the trunk, I jogged across the street, just as Pops stepped out into the front yard to tinker with the lights blanketed over the shrubs.

"Careful up there," I called as I approached. "Don't want you ending up with a cast to match Pops."

"Don't worry." He glanced down at me, holding a hammer in one hand and a clutch of nails in the other. "I've done this once or twice."

"That I find hard to believe."

"Oh, Elle!" Pops stepped back from the shrub lights, satisfied. He was sporting a red sweater to match his candy-cane cast. "Good to see you again."

"Hi, Pops. I see you've enlisted some extra help."

"Good sport, isn't he?" he said, nodding. "Lots to do. Don't want to get behind."

"Want to come hold this ladder?" Charles called sheepishly.

I jogged up the steps and put both hands on the wobbly metal ladder.

"Dang these lights. Every year I say I'm not going to get them tangled," Pops muttered to himself while he fished in a carboard box for the remaining decorations. "Then every year, here I am."

"Why don't you let someone else do that?" I told him. "Shouldn't you be resting?"

"No way. I've been in bed for two days already. I'm going stir crazy."

As Pops fought with the mess, determined to make himself useful, I looked up at Charles.

"Surprised to find you doing manual labor," I said.

"Pops and my grandfather used to do this every year when

I was a kid," he said, his eyes softening as he peered down at me. "I remember sitting on that porch swing over there, drinking hot cocoa, and watching them argue about the best way to hang the lights."

I smiled, imagining a younger version of Charles in this very spot. "Sounds like a nice tradition."

"It was." His gaze drifted to the inn's weathered facade. "When my grandfather passed, I was in college. Pops kept the tradition going, though, and now I guess it's my turn to help out."

There was a wistfulness in his voice that made me climb up and reach for his hand. He squeezed it gently, his warmth seeping through our gloves.

Pops joined us, carrying a spool of lights one-handed. "Charles, your dad mentioned you're gearing up to take over the company soon. How's that going?"

Charles hesitated, then shrugged. "It's . . . a lot. I like being more behind the scenes in Denver. Once Dad retires, I'll have to be front and center. That's going to change everything."

Pops nodded thoughtfully. "Big shoes to fill, but you've got a good head on your shoulders. Your grandfather would be proud."

I realized then that Charles was very much woven into the fabric of this town. Not just a spectator from high above on the mountain. He had roots here. Connections.

"Hey," I said, when Pops stepped back inside. "Can I ask you about something?"

"Sure. What's up?" Charles climbed down from the ladder and we both leaned against the porch railing.

"A few people have mentioned that this is your first time back in Maplewood Creek in years. I was curious as to why."

He was quiet for a few moments, gathering his thoughts. "My grandfather's death hit me hard. Coming back here after that made me miss him too much. So, I stayed away. Sort of in my grief, you know? This is the first year in ages I haven't wanted to just stay in bed and hide until the holidays are over." He took my hand and squeezed. "I think maybe you have a lot to do with that."

The blush rose hot and bright over my cheeks as I ducked my head to smother a grin. "I'm not taking credit, but I'm glad you're feeling a little better."

"Is there anything else you want to know?" he said, examining my face.

"Well, I don't want to pry, so you can tell me to shut up, but . . ." Ugh, this was awkward. "Well, I sort of heard something about a car accident?"

"Oh." His eyes widened, then his face fell with embarrassment. "Yeah. Not one of my finer moments. It was back in college. Just after my grandad died. I wasn't, let's say, coping well. Drinking, partying. All that." He glanced out across the snow-covered yard at the wooden Snowdrift Inn sign that sat among the shrubs near the road. "Plowed a Land Rover straight into that sign. Absolutely demolished it."

"Oh, wow."

"Yep. Spent the night in jail and everything."

"Was anyone hurt?"

"Oh, no," he said, with evident relief. "I mean, I was a little banged up from the air bag, but I got very lucky."

"Came back after he slept it off and apologized, too," Pops said, meeting us on the porch with a couple of coffee mugs held by the handle in his good hand. "Paid for that new sign there, and spent the rest of the season doing chores around the inn to make amends."

"Pops was gracious enough to forgive me," Charles admitted. "I'm grateful."

"Everybody deserves a second chance," Pops said cheerfully. "It's what you do with it that matters."

"Very true," Charles agreed. "I'm just glad to be enjoying a Maplewood Creek holiday season again. There's really nothing like it."

Truthfully, I felt exactly the same. This was the first time in a long while the holidays felt like something to look forward to. Usually, it just meant catering gigs and long hours. Microwave meals at home alone. This year, it felt special. Festive. And I couldn't have picked a better backdrop, or better people to celebrate with.

Back at the chalet, Charles helped me unpack in the kitchen. Every inch of storage space was packed full with supplies for the big event.

"You're really going to cook all this by yourself?" he asked, daunted by the prospect of everything we'd stuffed in the walk-in fridge.

"Kind of, yeah. Megan is bringing in a few sous chefs, but mostly they'll be on prep and plating."

He whistled, shaking his head. "I think I'd just curl up in a ball."

"Oh, I've already done that a couple of times since I've been here. A good stress cry in the shower does wonders."

"Seriously?" He grabbed me into a hug, kissing the top of my head. "Now I feel awful."

I shrugged in his arms. "Don't. In kitchens we refer to the walk-in as the crying pod. It sort of comes with the territory. Cooking is a high-pressure gig."

It was just about time to get started on tonight's dinner prep as we finished packing away the groceries. I pulled out my knives and began sharpening them. Charles watched me, cracking open a beer as he leaned against the island.

"You know," he said, fixing me with a mischievous grin. "You're awfully sexy in your element."

"Yeah? Knives are your kink, huh?"

He laughed to himself. "No, I think you're my kink."

I bit hard into my lip, shaking my head. He really did know how to lay it on thick. And it worked every time.

"You should probably go find something else to do," I told him. "Not sure I can concentrate while you're standing there."

"Distracting you, am I?" He swigged his beer and waggled his eyebrows.

"We've been over this."

Charles set aside his beer as I pulled a baking sheet from the shelf. He caught me in his arms, dipping his fingers beneath the hem of my sweatshirt to graze bare skin. That small touch sent lightning across my nerves, thoroughly erasing the careful order of tasks in my head. He picked me up by my waist and sat me on the island.

"You know, I'm going to have to clean this now," I told him, gazing at his soft lips that curved into a smile.

"Then might as well make it worth the effort."

Charles stepped between my legs to lift my chin and press his mouth to mine. He kissed me deeply, tongue gently caressing mine. His body was always so impossibly warm. Outside in the snow, or here in the chilly marble kitchen. It melted into me as I ran my hands down his back and pushed my hands beneath his shirt.

The faint clicking of stiletto heels on tiles echoed down the hallway. We shared a brief glance, then quickly broke apart as I jumped down from the counter.

Mrs. Hawthorne burst through the kitchen door to find us both a little red and flustered as I stood there with an empty sheet pan, floundering for something to do with my hands. She stopped short and leveled us both with a suspicious grimace.

"What are you doing in the kitchen?" she asked Charles.

"Just grabbing a snack."

"You're not wearing that to dinner," she said, thumbing her nose at his flannel shirt and faded jeans.

"Of course not. I was just leaving to change."

"Well, take a shower while you're at it. Your father has clients coming for drinks later, and I don't want you walking in there with your hair looking like you've been chopping wood under a waterfall."

Mrs. Hawthorne grabbed a bottle of wine from the rack. "I'm going to lie down. I have a terrible headache from the glare on the slopes."

At that she curtly turned and left. Charles and I shared a contrite glance before bursting into smothered laughter.

"A delight, isn't she?" he said. "I better bring her some aspirin and water."

He kissed my forehead before he left, setting butterflies loose in my stomach that lasted all through the dinner service.

Chapter 26

Dinner service that night went well, I thought. I even prepared a few light snacks that the waitstaff could put out if Mr. Hawthorne and his guests got peckish during drinks later. Back at my cottage, I sat in front of the fireplace in my pajamas with my phone and some mulled wine, posting new photos of my dishes to the Après Brie account. I carefully cropped out any identifying elements of the kitchen, as usual, and added a few cheeky captions. Then I went over my notebook again, checking off final items from tomorrow's event to-do list.

This would be the largest event I'd ever led. In the past, I'd been a line cook and a pastry chef, but never the sole head chef for so many guests. The current tally was over one hundred and it seemed every day Ali informed me of more last-minute additions. A mix of friends and business associates, I gathered. Honestly, I was growing more anxious as the big day approached, second-guessing my menu and worrying that I'd get so far in the weeds that the whole rickety house of cards that was my timeline to execute the food would collapse.

More wine helped chase those worries away, for now.

I was about to pack it in for the night when someone knocked at the door. I padded over to the front window in my thick, comfy socks and found Charles outside, looking cold and haggard in only a button-down shirt and trousers.

"Hey, get in here," I said, yanking him inside. It wasn't even twenty degrees out there. "You look terrible. What's wrong?"

He was breathing heavily as he charged inside to thaw by the fire. I filled a kettle with water and put it on the stove for some tea. Then back in the living room, I tossed some blankets and pillows on the hardwood floor and pulled him down to sit with me.

"Here," I said, handing him some of my mulled wine. "Have some and tell me what's going on."

I'd never seen Charles like this. He was edgy and frazzled. Like a thousand thoughts were colliding behind his unfocused eyes as he clenched his hands around the glass and stared into the flames. He took a swig and set it aside. Then, after several minutes of silence, his breathing slowed and he turned to me, brow knitted with frustration.

"I had a fight with my dad," he said simply.

"What about?"

"Same thing we always fight about." He huffed out a laugh, but there was no humor in it. "The business. It's the only thing we talk about anymore. The huge responsibility. His expectations. How I'm not taking this seriously enough. I've spent practically my whole adult life learning the company. Doing everything he's ever asked of me. Not once has he asked me what *I* want."

He grabbed for the wine again and took another heavy gulp

just as the kettle whistled. I got up and made us some chamomile tea, then brought the mugs back over to the fire.

"What do you want?" I asked, softly stroking his back with my fingertips.

He seemed to relax slightly, his muscles releasing some of their tension. "Honestly, just time to figure that out. While everyone else I knew was discovering their passions, I was following the plan Dad had laid out for me. The college he picked out, then business school. And it wasn't like I hated it, but I never had a choice, you know? I never got to fuck off for a year and travel. Take up piano. I don't know. Anything. Just to find out who I am before I become my father."

"What does he say when you tell him that?" I asked, passing him a mug.

The fire crackled, puffing out gentle sparks. The whole cottage smelled of rich burning pine. Charles shook his head, sighing. The lines deepened across his forehead as flickering shadows danced on the walls behind us.

"He says we have a responsibility to create a seamless transition. Thousands of employees counting on us to keep the gears turning. And the thing is, I know he's right. I've always been expected to take over one day, just like he took over for Grandad. The board, employee pensions, stock prices. All these things that represent real lives, you know? So, I guess I just feel trapped. Staring down the rest of my life feeling like I've never had a choice. It's daunting."

"Your dad must've felt the same way when he was in your position," I said.

Charles balked at that. "He's an old-fashioned guy. Still does business with a handshake over cigars and brandy.

Because that's the way Grandad did it. He was practically born in a three-piece suit."

I bit back a laugh. It was always hard for us to imagine our parents as people who had whole lives before we were born.

"I don't want to let him down," he said. "And I'm not saying I want to abandon the company. I just wish he would hear me out before automatically dismissing my feelings. I care about this company just as much as anyone. I just wish he'd give me a moment to breathe first."

As someone who'd worked for a lot of small-business owners, I knew something about the psyche at play there.

"Something I've learned throughout my culinary career is, people come to think of their businesses as children. Which are in turn like an extension of themselves. They get protective. Sometimes to a fault. And it gets hard to step back and hear other perspectives. Like a chef who suddenly has a kitchen full of line cooks. Some people can't give up control and they lash out. Nothing is ever good enough. They start to see every little mistake or suggestion as sabotage, because obviously no one will ever care for their baby better than they do."

"So, what do I do?" he asked me earnestly.

It was plain on his face that Charles desperately wanted his father's acceptance. He wanted it from both of his parents. They were each so accomplished and formidable. It must've been an impossible burden growing up in that shadow.

"I think you have to reassure him that you know what the company means to him. That you appreciate the legacy he's built. And that you want to honor that as much as he does. As much as he did when he took over from his father.

244

I think, ultimately, he wants to know that he's prepared you for this."

Charles collapsed back on the pillows, rubbing his face. "I'm not sure how to make him believe me."

"Time, I guess."

I lay beside him, brushing his hair off his forehead. Charles caught my hand and brought it to his lips, kissing the inside of my palm, then holding my hand to his face. It was an intimate gesture that made me feel closer to him than any time we'd spent under the sheets at the inn.

"Thank you," he breathed. "Sorry I came barging over here in the middle of the night like a lunatic."

"I'm glad you did. I've had one or two existential crises in my day. Several since I've been here, in fact. I'm sort of an expert now."

"What am I going to do when you leave for London?" he mused, looking up at the ceiling. His eyes landed on mine with a sober seriousness. "It just hit me that we're not both going back to Denver after this."

"Yeah." I winced slightly. Right now, I was barely looking a week ahead. Three months from now still felt like a very long time for me. "Weird."

Charles rolled over on his side. He tucked a few strands of hair behind my ear, then gently slid his fingers down the side of my neck. Where my oversized T-shirt hung off my shoulder, his fingers continued to graze the warm, bare skin.

"I think I knew the second I saw you that you'd change me," he said, almost as a whisper.

"Change you? How?"

"All I think about now is how to be wherever you are."

"Yeah?" A silly grin spread across my lips.

"Yeah," he said, twisting his fingers in the long strands of my hair that fell over my shoulder. "And all the places I want to go together. Things I want to show you. I saw you from across the room and it was like a whole future flashed before my eyes."

I shoved at his chest. "You're full of shit. But I like the way it sounds."

Charles held my wrist and pulled me to lie across his chest. His arm behind me lifted my shirt to trace patterns across my back. The sensation was like he was drawing on my skin with fire. It set every nerve humming.

"I'm not," he said. "I swear. I got one look at you and never turned back."

His arm curled around my back and he grazed his fingers along my ribs, barely brushing the side of my breast. With his other arm, he hitched my leg over his hips. As we kissed, I felt him grow hard against my thigh. His hand was tangled in my hair, holding me firm against his body while our tongues played, until he rolled me over to lie on top of me, settling between my legs. Charles kissed my cheek. The side of my neck. His hands found mine to extend out above my head among the pile of blankets and pillows that made our makeshift bed on the floor.

With both my wrists gathered in one hand, he returned his mouth to mine. The language of his kiss was deliberate and attentive. Not urgent or hurried, but sensual. Patient. Gently his free hand pushed up the hem of my shirt to lightly tease my skin before cupping my breast, making me arch into his touch.

"I've thought about touching you again every day since that first night," he said. "You have no idea how much I've missed this," he breathed against my mouth.

"Yes, I do," I told him confidently.

Because it was the same longing I'd tried to tamp down since I'd gathered the courage to leave that hotel room. There were armies of women out there who probably would've killed to switch places with me that morning. But I suppose things had a way of working themselves out.

As Charles hovered over me, I wrapped my leg around his hips, encouraging his hand that continued to tease my breast. The flames danced across his face, fire shimmering in his eyes while shadows painted patterns around us.

"You are so beautiful," he hummed, then sealed his mouth over mine again.

Finally, I pulled my hands free to unbutton his shirt as he peeled mine over my head. His mouth explored my chest, leaving warm kisses and gentle licks of his tongue, sucking one pebbled nipple into his mouth. The attention was almost excruciating, alighting every nerve and coiling my muscles into a single knot of overwhelming desire. I was wound up so tight I felt I might shatter.

Then he slid farther down my body, mapping a trail of kisses across my flushed skin. Sinking between my legs to spread my thighs. Reverent, he caressed his cheek against the tender flesh, starting at my knee and working closer, closer, until his mouth met my core. I shuddered beneath him. Too sensitive. Already teetering on the edge of self-control. My eyes snapped shut, teeth digging into my bottom lip while his tongue drew out my muffled moans. Charles hitched my leg over his shoulder, daring me to tumble over into ecstasy. This man made me delirious.

"What do you want me to do?" he whispered.

I couldn't speak. Could barely breathe. My heart was racing too fast. I knotted my fingers in his hair and writhed against his mouth. Encouraging him. Pleading. Racing toward that ultimate moment of exquisite release that washed over me like an avalanche. Quaking in response to his touch.

I dragged him up to unzip his pants and pulled down his boxers to take him in my palm. I had to get us closer. I wanted to feel all of him. Warm and safe in our secret retreat, where nothing else could find us. Not our fears or the world's expectations. In here, making love in front of the fire, we belonged only to each other.

Opening me with his hips, Charles reached one hand between my legs to caress me. It was almost painful, my body too sensitive. Yet I craved it, shivering in response to his touch. I bent my legs, urging him forward. Fingertips digging into the pulsing muscles of his back. Watching his eyes as he gazed into mine and entered me. That feeling of completeness. Of being exactly where I was supposed to be.

Nothing had ever felt so perfect. So right. Like we had been made to find each other. A thought that settled into my head and seeped into my blood. My heart. Growing with every kiss. Every thrust. I hadn't known I was capable of such strong emotion until that moment. Until Charles gave himself to me completely, and me to him.

Chapter 27

I was practically bouncing through breakfast service the next morning. Mostly because of spending such an incredible night with Charles. But also, because Megan and Hannah had finally arrived to help me execute this event. Deliveries started arriving at the chalet at 8 a.m. There were cocktail tables, linens, decorations, and so many boxes of dishware and cutlery. Thank goodness for Ali. She wrangled the whole circus while I pushed breakfast out, then hopped in the Land Rover to go check on my Denver girls.

"There she is!" Megan waved me over as I entered the dining room of The Snowdrift Inn. "Oh, it's so good to see you. I know it's only been a couple of weeks, but somehow it feels like forever."

She stood to hug me, until Hannah all but shoved her mom out of the way to get her turn.

"You look great," she said with a suspicious smirk. "Mountain air agrees with you, huh?"

I smothered a grin because, let's face it, she'd seen me stroll into work once or twice, a little hungover and a tad peppy after a hookup. And that was absolutely not a conversation we were having in front of her mother. I was supposed to be a good influence.

"This town agrees with me," I said instead, and took a seat between them at the table, where they were already enjoying their Snowbird Specials.

"I love it here, Elle," Hannah said, her eyes sparkling. "The snow, the lights—it's like a fairy tale!"

Megan laughed. "You've created a monster. She's already asking if we can come back next year."

Hannah's enthusiasm was contagious. She perked up even more when a young man in an apron strolled over from the kitchen.

"Extra side of bacon and two waffles?" he said, flashing a big white smile as he set the plate down in front of me.

"This for me?" It was always my go-to when they invited me over back home.

"I wouldn't forget," Megan said, nodding as she sipped her coffee.

"Hi, I'm Owen." The young man with dark curly hair and freckles addressed this mostly to Hannah. "Let me know if there's anything else I can get for you."

Hannah blushed, suddenly shy. Megan and I exchanged a knowing glance.

"Alright, Owen, wrap it up," Pops exclaimed, strolling through the dining room. "Those eggs aren't scrambling themselves in there."

Owen tucked his tail and returned to the kitchen as Pops came over to say hello.

"Picked up an extra pair of hands?" I asked.

"Nice kid. Helping out in the kitchen a few days a week over winter break. Gets a little distracted around the ladies, if you know what I mean."

Hannah turned her attention back to her plate and dug in, a little bashful.

"He's cute," Megan said, glancing back toward the kitchen. "Should I be worried?"

Pops laughed, swatting at the air. "Ah, he's a good kid. Harmless."

Once Pops started making the rounds to check on the other tables, Megan turned serious. "So, tell me. How's it really going up there? The job, the family, all of it."

I hesitated, then decided to be honest. "It's . . . intense. Mrs. Hawthorne is a bit of a dragon. But the work itself is rewarding, and Charles—" I stopped myself, heat rising to my cheeks.

"Ah, Charles," Megan teased, her eyes gleaming. "I wondered how long it would take for him to come up."

I sighed. "It's complicated. But honestly, what's been on my mind more is the Instagram account. It's taken off in a way I couldn't have expected. People love the behind-the-scenes look at life as a private chef in the Rockies."

Megan was already up to date on the new account. As a marketing tool, she thought it was genius. Only problem was, I wouldn't be able to tell potential clients it was me. A small flaw in the plan.

Megan nodded thoughtfully. "You've always had a knack for storytelling, Elle. And I think it informs your cooking. From what I've seen, it seems like you've been doing the best food of your life out here. I think Maplewood Creek has been good for you."

"It has," I admitted. "I'll be sort of sad to let it go when the season ends. Don't get me wrong, I'm still stoked for London. ACE has been my dream forever. But I'm really going to miss this place."

"That's the great thing about dreams," Megan said gently. "You never have to stop at just one. After you've conquered London, maybe Maplewood Creek could be a new dream for you."

Her words lingered with me long after we parted. And while my schedule for the day was tight, there was one more errand I wanted to see to.

I texted Mia on my way to the marketplace. She met me at the picnic tables outside the barn with some hot cocoa, and we both took a seat in the warmth of the nearby space heater.

"So, today's the big event," she said. "I figured you'd be neck-deep in butternut squash by now."

"I will be soon," I assured her, a little daunted by the scale of what was waiting for me back at the chalet. "But first, I wanted to clear the air about something."

"Uh-oh." Her smile turned a bit anxious. "That doesn't sound good."

"You and Charles. I know this is totally none of my business, but I have to know. What went wrong between you two?"

Much as I had told myself I wouldn't get involved in the gossip, things were different now. I cared about Charles. About where this thing between us might go from here. And if there was any possibility of a future beyond this season,

I had to know what I was getting myself into. For better or worse.

"Oh." Mia sighed. She took a sip of her cocoa while she deliberated over how much she cared to divulge.

A big part of me expected her to deflect. Or tell me outright to get lost. Whatever had happened, she was holding on to that grudge pretty tight. And by now, she probably had some inkling that Charles and I were together. So, it was conceivable I wouldn't be her favorite person right now.

"Believe it or not, we used to be close friends," she began after a while, looking out over the bustling parking lot and kids running around in the snow, while their parents chatted with other adults going in and out of the marketplace. "His grandparents and mine had known each other for years. We sort of grew up together."

I braced myself for the worst. A revelation that might shake the foundation of whatever I thought was growing between Charles and me.

"Anyway. I told you about my idea for culinary-inspired vacations to Maplewood Creek."

"Yeah . . ." That came from left field. Not at all where I thought this conversation was headed.

"Well, one year when he was up here on vacation from business school, I approached Charlie about the idea. To invest in the business, you know. Be partners. We were going to bring Pops and the Snowdrift in on it, as well as some of the other local businesses. I put together this whole presentation. He seemed excited about it. Said he'd bring it up to his dad and get us the funding to get started."

"So, what happened?"

She scoffed. "He blew me off. Was more interested in getting wasted and partying with his douchebag friends. Then he plowed his car into the Snowdrift sign one night. Got hauled off to the drunk tank. That was the last time he showed his face in town. Never heard from him again. Just left me hanging with all these promises I'd made to people. Got my hopes up and vanished."

"Oh, Mia. I'm so sorry."

"Whatever," she said bitterly. "Probably better off, right? To figure out who he really was, before it was too late."

I had prepared myself to hear that they were exes. That he'd cheated on her. Broken her heart. Somehow, this was almost worse. Not because I thought it made Charles a bad guy, but because it was such an enormous misunderstanding.

"He told me about the sign at The Snowdrift," I said. "And the drinking. His grandfather had just died and it really messed him up for a while. I know it's no excuse, but I think he was so wrapped up in his own grief, he wasn't thinking about anyone else. Still, I know if he understood how much he hurt you, he'd feel awful about it."

Mia shrugged. "I don't even care anymore. It was forever ago, right?"

She wasn't convincing anyone. Least of all herself. And I didn't blame her. I'd be pretty sore about it too, if someone blew up my dreams. I felt for Mia. I wanted so badly to make it right.

"Maybe you two could talk. Get it all out in the open and reconcile."

"I think it's too late for that," she said, standing. "Anyway. I've got to get back to my stall. See you around, okay?"

Mia was a proud person. It wasn't in her nature to ask for help. I understood how she felt. But I'd grown to care about them both. If it was in my power to help, I had to try. In the spirit of the holidays.

Chapter 28

Back at the chalet, I texted Charles to ask if he had a few minutes to chat. He invited me to one of the twin outbuildings on the property, used as guest suites, where he and Amelia stayed. I hadn't been out here before, since the waitstaff were typically in charge of running any incidental orders out of the kitchen. His suite was at least three times the size of the staff cottages; a smaller version of the main house, with the same rustic yet elevated architecture. There were huge, overstuffed sofas, lantern-style lighting fixtures, and antique skis and snow shoes on the walls.

"I'm up here," he called when he heard me arrive.

I followed his voice upstairs, past several framed nature sketches on the walls. Each one was an intricate, detailed depiction of local foliage and wildlife, including exquisitely rendered feathers and pinecones. I was mesmerized, examining each one until Charles poked his head out of his bedroom door to look for me.

"Hey, I'm in here," he said.

"I love these drawings. Are you a collector?"

"What? Oh, no. Um . . ." His eyes turned bashful as he ducked his head and smothered a sheepish grin. "I did those. Years ago. Grandad and I used to draw when I was in high school. It was one of our things. A bunch of his sketches are framed in the main house."

"You did these?" I took a closer look, admiring the line-work. "Wow. I'm impressed. You really have talent."

Charles shrugged. "It was a hobby. I did a minor in art at college."

Though the compliment embarrassed him, I could tell his art still held a great deal of meaning for Charles.

"So, what'd you need to talk to me about?" he asked, inviting me into the spacious bedroom with a huge four-poster bed and fireplace.

One whole wall of glass looked out on the mountain range, with a balcony where periodic snowflakes were beginning to accumulate.

"Mia, actually."

Charles stood in front of the mirror, wrestling with a bow tie.

"We used to run around together when I was younger," he said. "Your contest was the first time we've seen each other in ages."

"Well, I've gotten to know her a little bit, obviously."

"I noticed." Charles managed to get the bow tie under control, which was good, because I didn't know the first thing about tying them. He sifted through a leather box of cuff links to choose an appropriate pair.

"Yeah, well . . ." I sat on the edge of the king-size bed, made up with too many pillows and blankets. Obviously, his mother's decorating and the housekeeper's doing. "I, uh, sort of pried some stuff out of her."

His eyes caught mine in the mirror. "Sounds ominous."

"I don't suppose you remember her talking about a business venture years ago? Sort of a farm-focused vacation thing."

Charles fit one cuff link through his sleeve, then the other, brow furrowed while he searched his memory. "That does sound familiar. Yeah. I remember being pretty into the concept. She wanted to draw in several local business owners to partner on it with her. Create a little industry around food and wine."

"Right."

Then a look of horror captured his face. His eyes widened. "You know what I just remembered?"

"I have a pretty good feeling I do."

Charles turned to look at me. "I'm a bastard. I swear I hadn't thought about it in probably a decade. No wonder she wouldn't talk to me at the Thanksgiving Throwdown." He sighed, dumping himself on the bed next to me to hang his head. "I promised to talk to my father about making an initial investment. Getting her the startup funds she needed."

"Then you ghosted her."

"She must hate my guts. I was going through so much shit with my family and I just forgot all about it." He blew out a breath, raking his hands through his hair. "Wow, that sounds awful."

I took his hand, squeezing gently. "It sucks, but it's understandable. And know she'd forgive you if you talked to her about it. Let her know what you were going through."

"I don't even know where to start to approach her." Charles placed his hand over mine, bringing them to rest on his lap and running his thumb absently over my knuckles. "Mia was the kind of girl who scared the hell out of all the boys growing up."

"I think maybe if you sent her a letter. Wish her happy holidays and maybe invite her to dinner. You'd probably be surprised at how far the gesture would go with her."

He smiled, lifting my hand to his lips to plant a soft kiss. "That's a great idea. I'd really love to catch up with her. Make this right."

"Good. Now that I've done my good deed for the day, I've got to run before Ali sends a search party after me." I pressed a quick kiss to his cheek and darted out of the room.

I was only thinking about menus and to-do lists when I jogged out of the guest suite and across the courtyard. So, it barely registered that there might be anything to worry about when I spotted Amelia leaving her own suite next door.

Back at the main house, it was all systems go. Ali and I had a meeting with the additional staff Megan had hired for the event. We coached them through the timeline and how the hors d'oeuvres would proceed through cocktail hour, before a plated dinner in the ballroom.

Next, I gathered the kitchen team to begin prep. We only had six hours to prepare, cook, and plate 600 canapés, plus a six-course sit-down dinner for nearly 200 people. Every time I said those numbers out loud, I felt my stress level ratchet up again.

Mrs. Hawthorne had insisted on an autumnal-inspired

menu. Their Thanksgiving party was legendary, and every year guests expected she'd outdo herself to be even more elaborate than the last. I'd wracked my brain for days and endured several heavy edits by Mrs. Hawthorne until we arrived at a satisfactory menu.

First up were harissa-spiced tiger prawns in filo dough cups. Then cranberry and ricotta-stuffed endives with walnuts. We had lamb meatballs with mint chimichurri, brie crostini with bacon-plum jam, pumpkin pinwheels in a saffron puff pastry, and finally, crumb-topped caramelized butternut squash with sage and brown butter.

For the dinner service, we had tomato and peach carpaccio, soy-glazed tuna, potato gnocchi, veal meatballs with cranberry chutney, squab served on a bed of mushroom risotto and topped with haricot vert sautéed in brown butter with almonds, and finally, individual apple tarts with miso caramel, chili flakes, and homemade vanilla ice cream.

Most of our day was spent dicing up vegetables, cleaning and deveining prawns, stuffing squabs, and baking like mad. There was so much food, we had to rent three rotisseries and a whole truck of ovens running off a generator outside the staff garage. I was constantly sprinting back and forth between those ovens and the main kitchen, checking temperatures and watching my dough rise. Everything had to be perfect. There was zero room for error.

As I was jogging from the ovens toward the kitchen, skidding past the drawing room, I heard raised voices and realized I'd accidentally stumbled on a heated conversation between Charles and his parents. I would have minded my manners and been on my way, but I tripped over a power cord and nearly dove headfirst into a table with what I'm sure was a priceless heirloom vase perched on top of it. While I steadied the decorative vessel among the dozens of staff marching back and forth with boxes and folding chairs, I couldn't help but overhear part of their argument.

"You two haven't been fooling anyone," Mrs. Hawthorne sighed. "Sneaking around the house at all hours."

"Who's sneaking?" Charles shot back, his voice rising and clearly agitated. "I'm not a teenager."

"Exactly. There's no excuse for such careless displays, running around town with that girl."

"You watch the way you talk about her," Charles snapped.

"Charles, don't raise your voice to your mother," his father interjected.

The venom in Charles's voice made me a little sad. I also got a tiny thrill out of the way he jumped to defend me. Still, I didn't want to be a wedge between them, especially when their relationship was already strained about this major transition for the business.

"Charles, listen to me," Mrs. Hawthorne's icy voice insisted. "You're about to be thrust into the public eye. How does it look for a new CEO to be fooling around with the help?"

"The help, Mother? Really?"

"You have to see we have a greater responsibility here," Mr. Hawthorne implored him. "Appearances matter. I'm sure she's a lovely girl. Understand this isn't about her. But you have to be careful about the message it sends at such a delicate time for the company."

"What about my feelings?" Charles shot back. "Does that matter to either of you at all?"

"Of course, son," his father said. "We want you to be happy. But right now—"

"You aren't a child anymore," Mrs. Hawthorne interrupted. "Stop expecting to be coddled. This little romance of yours is over when the season ends. After the holidays, you must refocus your attention. Buckle down and start thinking about what kind of image you're projecting."

Wow. I really had forgotten my place, huh? The help. Another nameless, faceless servant to the Hawthorne empire. I was kidding myself to think that I was anything else. I turned and ran back the way I'd come, bursting outside the back door into the frigid air to catch my breath.

I tucked myself against the wall, around the corner to hide from the constant stream of traffic in all directions as the party preparations continued around me. I wanted to sink into the ground. Be swallowed up and emerge on the other side, anywhere else. Away from here. Somewhere they'd never heard the Hawthorne name. This must've been that look I'd seen in everyone's eyes at the first mention of the family. Behind the practiced veneer was the same spoiled sense of self-righteousness and entitlement as every other rich asshole who looked down on us.

The help.

Whatever. Better I figure this out now. Before I'd deluded myself into thinking this silly affair would turn out any other way.

Chapter 29

Brushing away my tears, I resolved to refocus my priorities. Stepping back into the kitchen, I told myself I would freeze Charles out. A clean break. It was better for both of us that way. He could make his family happy, and I would chase my culinary dream. No more detours.

"Where are we on the prawns?" I shouted, jumping back into the scrum among the sous chefs in white coats working at the counters on the mise en place.

"Prawns are cleaned and marinating, chef," the short female sous answered, carrying a sheet tray of soaked prawns to the fridge.

"Good. Let's prep the tuna next."

"Yes, chef."

I tightened my hair into a thick bun on the top of my head, and went back to the sink to wash my hands again.

"How's the texture of the lamb?" I said, looking over the shoulder of a man standing at the meat grinder.

"A little lean. Should we add more pancetta?"

"I think we should have just enough. How many pounds have you done without it?"

"Only two so far," he said.

"Send it through the next batch and combine them before you portion into the fryer."

"Yes, chef."

In the kitchen, I was fully in my element. This was where I knew myself. Where things made sense. And it was here I would put my energy.

Two hours before the guests arrived, we tested a few rounds of the canapés, experimenting with the perfect construction before we started on the big batch.

"Chef?" One of the women approached me quietly at the island where I was chopping morels for my risotto. "I can't find the sage."

"You checked the walk-in?"

"I did. And the pantry."

"Everyone look around," I called out to the other three sous. "Who has sage at their station?"

They all dropped what they were doing and searched. I darted around the kitchen, checking shelves and cabinets.

Fuck.

It wasn't here. Not a single tiny sprig. I didn't know what had happened. Maybe I'd left it behind at the market. Or forgotten it entirely. There were so many things on the list and I was on my own with so many components running through my head. But we were too deep into prep now. I definitely couldn't leave, and I couldn't spare a set of hands to send them down the mountain and back.

Shit!

"Stand by," I barked.

I grabbed my phone and stepped outside, frantically dialing Megan. It had started snowing harder sometime in the last couple of hours, and already it was several inches deep, coming down in thick puffs like cotton balls. The wind blew sideways, piling the snow up against the house. I hadn't seen it snow this hard since the blizzard, and I wondered if the guests would even make it up the mountain before they closed the road.

"Hello?" Megan answered on the second ring.

"I have an emergency," I told her, nearly hyperventilating at this point. "Sage. I need a fuck-ton of sage. However you can get it, and run it up to the house. Tell them I sent you and to put it on the Hawthorne account. I'll settle up first thing in the morning."

"I'm getting in my car right now," Megan said. I heard the jingle of her keys and a door slam behind her. "Don't worry, Elle. I've got you. See you soon."

I dashed back to the kitchen. "Sage is coming. We've got to push now."

"Heard," they collectively shouted back.

In the meantime, I started reducing my figs with sugar in wine, while my bacon rendered on the stove.

Eventually, Ali came into the kitchen to announce guests were arriving.

"How's everything going in here?" she said, dressed in a tailored black suit with her hair pulled back in a tight French twist.

"Great," I lied. "Right on schedule."

I caught a few wondering eyes from the sous chefs, but chose to ignore them while we all put our heads down to work.

"Let's line up the plates for the canapés," I told them.

Twenty at a time, we plated the prawns, endives, meatballs, crostini, and pinwheels. Everything but the damn squash that was sitting on the stove waiting for sage breadcrumbs.

"Wow, it's getting hectic in here, huh?" Charles entered the kitchen, looking dapper in his tux. I felt him strolling among the sous behind me but I didn't turn to acknowledge him. "Need me to jump in on some mac and cheese balls? I think I'm ready for the big leagues, coach."

He came to stand beside me, so I darted away to find something that needed doing in the pantry. Still, he followed me.

"Hey, are you okay?" he asked, trailing behind as I went to the walk-in fridge and then back to the stove.

"Pretty busy," I said curtly.

"Alright. Just wanted to wish you good luck." His voice was confused. "Or, break a leg? I'm not really sure of the kitchen lingo."

"Yep, thanks."

"Elle?" He put his hand on my arm and I pulled away. "What's going on?"

"I'm working," I told him sharply. "I need you to leave."

Charles recoiled. He watched me for a moment, visibly wounded by my coldness. I'd be lying if I said it didn't pain me to ignore him, but I'd already made a promise to myself. This was the way it had to be.

"Alright," he said, backing away. "I'll leave you to it, I guess."

Then my phone vibrated in my pocket with a text from Megan:

> **Megan:** The parking lot's snowed
> in. I'm still trying to dig out my car.

Damn it. If I didn't send out the squash, Mrs. Hawthorne would know something had gone wrong. She'd rip me to shreds. I had no choice.

I chased after Charles, into the staff corridor and outside into the freezing snow.

"Wait!" I called after him.

Charles abruptly turned, snow hitting him sideways. He wasn't even wearing a coat, and I wondered why he hadn't left through the house, where it was warm and protected.

"I'm really in the shit," I confessed, pleading as I stood in the whirling snow, my feet soaked and the moisture seeping into my black chef's coat. "I forgot the sage for the hors d'oeuvres and Megan is snowed in at The Snowdrift. If your mother realizes I've fucked this up, I'm fired. What do I do?"

"How much time do we have?" he asked, standing in the blizzard like it didn't affect him at all.

"I don't know. Like, thirty minutes before she realizes something's up?"

"I'll be back in twenty," he said.

"Wait! What are you going to do?"

Twenty minutes wasn't enough time to get down the mountain and back up again, even in good weather. If The Snowdrift was snowed in, there was no way he'd make it to the market. Even in the Land Rover.

"Trust me," he said.

And in that moment, I had no choice.

Chapter 30

The first five canapés started to go out at a steady pace, while we fired the first dinner courses. I anxiously watched the clock over my shoulder while furiously stirring my risotto. Any minute, I expected to hear the click of Mrs. Hawthorne's stilettos on the tile. Instead, it was Amelia who burst into the kitchen.

She strode up to me in a sequined black gown, her bouncy curls pulled into a loose updo with tendrils framing her face.

"Can I speak with you?" she said, her eyes urgent behind black eyeliner.

"Can we talk after dinner? I really have to keep an eye on this risotto."

Her posture stiffened. Something was off. Amelia seemed troubled and not her usual bubbly self. I called one of the sous over to the stove to take my place and walked Amelia out to the corridor and around the corner. From her sequined clutch, she pulled out her phone.

"This is you, right?" She opened Instagram and showed me the screen, her tone sharp. "Après Brie?"

My stomach dropped. It felt like all the oxygen had been sucked out of the room.

"I don't know what you're talking about," I said, my voice too soft to be convincing.

Her expression hardened. "I've seen the posts. The witty captions. The not-so-subtle digs at the lifestyles of the 'rich and pretentious.' It's all there."

I swallowed hard, my pulse pounding in my ears. "I haven't said anything—anything bad about your family. It's just food, Amelia. Just . . . my perspective on the job."

"Stop." She held up her hand, shaking her head. "You can try to justify it all you want, but the fact is, you've been using us. Using *Charles*. You've been building your brand off our backs and taking pot shots at us all the while."

Amelia sounded very much like her mother in that moment. Icy and intimidating.

"I haven't—"

"Why?" she interrupted. "I thought we were friends. Were we really so awful? I understand blowing off steam, but do it in private. That was the only thing we asked. Instead, you drag this family all over social media. How is that fair?"

"Amelia, no. It's not like that."

"You're finished here. When Charles gets back, I'm going to show him everything. You're just another social climber, using him for his name and his connections."

My heart thudded painfully against my ribs. "Amelia, please," I said, my voice cracking. "That's not who I am at all. The account isn't about him, or your family. It's about me—my journey as a chef. That's all."

"I'm sorry, Eleanor. I really am. I liked you. But this is a gross breach of trust. I have to tell my mother."

I felt like the walls were closing in around me. My mind raced with potential defenses, explanations, but none of them would suffice. Amelia was right about one thing—this wasn't just about the Instagram account. It was about my place here, about the delicate balance I'd been trying to maintain between my personal goals and my professional obligations. And now, it felt like it was all crumbling.

"You don't have to do this," I said, my voice trembling. "I've worked hard, Amelia. I've done everything I can to make this party a success, to prove myself—"

She raised her chin. "I'm sorry. You should have thought about that before."

She turned on her heel and walked out, leaving me standing there, shaking and struggling to breathe.

I leaned against the wall, my hands trembling as I tried to steady myself. Ali soon came around the corner, her face creased with worry.

"What's wrong?" she said. "Mrs. Hawthorne's asking about the butternut squash."

Of course she was.

I was nearly in tears. Still, I couldn't curl up in a ball now. One way or another, I had to complete this dinner service.

"All good," I said. "Amelia was just asking me a question. I'm headed back in there now."

When I got back to the kitchen, I stopped in my tracks, dumbfounded. Charles was standing there with his jacket off and the sleeves of his crisp white tuxedo shirt rolled up to his elbows as he stirred my risotto.

"What the hell's going on here?" I said, overwhelmed with the entire evening.

"Breadcrumbs just came out of the oven," Charles said.

At the island, the sous worked quickly, assembling the squash canapés.

"You got the sage already?" I went to the island, checking on the plating. "How?"

"Drove to the neighbors," he said, with a searching smile that hoped he'd done right. "Their chef had plenty of sage."

I went up to him and took the wooden spoon to continue stirring the risotto. "You saved my life," I told him earnestly. "Again."

"Anything for you."

He said the words with such heartfelt sincerity, I nearly broke down in tears.

I touched his arm, wanting desperately to explain, and yet completely at a loss for words. This would likely be our last night together. Very soon, Amelia would tell her mother what I'd done. If not for the snow, I'd probably be out tonight. All that was left was to finish the party. It was the least I could do.

"Charles." I froze at the sound of Mrs. Hawthorne's voice. She stood in the doorway in a navy-blue gown. "What are you doing in here? You should be with the guests."

"They'll survive without me for a bit," he said firmly, grabbing a cutting board to lend a hand.

Waiters came in to collect the squash canapés. She eyed them carefully as they were loaded onto the serving trays.

"Fine," she said reluctantly. "Don't be long."

I held my breath until I heard her heels clicking back down the hallway. Not long after she left, Mr. Hawthorne appeared, looking bemused to find his son elbow-deep in squab.

"What's all this?" he said.

"Helping Elle with the prep," Charles replied without looking up.

To my surprise, Mr. Hawthorne stepped forward. "Well, I can't let you two have all the fun. What can I do?"

I handed him a knife and a pile of herbs for garnish, and he got to work, his movements surprisingly deft. As we worked side by side, he glanced at me.

"You know, Elle, I wanted to go to culinary school once."

I blinked. "Really?"

He nodded, a wistful smile tugging at his lips. "But my father had other plans. The family business came first."

He looked over at Charles, his expression softening. "You're doing a good thing here, son. You always put people first. That's what will make you an excellent CEO."

Charles paused, clearly moved by his father's words. "Thanks, Dad."

Mr. Hawthorne turned back to me. "Maybe it's not too late, you know. Culinary school. I've been thinking about it more and more lately. Maybe it's time, after I retire."

I grinned. "Escoffier would be lucky to have you."

Once we had things under control again, I kicked the Hawthorne men out of the kitchen so we could start serving the dinner courses. And once dessert had been served, I took a walk to the ballroom to finally peer in on the meal.

The way through the house was lined with rustic lanterns lit with electric votives. Autumn leaves created a festive red-carpet effect to the ballroom's entrance, where guests were met with the fragrance of cinnamon and apple spice. There was a photographer taking photos in front of a vintage sled, adorned with faux-fur blankets against a backdrop of real coniferous trees. Inside the ballroom, waiters in white tuxedos passed silver trays beneath hundreds of hanging tea lights in crystal ornaments. More autumn leaves and boughs of pine dripped from the ceiling, creating the illusion of walking beneath a forest canopy on a starry night.

A jazz band played while the diners sat at numerous tables set with gold-trimmed china. Decorative gourds and flowers in every hue of red and orange made up the centerpieces, with tiny flickering candles that made the entire room shimmer and shine with the reflection on the crystal glassware.

I stood back and watched Charles as he chatted animatedly with his father and several older gentlemen who could've been family friends or business associates. He commanded the attention of the table with his easy confidence. Much as he was reluctant to become his father too quickly, he really was born for it. It just came naturally to him. I knew, fight it as he might, he'd be good at it. CEO. Man of industry. This was his world. In the same way that mine was the kitchen.

As I watched the guests savoring the food, I couldn't help but feel a sense of pride. Nothing made me happier than people enjoying my food. Guests made appreciative faces as they tried each element on their plates, nodding and smiling at every bite. Somehow, I'd pulled it off. And although Mrs. Hawthorne's approval still eluded me, I didn't care. In that moment, I knew I was on the right path. Maybe it wouldn't be in Maplewood Creek. Or in the state of Colorado, once Amelia told the family about my posts. But across the pond, I could start over. Reinvent myself. It was something to look forward to. Far away from Charles and the chalet. Far enough to forget him, I hoped.

Chapter 31

It was well after midnight before we finished washing and putting away all of the dishes. The sous and I scrubbed the kitchen from top to bottom, then shared a toast with a little brandy I'd purchased for the occasion.

"You all did excellent work," I told them, passing out the paper cups of amber liquor. "Thank you for all your efforts. It really meant the world to me. I know it got a little bumpy there for a bit, but we pulled it out the bag. Well done."

We raised a toast and knocked back our shots before saying our goodbyes. The snow had stopped a couple of hours earlier and the Hawthornes had already arranged for plows to clear the road down the mountain and back through town, to help their guests and crews make it home.

I was considering a final stress-cry in the walk-in when I heard the tell-tale click of Mrs. Hawthorne's heels approaching.

This was it, I told myself. Time for my firing. And with the roads clear, I didn't have an excuse to wait 'til morning to clear out. With any luck, Megan was still awake, and I could crash with her and Hannah at The Snowdrift tonight.

As Mrs. Hawthorne entered, I saw that she had someone else with her. My heart leaped into my throat.

"Eleanor Evans," she said, gesturing to me, then her guest. "This is Chef Marcus Lee. We were fortunate enough to have him as a guest tonight, and he asked to meet you."

"Chef," I said, absolutely starstruck as I held out my hand to shake his.

"Call me Marcus." The Japanese-American man in the impeccable purple velvet suit took my hand with a beaming smile. "Your squab was perfection. The sweetness and heat were perfectly balanced, while not overpowering the umami. Where did you pick up that recipe?"

A blush bloomed across my cheeks. I wasn't even sure I was still standing upright, totally bowled over by the compliment.

"It's a play on a few different recipes. But with my own twist on it. I sort of improvised."

"If you don't mind, you must write it down for me. I'm definitely stealing it for my next dinner party."

"Of course," I stuttered. "I'd be honored."

"I understand you live in Denver. I'll be there for a friend's pop-up in July. You must join us."

"I'll actually be in London." If I found thirty grand lying on the street somewhere. "I'm set to attend culinary school at your alma mater."

"Really?" His eyes lit up. "That's excellent news. They're lucky to have you. You must keep in touch."

"Certainly. Thank you, Chef. Marcus."

"It was a wonderful evening, Caroline." He kissed her on

both cheeks, then squeezed her hands. "I better run. Timothy is probably furious with me."

Once Marcus had left, Mrs. Hawthorne cleared her throat to address me. I braced myself for what I expected would be a truly historic ass-chewing.

"Well, Miss Evans. I told you I expected perfection."

"Yes, ma'am," I said, staring at my shoes.

"And if Marcus Lee says your meal was perfect, far be it from me to contradict him."

"What?" My eyes lifted to hers. I was completely at a loss. "Thank you, but . . ."

"I know I've been hard on you, but you've proven yourself capable. Some people crack under pressure. You've risen to the challenge. I admit I had my doubts. Nevertheless, I think we'll be pleased to have you around for the season. Good work."

I was dumbfounded. As Mrs. Hawthorne left the kitchen, I staggered back against the island. Clearly Amelia hadn't caught her mother yet to tell her about the Instagram posts. Maybe she was waiting until morning to bring it to her. In which case, the forthcoming ass-chewing would be twice as bad.

For several minutes, I stood in the kitchen nursing that bottle of brandy, almost too shellshocked to move. Until Charles crept in, with something concealed behind his back. He'd discarded his tuxedo jacket and bow tie, and his smile was hesitant.

"So, that was something, huh?" He edged his way into the kitchen. "I got you a little something. To say congratulations. And, I guess, as a memento."

Charles placed the small turquoise box in the center of the island and pushed it toward me. Inside was a silver link bracelet with a heart pendant.

"There's an inscription," he said.

I turned over the pendant. On the back it said, "We'll always have the blizzard."

At those simple, silly words, I burst into tears. Charles was at my side immediately, scooping me up just before I sank to the floor.

"Elle, hey." He brought me into his arms, holding me tight against his chest. "Hey, what's wrong? Shh. It's okay. Tell me what happened."

"I heard you fighting with your parents today," I muttered against his chest between sobs. "How they said we were only for the season and you had to get your priorities straight. That it wasn't appropriate to be dating the help."

"Oh, no. Elle." He kissed the top of my head, squeezing me tighter while my tears soaked into his shirt. "No wonder you were giving me the brush-off. Hey, don't listen to them, okay? Honestly, I almost never do. They like to huff and puff, but I'm my own person, got it? I make my own decisions. And they usually come around to find a way to live with them. It's not like I'm out there trying to start an alpaca farm or something, right?"

I laughed into his shirt, wiping the snot from my nose. "Alpacas?"

"Yeah, I don't know. It was the first thing that came to mind."

"Alpacas are cute."

He chuckled and I felt the vibration of his chest against my cheek. "You want one? I can find you a flat in London that allows pets."

"I'm not going to London," I said, sniffing. "Your mom's going to fire me when Amelia tells her what I've done."

"What?" Charles pulled away to meet my eyes, his arms still locked behind my back. "What are you talking about? Mother said she was thrilled with how the food turned out. She couldn't stop bragging about you to everyone at the party."

Really?

"I created this Instagram account," I told him. "It's just a stupid little food thing, basically. I post what I'm cooking, about my job, and some reviews about places in town. It was supposed to be anonymous, but I guess I didn't do a very good job hiding it because basically everyone figured it out. Only Amelia took offense to some of the things I posted. And I swear I didn't mean anything by it, but—"

"That's what you're upset about?" He smiled sympathetically, wiping the tears from my cheeks with the pad of his thumb. "Amelia is sort of a busybody. She tends to get hung up on stupid stuff and moves on just as quickly."

"She was really upset," I insisted, wiping my nose again and feeling like a disgusting, sniveling mess. "She said she would tell your mother that I broke the NDA and have me fired."

"Not if I have anything to say about it."

"No," I sniffed. "She's right. I was totally out of line. She warned me about discretion and I ignored it. I knew even when I started it that I was tempting fate. It was stupid and I feel awful about it."

"I know there's no way you meant anything malicious."

He held me in his arms, gently rubbing my back. Which only reminded me how sweaty and disgusting I felt after being in the kitchen all night. "I'll make her understand that."

"I just feel terrible," I said, dropping my head against his chest. "She looked so betrayed."

"My sister's been burned before. She had a hard time making friends because, for a while there, it always felt like they were only using her for trips or connections. Especially when we were in college. People would post photos with her for clout, then turn around and talk shit behind her back and whatever."

I nodded, sympathizing with her. "Girls can be cruel."

"We all make mistakes," he insisted. "But Amelia doesn't know you like I do. I'll make her understand." He pulled me once more against his chest and tucked me under his chin. "I'll talk to her. And Mom if I have to. I'll make them understand."

"How?" I asked.

"Simple. I'll tell them I'm in love with you."

The words washed over me like the first rays of morning light after a storm. Warm and comforting, filling the empty spaces of my heart with elation. Because I realized that I felt the same about him. Only I had to be sure he wasn't doing this out of some misplaced desire to protect my job.

I looked up at him, searching his eyes. "You don't have to say that."

"Why not?" He shrugged, a warm smile spreading over his face. "It's the truth."

"We barely know each other."

"That's not true." He leaned back against the counter, watching me with amusement, like a huge sense of relief had washed over him. "I don't care how long it's been. You see me. And I see you."

"You're out of your mind," I said, biting back a laugh. Something about his disposition, almost effervescent, was infectious.

"Maybe," he said, nodding. "But my heart knows exactly what it's doing."

"Oh, really?" I hoisted myself up on the opposite counter to sit. "And what's that?"

"Well, I think that probably starts with making you my girlfriend."

My lips curled. "That's so cringe."

He barked a laugh, shaking his head. "You really are going to make this difficult for me, aren't you?"

"What about your parents?" I said, practically bouncing on the countertop because the excitement bubbling in my stomach was almost too much to contain.

"They love you too. Or they will. Maybe it will take them some time to grow into the idea. But I've got a solution for that."

"Oh, really? I'm dying to hear what that is."

"I go to London with you."

If I'd been drinking, I would have spat it out all over him.

"No way your dad goes for that," I told him.

Still the thoughts rushed through my head. Exploring the city together. Cozying up in a little flat above a charming cafe. Mornings in bed with tea. I'd never had a real adult relationship, and it almost felt like too much to hope for. I guess I'd let myself believe it was something for later. After I was settled. Established. Had myself on firmer financial footing, and

I could start entertaining the idea of being responsible for anyone but myself. I'd never dared even get a houseplant for fear it would shrivel from neglect.

"I don't plan on giving him a choice," Charles stated emphatically.

He was starting to look a little punch-drunk and I worried about how much he'd had to drink. The man was seriously delirious.

"I'm going to tell him I want to take a year's sabbatical from the company. Figure a few things out. I need this time before I can fully commit to taking on a bigger role in the family business. I can't become the CEO if I still have all these questions about my future."

"Wow," I said. "You've really thought about this, huh?"

He came to stand between my legs, brushing errant strands of hair from my face.

"I have," he said. "Even before I met you. But especially since our first night together. If you hadn't turned up here the next day, I was going to find you. I knew it the second we woke up together. There was no way I was letting you slip through my fingers."

I ran my hands down his chest, smoothing the wrinkles from his shirt. "I never stood a chance, did I?"

Charles shook his head, grinning. "Nope."

I draped my arms over his shoulders, running my nails through the soft hair at the back of his head. "I can't believe this is really happening."

"There is just one thing I need from you," he said.

"Yeah, what's that?"

"Well, I mean, I told you how I feel . . ."

I breathed out a laugh, sucking my bottom lip between my teeth. He was so cheesy. And I was so happy.

"Well, duh," I said, locking my ankles behind his legs. "I must be in love with you. I don't go skinny dipping with just any guy."

Charles laughed, cupping my face in his hands to press his warm, soft lips against mine. Tender and sweet. I hugged him closer, comforted by the beating of his heart against my chest.

"So, London," he said, pressing his forehead against mine.

"London."

"Well, this should make for an interesting family breakfast in the morning."

Chapter 32

Charles thought it was best he speak to Amelia alone the next morning, which was fine by me. So, following breakfast service, I met up with Megan and Hannah at the marketplace. They were seated at a picnic table just inside the barn, with cups of cocoa and fresh pastries, and a mountain of shopping bags beside them.

"Wow, you two have done some damage, huh?" I said, folding myself in beside Hannah, who was bundled up in a thick green knit scarf and matching cap I recognized from a local handmade goods store. "Must've gotten an early start."

"There are so many cute shops around town. We've been hitting up all the great spots you posted about on Après Brie."

"I can see that," I said, laughing at their haul.

"Just a few souvenirs and Christmas gifts," Megan added, picking off a flaky bit of croissant to pop in her mouth. "Might as well take advantage of the sales, right?"

"Well, on behalf of the local economy, thank you for your business."

"Oh!" she said then, waving her hands in mild panic. "What

happened with the party? I hope it wasn't a total disaster. I couldn't believe how quickly the snow shut down everything last night."

Just thinking about that damn sage got my blood pressure rising again. I'd have stress dreams about that dinner service for months.

"Actually, it all worked out. Charles really came to my rescue. Trudged out to the neighbor's house in the middle of the blizzard in his tux to scrounge up just enough. Then he and his dad jumped into the kitchen to lend a hand."

"Really?" Megan sat back, impressed.

"And I almost forgot . . ." The whole night was sort of a blur. "I met Marcus Lee!"

"Whoa," she said, eyes wide in awe. "What was he doing there?"

I shrugged. "Good friend of Mrs. Hawthorne, apparently."

"Well, what'd he say?" Hannah demanded. "What was he like?"

"Very nice. Way more handsome in person. Said he loved my squab and to stay in touch while I'm in London."

Hannah whistled, brushing off my shoulders. "Check out who's moving up in the world."

"Definitely one of my strangest days in the kitchen. That's for sure."

"So . . . Charles." Hannah accentuated his name, bouncing her eyebrows at me. "Kinda sounds like he's obsessed with you."

Much as I tried, I couldn't smother my silly grin. Just the mention of his name had me beaming.

"Ugh, look at you," she laughed. "Who is this person? I

barely recognize her. Smiling? Giddy? Where is my neurotic, curmudgeonly Elle and what have you done with her?"

"She's taking some much-deserved time off," I said. "Though there is one unresolved catastrophe from last night."

"What's wrong?" Megan asked, her smile dropping.

"The Instagram account. Amelia Hawthorne saw it and wasn't thrilled I'd been using her family for content."

"But you don't even mention their name," Hannah argued.

"No, I know. But I get the impression she's sensitive about this kind of thing. She feels like I betrayed their trust. And I'm not sure she's entirely wrong."

Suddenly, I watched their attention rise over my head and both their faces go a little slack. I turned to see Charles striding up to our table. Yeah, he had that effect on people.

"Morning, ladies." He bent to place a kiss on my cheek, the scent of his shampoo now a trigger that made my stomach flip and my brain turn to mush.

"Hey," I said. "This is a surprise."

"Hi," Megan and Hannah both said in unison, all starry-eyed.

"Charles, this is Megan and Hannah. They don't usually stare this much."

"Pleasure to meet you," he said, flashing that charming grin. "Elle talks about you both all the time. How are you enjoying your visit so far? Hopefully that storm wasn't too rough on you last night."

"We love it here," Hannah gushed. I thought I might have to restrain her. "Can't wait to come back for Christmas."

That snapped Megan out of her trance. "We'll see."

"Sit with us," I told him, moving over to let him slide in beside me. "What are you doing here?"

"Actually . . ." He glanced toward Mia's stall through the crowd of afternoon shoppers. "I came to talk to Mia. Thought I'd take her out to lunch, so we could hash some things out."

"I love that," I told him, taking his hand to squeeze.

I knew he was nervous about reopening the past, but it was closure they both needed. And hopefully this would be a small step toward mending their friendship.

"And I talked to Amelia," he said.

Megan and Hannah shared a quiet look.

"She's a little peeved, but I think she's calmed down after sleeping on it. And I explained there was no ill intent behind it. Told her it'd mean a lot to me if she could see her way to forgiving you. I thought it might be nice for the three of us to spend some time together this week. Give you two a chance to get to know each other better."

"Absolutely," I agreed. "If you think it'll help. I really don't want her to hate me."

Not just because it would make working in that house a nightmare. This relationship with Charles was really a nonstarter if his sister and I couldn't be friends.

"Trust me," he said. "Amelia has a good heart. I have a feeling you'll both be laughing about this in no time."

"So . . ." Hannah cleared her throat, turning to level Charles with narrowed eyes. "What are your intentions with our Eleanor?"

"Okay." I smothered her face with my hand. "That's enough meet-and-greet. You better leave while you still can."

Charles laughed, climbing to his feet. "Catch up later?" he

offered, glancing at Megan and Hannah. "Maybe I'll swing by The Snowdrift for cocktail hour."

"I'd love a cocktail," Hannah said, removing my hand from her face.

"Nice try," her mother grimaced, scolding her daughter with a glare. "Wonderful to meet you, Charles."

As intros to the family went, I thought that had been a good one. It was easy with Charles. He had a way with people. Effortlessly approachable and charismatic. It didn't hurt that he was gorgeous, either. Now, if only I could secure myself in the same good graces with his family, starting with coming clean to Mrs. Hawthorne.

After I left the marketplace, I returned to the chalet and asked Ali if I might find some time with Mrs. Hawthorne today. I was surprised when she came back minutes later to say she would see me in the gym.

In a wing of the main house I hadn't visited before, I found a room almost entirely enclosed by windows on one side and mirrors on the other. There was every imaginable piece of equipment arranged around the room, with a large space by the far wall with rolled-up yoga mats and large inflated balance balls. And off a short hallway, a sauna and steam room too.

Inside, Mrs. Hawthorne, wearing black leggings and a zip-up athletic jacket, lay on an elevated table while a man in a polo shirt manipulated her back and legs through a series of stretches. I knocked on the open door, hesitant to disturb her.

"Come in," she called from the table. Mrs. Hawthorne lifted one hand to wave me over. "What can I do for you?"

It was a strange departure, encountering her like this. So

casual. Every other time it had been in the kitchen or her office. Always pressed and proper. Buttoned up and impeccable. Now she wore her hair in a simple pony tail and sweat beaded her forehead.

"It really isn't urgent," I said, feeling like an intruder. "We can talk later."

"Nonsense. You're here now. Say what's on your mind."

I took an unsteady breath and glanced at the man who continued to flex her knees and roll her ankles. He kept his attention firmly on his client, blending into the scenery. Something I supposed came with practice.

"Amelia mentioned to me last night that she'd found an Instagram account I started. Après Brie." It was mortifying having to explain this to a woman like Mrs. Hawthorne. It felt infantile and silly and I wanted to sink into the floor as my mouth dried up and my hands went clammy. "Sort of a food blog kind of thing, I guess you could say. I post about cooking and also some reviews from places around town and—"

"I'm aware." Mrs. Hawthorne sat up abruptly and reached for a towel, wiping her forehead.

"Oh." I braced for that long-awaited ass-chewing.

Instead, her trainer handed her a bottle of water and helped her down from the table. He handed her an elastic band that she placed around both ankles, before proceeding to put her hands on her hips and balance on one leg while extending the other to her side, repeating the action.

"I think it's marvelous."

"What?" I couldn't be sure I wasn't hallucinating.

"It's quite entrepreneurial. Everyone was talking about it at the party last night. I do hope you'll post photos of the event. I can have our photographer send over some shots."

"Really? Oh." I was totally at a loss for words. The panic was now turning to utter confusion. "It's just, I know it technically violates the NDA."

She switched to balancing on the other leg.

"I don't consider my dinner china a matter of national security," she said, flicking her eyes to me with the slightest hint of a smile on her otherwise pencil-straight lips.

I was pretty sure that counted as a joke and it hit me sort of sideways. I didn't know Mrs. Hawthorne had a sense of humor.

"My friends are all terribly jealous," she said, moving on to squats. "Seems like everyone has a spread in *Architectural Digest* now. None of them have a viral chef."

Wow. I didn't know I was such a trendsetter.

Her trainer then spread out a yoga mat on the floor with more elastic bands, instructing her through a further series of stretches and joint exercises while I stood off to the side because she hadn't dismissed me yet.

"Since you're here," she said, lying on her back to lift her hips off the ground with one foot planted on the floor. "We might as well discuss my son."

I swallowed the heavy lump in my throat.

"He tells me he's quite taken with you."

Her words from their argument still echoed in my head, the sting as potent as when they'd first come from her mouth.

"He's always been impulsive," she said. "Tends to leap without looking. Got him into a fair bit of trouble in his youth."

So I'd heard.

"And he's stubborn. Once he's set his mind to something,

there's no use arguing with him. I suppose he gets that from me."

That was a trap and I knew better than to open my mouth.

"But my son isn't frivolous and he doesn't easily give his heart away. If you've captured his interest, he must see something special in you." Mrs. Hawthorne sat up, reaching for her bottle of water. "And you feel the same about him?" she said.

"I do. I know this presents all sorts of thorny issues with my employment, and I'm so grateful to have a job here, but . . ." I shrugged. "I think he's pretty special, too."

"Let me give you one piece of advice," she said, taking another sip of water and wincing at some pain as she flexed her knee. "Never get old."

I smothered a laugh.

"I've had two knee replacements and hip surgery," she said. "Looking back, I'm not sure skiing was worth the damage it caused."

Her trainer handed her another elastic band to wrap around her toes as he led her through another exercise. It felt like I was learning more about her in this one conversation than I'd gleaned from all the time I'd been here combined. This felt intentional. Like she was bringing me into her world. Letting me see the real her.

"But you must've loved it a little," I said. "All the trophies and titles."

Again, a slight smile teased the corner of her lips. "I was something back then."

"We get so little time to be great at anything," I offered. "Some people never find their thing. I don't know. Maybe

I'm naive, but I think being great for even a little while is still better than never at all."

"I suppose you're right." She considered that a moment while her attention remained focused on her trainer. "I have no doubt you're well on your way to being a truly great chef, Miss Evans. Eleanor."

A compliment from her felt like winning a gold medal. Little fireworks went off in my chest while I tried to maintain my composure.

"My son's romantic intentions are his own business," she said then. "I don't intend to interfere. But between us, he could do worse. I think you'll be good for him."

I smiled to myself. Caroline and I weren't about to become best friends overnight, but that was the closest thing to a ringing endorsement I could expect. More importantly, it felt like we understood each other now. She'd let me into her circle of trust. Even if just the outermost layer. It was the first step.

Epilogue

One Year Later

In the ACE kitchen today, we were preparing beef Wellington. I decided to experiment a little and prepare a chorizo-spiced duxelles from a Marcus Lee recipe. He'd sent me a signed cookbook recently, with a note urging me to invite him to my graduation. I guess that sort of made me friends with a celebrity chef. Which certainly didn't suck.

To prepare my tenderloin, I seasoned and seared it briefly in a cast-iron pan with butter and aromatics, then wrapped it tightly in plastic wrap to cool in the blast chiller. For my duxelles, I finely chopped a mixture of wild mushrooms and fried them in a pan with chorizo until they became a luscious paste. Next, I laid out paper-thin slices of spicy Iberico ham and spread them with my duxelles. I unwrapped and seasoned my chilled tenderloin to fully envelope with the ham and duxelles, then tightly wrapped it again and put it back into the blast chiller. While that set, I rolled out my dough and brushed the pastry with an egg wash, before applying first a base layer over the tenderloin, then an intricate lattice design that allowed me to show off some of my finer pastry skills.

It was a process that took several hours, a dozen of us toiling away in the kitchen while our instructor hovered over our shoulders. It was more than a little nerve-wracking, knowing every move we made was being evaluated. Though after a few months under Mrs. Hawthorne's discerning eye, this was nothing. It was in these moments, watching my classmates nervously fret over fallen dough, hands shaking over intricate knife cuts, that I realized I'd come away from the chalet with a new confidence in myself. Ascended the mountain, so to speak. Maybe caught a couple of bumps and bruises along the way, but I was here. Not an anxious wreck. Not crying in a bathroom stall. Thriving.

When my Wellington was baked and ready for presentation, I sliced a medallion for the instructor and drizzled it with a chimichurri of cilantro, parsley, and oregano, with olive oil, red wine vinegar, red pepper, and a hint of lemon.

She raised the plate to her nose, taking in the aromas before cutting a piece and dragging it through the sauce.

"A Latin-inspired approach," she said, without a hint of whether that was a horrible miscalculation on my part.

"Yes, chef. Chorizo and Iberico ham. I really love the bold flavor they impart."

"A nice palate cleanser after so many pan jus," she said. "Nicely done."

That feeling never got old. It reminded me that I was on the right path. That this dream was worth every sacrifice I'd made along the way. Even when it meant leaving my life back in Denver to step out on a limb. Because in food, I'd found myself. And I was damn good at it.

After class, I walked to Hyde Park and stopped at a cart for something called a chimney cake. Friends at school were raving about them, so after finishing up my last day of class before winter break, I had made a special trip to track one down. They reminded me of churros, but shaped like a spring, and served wrapped in paper like an ice-cream cone, then filled with banana and Nutella and topped with whipped cream. The pastry, dusted in cinnamon sugar, was the perfect complement to a piping hot cocoa.

It was a gorgeous winter day, with a light dusting of snow blanketing the ground. The annual Winter Wonderland festival was in full swing, bringing carnival rides, pop-up eateries, games, and a Christmas market to the park. Families strolled with their children bundled up, little waddling marshmallows amid the melodies of Christmas music from live performers on a distant stage.

It made me miss the mountains. The expansive vistas that stretched to the horizon. Mulled wine and a roaring fire. Maplewood Creek had gotten under my skin and wouldn't let go. It had been a year since I left, and while I still talked to the girls online now and then, it wasn't the same. Not like popping down to The Snowdrift for breakfast with Pops. Strolling the shops among the twinkling lights. That perfect storybook village, like something out of a dream. Here, in the shadow of skyscrapers and the noise of traffic, it almost didn't seem real. Like a dream getting smaller in my mind the farther I got from that place.

From the park, I walked back to my apartment. I tossed my

keys in the tray by the door and kicked off my boots, jumping straight into the shower to rinse the smell of the kitchen out of my hair, and put on some comfy sweats and slippers. Ten hours on my feet really did a number on my muscles. My shoulders ached and my feet were sore.

In the kitchen, I gulped down a sparkling water before putting some music on the Bluetooth speaker and padding into the office. Charles was sitting at his desk in front of the computer, his glasses sliding down his nose as he typed.

"Hey, babe," I said, coming to sit on his lap.

"Good day?" He wrapped his arms around my waist and kissed my neck while I read the screen.

"Yeah, not bad. Instructor liked my Wellington."

"That's great. Glad you went for it?"

"Definitely. So, how's it going in here? Getting any packing done?"

"Nope." He laughed at my admonishing grimace. "Just following up on Mia's emails from last night. She's starting to panic a little. The time difference isn't helping."

We were flying back to Maplewood Creek in the morning to see his family for Christmas. Megan and Hannah were making the drive too. Thanks to the Hawthornes, Megan had almost more clients now than she could handle. But the real news was the official launch of Après Creek, Charles's business venture with Mia. After their talk last year, Charles decided the best way to make amends was to simply pick up where they left off. It took her a few weeks to believe he was serious, but after she dusted off the old business plan, he cut her a check and they were partners again. For better or worse. Only now that the big day was fast approaching, Mia was a ball of nerves.

"Just remind her that we'll all be there to lend a hand. We won't let anything fall through the cracks. And tell her she's got this!"

"I will," he said, resting his chin on my shoulder.

"Did you have class today?" I asked.

"Mmm-hmm. I'm still no better at watercolors than I was a month ago. Not sure it's my calling."

Charles had managed to convince his father to let him take the sabbatical from the company. And even though he had Mia and their business to tend to, he needed something to occupy his time while I was at school. I had encouraged him to find an art class. It was something he was passionate about, after all.

"Hang in there," I told him teasingly. "Maybe pastels will be more your thing."

"Speaking of pastels, I talked to Amelia. She's bringing her new guy," he said. Charles transferred his hands to my shoulders, digging deep into the stiff muscles. "So, we get to relentlessly grill him for the next two weeks."

"Can't wait."

Amelia and I had grown closer over the last year. We began by FaceTiming and exchanging emails. Then she came to visit for a couple of weeks over the summer, which gave us a chance to bond over good restaurants and shows in the West End.

"And I was thinking," Charles said. "There's supposed to be bad weather in Colorado late tomorrow. I'd hate for Megan and Hannah to end up stuck on the roads. Why don't I send a plane? Get them up there first thing in the morning, so you all have the whole day together."

I twisted my lips, hesitating. "It is an awfully long drive in bad weather."

Charles's constant insistence on paying for everything was always a point of contention, but I had to admit it was a very tempting offer. And I knew Hannah would never let me hear the end of it if she found out I stood between her and a ride in a private jet.

"Please. Let me do this. It's Christmas and I want to spoil you," he insisted, kissing the tip of my nose.

Charles usually got his way on these things. Not because he was right necessarily, but he was ruthless with the puppy-dog eyes. It made him happy, so I tolerated it. For now.

"Fine. What do you think you want for dinner?"

"Takeout?" he said.

"Right answer."

"Are you ever going to cook for me again?" he said, lifting me off his lap to go hunting for his phone.

"Nope."

Not until he put a ring on it, at least.

Just before I left the office, he caught me by the hand. Charles pulled me into his arms and tilted my chin up. Then, just before he leaned down to kiss me, his shimmering eyes paused on mine.

"I love you, Elle. That blizzard really was the best thing that ever happened to me."

"To both of us," I told him. "I love you, too."